*The Disc*

Tom Ackland was born in 1955. After the
University of Oxford he worked first in
London in the Overseas Development
Administration, then in Brussels, London
and Paris for the Foreign and Common-
wealth Office. He has also lived in Stock-
holm, where his second novel is set.

# TOM ACKLAND

## *The Disobedient Servant*

INDIGO

First published in Great Britain 1996
by Victor Gollancz

This Indigo edition published 1997
Indigo is an imprint of the Cassell Group
Wellington House, 125 Strand, London WC2R 0BB

© Tom Ackland 1996

The right of Tom Ackland to be identified as author of
this work has been asserted by him in accordance with
the Copyright, Designs and Patents Act, 1988.

A catalogue record for this book is
available from the British Library.

ISBN 0 575 40036 6

Printed and bound in Great Britain by
Guernsey Press Co. Ltd, Guernsey, Channel Isles

All rights reserved. No part of this publication may be
reproduced or transmitted in any form or by any means,
electronic or mechanical including photocopying,
recording or any information storage or retrieval system,
without prior permission in writing from the publishers.

This book is sold subject to the condition that it shall not,
by way of trade or otherwise, be lent, resold, hired out, or
otherwise circulated without the publisher's prior consent
in any form of binding or cover other than that in which it
is published and without a similar condition including this
condition being imposed on the subsequent purchaser.

97 98 99    10 9 8 7 6 5 4 3 2 1

*For the real Tom . . .*

'An Englishman's mind works best
when it is almost too late'
Lord D'Abernon

# Chapter One

Had there ever been a November so wet? Ever been mornings and evenings so dark, trains so full, lights so inviting, umbrellas so menacing?

Life in London had taken on the look of a watercolour left out in the rain. There was a subaqueous sheen to surfaces, as if the sky were a pool spotted by rain, filtering down beams of watery light to play upon the submerged objects beneath. The moisture dampened sound and added a faint dank hiss to all noise. A seamless cloud hung over the whole city, possibly over the whole island.

It was Guy Colchester's secret delight to watch the morning rain glistening on the railway tracks. He liked to imagine the deadly mixture of water and electricity held from the passengers by steel and rubber. Throughout the network there coursed terrific charges of power, restrained and controlled by machines. Although he carried a newspaper, on mornings like this when the train was full it was impossible to read and he would fall to musing quietly.

When travelling he particularly loved to think about systems and links. There was something oddly satisfying about being on a train and thus part of a larger network of other trains each slotting into place. When this morning, as on most mornings, his train was held up briefly outside Waterloo he made a point of not showing impatience like the other passengers. Instead he thought about the signalling and switching which was taking place – flashing lights in the pouring rain – allowing some other train to take priority. This ordering of things pleased him, reminding him of the way he too belonged to a wider society. It was not lonely at all, the solitary existence he was forced to lead in London; his family were all around him, strangers but brothers.

When his train started up again and ran through a tunnel he

peered critically at his own reflection back-lit in the carriage window. The hopelessly optimistic square face topped with fair hair. The slightly blunt, slightly too large, slightly off-centre nose. The blue eyes that caught his gaze as if surprised. Perhaps the face of a young man a little bit puzzled about the turn of events. But certainly ready if need be to make the best of a bad job.

It took twenty minutes to walk from Waterloo to the Ministry of Exports on Northumberland Avenue. Colchester always took Waterloo trains, relishing the brisk walk across the river. He checked in at nine-twenty, showing his security pass. This was a weather-beaten brown card in a plastic folder with a diagonal purple stripe. In one corner a tousled criminal face stared out and the guard checked that this was indeed Colchester. (There had been the recent case of a junior member of staff who for a week had gained entry by sporting a likeness of his family bulldog.) Once in Colchester waited patiently with the others for the lift. He nodded to acquaintances from other floors.

'The month of the drowned dog,' he observed to Fulbright's young and rather vivid secretary, Molly, in passing her open door on the tenth floor.

'You said it,' she replied, a smiling blonde with a flash of blues and greens.

'Not me. The poet laureate.'

'All right. He said it.'

Colchester went off to start his day's work.

His co-worker Stanton was already at his desk when he arrived. The office they shared was functional, spartan, stripped for action. As was his custom, Stanton was drinking a cheering mug of Oxo and consuming a bar of chocolate for his breakfast. Something of the wartime spirit of austerity seemed to cling to him, although he could hardly have been alive at the time. Stanton was measured and dogged at his work, displayed a knowing cynicism regarding bureaucratic ways and a wealth of knowledge of the myths and legends of office life. It was said that out of office hours he looked after a mad father. He had worked there for as long as anyone could remember.

'T-G-I-F,' said Stanton as Colchester shook out his umbrella. He jerked his biro at the calendar showing a picture of Windsor Castle. 'Thank God It's Friday.'

'Y-C-S-T-A,' replied Colchester. 'You Can Say That Again.'

Stanton waited until Colchester had settled himself before springing the bad news.

'Fulbright is going round in circles. He's forgotten it's Molly's birthday. And he wants us all to work over lunch after the PC.'

'Predictable, I suppose,' replied Colchester.

'Yes, but lunch! I'm not paid to work over lunch and neither are you.'

It was all true. There was indeed much fluster this morning, with only one hour to go before the Projects Committee met. Fulbright's department had five projects up this morning, two belonging to Colchester.

Fulbright was sitting in his head of department's office, puffing angrily on his pipe and working himself up into one of his states, sending for everyone in turn and rehearsing familiar arguments or demanding enlightenment on obscure details. He was nearing retirement and his appearances before the committee always tried him sorely. He was convinced that part of the committee's purpose was to provide an opportunity for the senior officers to trip him up. It seemed a rough way to treat an old soldier like himself. He quizzed Colchester closely on his two projects, probing for the weaknesses, the faultline that might prove a source of embarrassment. Colchester was packed off to unearth some Middle Eastern trade flow figures, the dollar/drachma exchange rate and the times of high tide in Alexandria.

Half an hour after Colchester arrived at the Ministry of Exports another worker presented himself at the entrance to begin the day. His car – a new black Rover (replacing the horrible old wedge-shaped Princesses) – purred through the ragged remnants of the rush hour mêlée and came to rest on the double yellow lines outside the front, just beside the 'No Parking' sign. The light over the rear seat snapped off. A youthful, bespectacled face peered briefly out of the rain-spattered window at the crowds of tired and wan faces passing by, then turned back.

'So, three o'clock at Jenny's, and the House at four?'

The driver, a woman in a bottle-green uniform, nodded.

The passenger, body long and thin, clad in an angular pin-striped suit, sorted out the papers cascading all over the back seat. A mass of green official paper – best-quality parchment – had fanned out of a folder and spilled on to the floor. He had scribbled on the top sheet in red ink. One of the drawbacks to living in central London was that one had so little time to work in the car. When he had refilled his box-like briefcase, he gingerly opened the car door. It was still raining. Before he could step out a security guard came forward to hold an umbrella over his head. The passenger smiled gratefully and allowed himself to be escorted the six feet from one side of the pavement to the other. One or two commuters lifted their eyes and looked at him with faint interest. The special glass door beside the revolving doors opened to receive him.

Timothy Warwick had arrived at the office.

'Good morning, Minister,' came a chorus of voices from behind the reception desk.

Warwick gave a genial wave to all. Another security guard was standing by one of the lifts. The door was open, the lift immobilized by a key in the control panel.

'Morning, Bill.'

The two got in. The doors slid to. Going up. And to the top.

Jill, his principal private secretary, big-boned, lank of hair, serious, was waiting when the lift door opened on the twelfth floor. She would have been there at least two hours before him, and would work at night for at least an hour after he left. They had already spoken three times the previous evening by telephone. Warwick thought it best not to ask what happened to her own private life. A wise virgin, he suspected.

'Hello, Jill. I forgot, can you ask Mark to put back the surgery?'

'I already have, Minister.'

Warwick nodded. He should have known. There was not one minute of the waking day – or at least the official part of it – that Jill did not regulate. It had frightened him at first to see the hours, days, weeks stretching ahead in his diary, all filled up with engagements, meetings, commitments of one sort or another, all planned, programmed, cut and dried; his entire life given over to performing his public duties. But now he was learning to enjoy it, the comforting sensation that wherever he went, whatever he did, someone was looking after him. It was like having a high-powered valet service, quietly and efficiently removing the element of risk from one's life.

But it was still important to keep one jump ahead.

'Did you manage to look through the speech in the end?' Jill asked as he walked briskly in front of her along the corridor.

She had taken from him the box of papers that represented his evening's work.

'I did.'

'And?'

Warwick paused on the threshold of the private office. The three secretaries within were standing to attention.

'You know I cannot seriously be expected to stand up in the House of Commons and say that.'

A momentary hush.

'No, Minister. I suppose not.'

Jill followed him thoughtfully into the office, already mentally rescheduling the morning's work programme. Someone would have to do more work on the speech. And that meant her. It always did. In the end, at the fifty-ninth minute of the eleventh hour, they would work out an acceptable text. They always did.

'OK,' said Warwick briskly. 'Diary meeting. Let's see what the fixture list looks like.'

Jill and the diary secretary – a middle-aged spinster named Margaret – trooped into Warwick's personal office behind him, their arms full of papers. Warwick went and sat behind the pleasant mahogany desk he had had installed – a memento from the bank he had recently left – and relaxed with his ministerial folder in front of him. Someone had already switched the overhead lights on. Someone had already switched the desk lamp on. Someone had already put the coffee in a china cup on his desk. The frames of the pictures on the walls glistened and gleamed with polish. A signed photograph of the Prime Minister beamed down on him with approval. Beside it was an original of a political cartoon, depicting an owlish Warwick as a boy scout brandishing a pen-knife, with one foot on the corpse of a huge black bear that represented backwardness, reaction, sloth or some such vice.

Warwick peered over his spectacles, a boyish thirty-eight-year-old. 'Shoot.'

Margaret dutifully ran through the day's programme. Five minutes for this meeting. Ten minutes for letter signing and case-work (decisions which the department felt he should take). Then morning prayers with the senior staff. Then EX(3) Committee in Whitehall . . .

They were already running late. Warwick could hear a rumble of footsteps out in the corridor, the senior staff milling about. As

13

the day progressed the programme would become increasingly unstuck, to the mounting distress of his private office.

Margaret wound down.

'Another coffee, I think?' said Warwick, and ignoring the sounds outside turned to the folder of neatly stacked papers in front of him. He was looking forward to the weekend. Even in the filthy weather there would be plenty of birds. Good shooting. Good drinking afterwards in the castle. The new intake and the old troopers. Good talk. Politics. Finance. The art of the possible. Miriam slipping in and out the room, Miriam pulling a face when her father started one of his stories, Miriam putting her foot on his under the dinner table as the talk got riotous and Bill did his impersonation of the Foreign Secretary at the Party Conference. Miriam coming to his room that night, a room he knew she had specially chosen for ease of access . . .

Well, why not? She would be a good wife, once her divorce came through. It was not that side of things that bothered him. He could always square that with the PM.

No, it was something else entirely that from time to time made Warwick wonder who or what was not quite on his side. Warwick knew that all his official correspondence was read by his assistants, was routinely processed around the department by the machine which looked after him. That came with the job. Private secretaries wrote letters for ministers to sign and opened letters signed by other ministers that were in fact written by other private secretaries. He had no illusion there.

But private correspondence was another matter. The machine was supposed to be able to distinguish between the two. He received in his box many personal notes: from colleagues, from friends, from his assistant in the Commons, from his political agent, even sometimes from the PM. Why then did he have the impression – which he could not yet prove – that someone was reading his private mail too? And if they *were* doing so, on exactly whose behalf were they doing it?

Jill came back in.

'Do you really want to have the meeting now, Minister? Or shall I ask Garrick to go away and come back again with the staff in ten minutes?'

'No, Jill,' said Warwick. 'Let us pray.'

\*　　\*　　\*

The Projects Committee was not in the end a great success. Four out of five of Fulbright's projects were rejected and, like horses made to try again after refusing a jump, would have to be re-presented at the next session. One of them was Colchester's. Fulbright had suffered great indignities when it became clear that some routine consultation of interested departments had not taken place. He spent the rest of the day in a poor temper composing letters which sought the necessary clearance but also contrived to obscure the precise reason for doing so.

The light faded early in the afternoon. Colchester, busy compiling yet further memoranda, reflected, as so often after a committee, on the timeless nature of the work. Experience showed that it was useless to take reverses too seriously or rejoice in successes overmuch. Over time all was as one. In some ways it was comforting to think of thousands of others throughout London performing similar tasks; cohorts of functionaries sending messages to one another, phoning one another, keeping in play the vast communication system that comprised this city of government, while outside the rain continued to fall on the darkening world.

Yet, in his heart of hearts, Colchester had the growing feeling that perhaps he might have made a mistake. When his father, two years ago, had insisted that his only son should continue the family tradition and do a kind of apprenticeship in the public service Colchester had not really been in a position to object. His father, who was now nearing retirement from a prosperous medical practice in the Midlands, had been young and hopeful in the days of Beveridge and free milk. He saw his son as following in the footsteps of a grandfather who had once governed a small but lucrative segment of West Africa for the Colonial Office. Edinburgh University, thought his father, would teach Guy the stoic creed, ever more necessary for a tribe of servants of the Empire now turned inward to administer a country which was the last patch of normality left on earth. Not redbrick but grey granite, his father had specified. The last of the Romans, his mother had once called his father.

And so Guy Colchester had fetched up in this job, primed and ready to fulfil his destiny. The trouble was, the public sector in the late 1980s did not seem remotely like his father's view of it. Working on behalf of the nation, his father would say, is both a privilege and a responsibility. And Colchester reminded himself of this when every day brought its fresh load of administrative chaos. Individual actions are not of themselves meaningful, his father would repeat, but if they are part of a structure dedicated to the public good they take on a *sublime quality*. Colchester had thought about this when, on his first day at the office, a plump and earnest under secretary with ginger hair and a smile like the Cheshire Cat had said to him that the Civil Service encompassed the drafting of important policy papers for perusal by ministers and at the same time the tying together of those documents with bits of string. Each had its part in the scheme of things.

The Friday afternoon slid into Friday evening. Colchester packed a briefcase full of papers in case he was bored at the week-end and left at six o'clock, edging cautiously past Fulbright's office. Fulbright was bristling on the telephone because Molly could not locate an errant member of the London Chamber of Commerce. With his white jutting little beard and frowning, blinking eyes Colchester thought how much Fulbright resembled a slightly perplexed badger. He managed to slip past unnoticed, making a semblance of a farewell to Molly through the open door.

The crowded twenty minutes back to Waterloo were like a battle conducted at night, or perhaps a retreat from a massive engagement by cover of dark and rain. He blended into the dense moving crowd of commuters and drifted with the tide down pavements and over streets. But he did not blend so well that the individual who shadowed him from office to station could not follow him.

The following morning, however, the rain had lifted slightly. Back at the one-bedroom utility flat in Croydon (another consequence of his father's career planning) Colchester prepared the apparatus for the day's events as the coffee percolated. Into a waterproof rucksack he stuffed a note-pad, miniature tape recorder and a tiny pair of binoculars. He went outside, heaved the tarpaulin from his battered old Toyota and with some difficulty coerced the tired old oriental engine into life. It lumbered up through the gears and set off in a southerly direction.

The jack snipe pottered aimlessly about in the marsh. It paused briefly to extract an unwilling worm from its shelter below a clump of grass and then made off noiselessly, retiring behind a bank of reeds to digest its food. This done it stood on one foot for a while, as if enjoying the ray of autumn sunlight which broke through the clouds marching to the west. After five minutes of inaction it suddenly trembled, immediately aware that it was being observed. Uncertain in which direction the danger lay it took off, crossing the marsh with a low zig-zagging flight designed to evade the sights of the waiting hunter.

Silent, and also standing on one leg, Colchester held his breath as he followed the movement of the bird through his miniature binoculars. He watched it swoop back and forth, skimming the surface of the reeds and darting in and out of the low sunken trees until it was finally lost in the easterly morning haze. He put down his binoculars and made some annotations in a notebook slung around his neck.

On the other side of the marsh, also silent, and with no need to break off observations by writing things down, another watcher of events held Colchester long in a telescopic gaze, seeming to derive much satisfaction from what little action could be made out.

# Chapter Two

The City dominated the skyline to the west. The immense stacks and towers of the money factories loomed a mile or so away. On a summer's day the setting sun would catch the silhouettes and light up the odd crevice or crenellation, illuminate some glass facet for a minute. But most of the time the blocks reared up like mountains and blotted out the light. As now, on this late Saturday afternoon in November, the lowland to the east of the City was starved of light.

The wind chased bits of paper, fruit and orange peel around the streets. Scarcely a tree, scarcely a blade of grass, came between concrete and brick. This urban territory, in the shadow of the City, was entirely man-made. Man-made and largely forgotten. Except by those impov rished settlers who came to England from the old colonies and who found here a cheap stopping-off point for a generation or two; before sons and daughters moved to the promised land of the suburbs. And except by those whose business was running on a shoestring, or whose accounts might not stand scrutiny, who found the black economy on the edge of the City a good place to hide, or disguise themselves. No questions asked.

A revolving orange light burned twenty-four hours a day outside Jasper's Cabs. The office entrance was small, the number of paying customers who came in that way few. Down a cul-de-sac larger doors gave on to the garage. Cabs trundled up and down the street.

Cigarette smoke hung in the air in the drivers' waiting room. Four or five drivers lounged around, two playing cards, one staring intently at a newspaper. The loudspeaker on the wall emitted tinny pop music, broken every few minutes by static and messages to and from base.

Cowboys. Waiting for the football results.

The waiting room had a connecting door leading to the radio centre. Elphick, the radio operator, sat beneath an immense instrument pouring out a stream of messages, instructions and abuse to the network of cabs. He favoured country and western music for his own working environment. The whining of guitars and the simple moral songs of faithless husbands, drunks and Jesus filled the air.

'Citizen standing outside Baker Street tube, number four. Deliver same to own doorstep, Balham. Take him back some day, come what may, to Blue Bayou . . .'

'Got that, Elvis,' came a voice on the airwaves from across London. 'On my way. But stuck in traffic, my old son. He'd be better off with a bus.'

'You still at Heathrow, number thirteen? How about flying back to Hounslow and shipping cargo?'

This time another voice, more distant, out on the edge of the radio universe.

'OK, white trash. Moving on and moving out.'

Elphick gave his usual exhortation. 'Move the punters around faster, boys. Nobody pays us for standing still.'

Fifteen cabs jammed the airwaves with obscene replies.

In the accounts office next door Clive, the assistant manager, was doing some creative work with the previous day's inflow of cash, little of which would end up in any ordinary bank account. Outside, in the street, three cabs were throbbing, bonnets up, engines ticking over, receiving a cursory check and a perfunctory polish from one of the handful of mechanics, none of whom seemed over-occupied. An accountant – if they had used one – might have said there seemed to be an excess of supply over demand.

Over in Soho, Flynn the driver – today's man of the match – put down his cheese sandwich and looked at the watch on his podgy wrist. He carefully examined the wet streets outside the stationary cab, gauging speeds, distances, forces of acceleration and deceleration. He was a burly, nervous, Labrador dog of a man in his late forties, running to fat, under-exercised and, right now, over-tense. He was the type you saw everywhere behind the wheel, eyes focused elsewhere, attention devoted to some inner worry. He and his vehicle were as bogus as everything else about Jasper's Cabs: but no one ever noticed.

The radio crackled, on cue.

'You're on, number eleven,' said Elphick quietly. 'Make your

19

own way over. The customer is waiting for you on the steps of the hotel.'

Evening was falling in the West End. Flynn had no need to jot down this message from out of the east. The cab nosed into the traffic. Headlights dipped. One of a thousand cabs moving through the heart of the city, black and gleaming in the November dusk. Just another job.

The cab circled round Soho Square. Past the film distributors and television companies. Down Frith Street. Into the moving river of lights on Shaftesbury Avenue. Bookshops, theatres, construction and destruction.

Held up for ten minutes around Piccadilly Circus. A blockage of cars, people and scaffolding. A policeman waving on the traffic, little dumper trucks scuttling up and down between the gaps. A supporting cast of thousands.

To the seasoned driver a delay is as good as a rest. No hurry. Money in the bank already.

Flynn eventually broke free and accelerated down Piccadilly. The radio crackled; Elphick arguing with another driver. Flynn shut it down. No distractions. Not this evening.

He stopped three times at the lights on Piccadilly. But each time his moving off was more abrupt.

When he reached Hyde Park Corner he had to make a conscious effort to slow the taxi down. It was going too fast. Since when did an empty taxi hurry anywhere? He must blend into the night, move calmly with the rhythm of the traffic. Find safety in anonymity.

Hundreds of vehicles were revolving around Hyde Park Corner. Dozens of taxis. Flynn slipped out at the Knightsbridge exit and turned along Kensington Road. The park lay to the right-hand side, a dark space in the centre of London, with trees picked out briefly by passing lights.

A left turn and there he was. On Gloucester Road. Crawling along. The lights dimmed. The meter off. Side window down. The hiss of evening drizzle. Silenced pistol protruding only very slightly.

Something happened outside the Friendship Hotel. Something strange. One moment everything was normal. The traffic going slowly past. The crowds moving along the pavement. Visitors to the hotel mingling round the lobby. Cabs pulling up to the kerb.

It was the shout that was the first odd thing. It was that which stayed in the memories of the witnesses when later they tried to explain what had happened. A shout. A moving taxi. And then an absence, a gap. A space where a man had been. A curious disappearance. Except that he was still there. On the ground. An Arab. By the kerb. A briefcase beside him.

Flynn was fifty yards away, part of the ever-flowing, un-stoppable stream, before the first scream rang out.

# Chapter Three

Fulbright liked young Molly to be in early. She had worked for him for eighteen months. She knew his likes and dislikes. His anxieties about his position. She knew that when he went home it was to a wife who made a point of being out most evenings. She knew that Fulbright viewed retirement with trepidation because it meant he and his wife must spend more time together. Fulbright had once said, in a roundabout way, that he saw more of Molly than Millicent, and she knew that he meant her to guess that he preferred it that way.

Molly could cope with Fulbright's crablike advances. She could see off the occasional blustering gallantries. The furtive glance out of the corner of the pink eye. It gave her a certain power over him.

She stood at the window, waiting for Fulbright's electric kettle to boil. The lights of the office were reflected in the panes of glass. Outside, Monday morning was still a shadowy, clouded thing, an almost hostile presence. The skyline was close since the office was on the tenth floor. The rooftop of the adjoining hotel was a jumble of outlets, struts, pylons, antennae, all mixed up with the reflections in the naked window.

She could see almost as far as Waterloo Bridge. The morning crowd advanced before her eyes, edging along the pavement one hundred and fifty feet below, spilling over into the street as umbrella met umbrella, but swiftly shepherded back into place by the traffic. The in crowd, they called it.

The kettle boiled. Fulbright was absorbed in his mail, scratching his beard for inspiration. Molly switched off the kettle, but she did not unplug it. Instead she rattled the mugs and spoons for a while, and then took a jug of cold water and doused the plants along the windowsill.

Colchester was late. He was always late on Mondays. She had looked up the train timetable. He could catch a different train seven minutes later and still be here just after nine-thirty if he ran from Waterloo. Was it worth it, she thought. Why not plan your life better? Why run when you can walk?

She tried to picture Colchester first thing in the morning, lumbering erratically around his flat, running a comb through his disordered hair, those frank and rather nice blue eyes darting to and from the clock while he gulped his coffee. It was pleasant for her to think idly of him in this way. But at the same time she often wondered what impulse it was that had brought him to this office in the first place.

A familiar figure appeared at the end of the street, three hundred yards away. In with the in crowd. Large. Bluff. Fair-haired. On the home straight. She switched the kettle on again and puffs of steam rose towards the ceiling.

Colchester, ascending in the lift, shook off the water clinging to his umbrella and overcoat. His briefcase contained a mass of undigested papers as well as a plastic lunch box, filled with sandwiches and fruit, prepared the previous evening. Yet it was not the weekend's incomplete work that nagged at the back of his mind. Nor was it the thought of tasks yet to perform this morning.

He passed Fulbright's office, noting with relief that Molly had engaged Fulbright's attention in making coffee, and swung into his own. Stanton's desk was laden with files sent up that morning from central records in Harlow. Stanton grunted, barely lifting his head from a ten-year-old tome. He had been commissioned by Fulbright to write a summary note of some Anglo-Italian trade talks and could spend days happily busy at this pointless task.

The question that nagged Colchester was: would that strange man ring today? Twice last week someone's secretary had rung him. Someone had spoken very briefly, been interrupted, and said he would call back. Someone who seemed to know exactly who he wanted. Who was reluctant to leave a telephone number. And who had finally said he would call back the following Monday.

Colchester unpacked his briefcase. Next he went to the safe he shared with Stanton and pulled out the files on which he had been working. He swiftly surveyed the subjects. More letters from members of the public about difficulties encountered trading overseas. Problems trying to get local officials to understand simple English. The outline of his contribution to the department's annual strategic plan for export promotion. Most urgently, and marked with a bright red 'Immediate' tag, a letter from a member of parliament to the minister complaining that a firm in his constituency, with which he had some personal connections, had not received all the support it might in bidding for – and failing to win – a contract in Turkey in the teeth of Italian competition. The draft reply to be up today.

Create a Ministry for Exports and you create a resting place for half the frustrations of British industry, Colchester reflected.

The telephone rang.

'Good morning, sunshine,' said Molly. 'Stay at home over the weekend, did you?'

'Here and there,' Colchester replied. 'In and out. Work on the bathroom ceiling.'

'Chasing the birds?'

'And that. Those that came out in the weather.'

'Which ones are those?'

'Tough ones. The all-weather types. Waterproof feathers.'

'Himself wants to see you. Not now. This afternoon. Three o'clock. Put it in your diary.'

Colchester had a go at drafting a reply to Alfred Weatherby MP. The trick was to catch the right tone. Everything possible being done. Hint at unfair advantages elsewhere. Possibilities of future business. Recollect past successes. Government can only do so much. Then up to individual companies. Will look out for further opportunities. Suggest keep in touch.

Stanton remained engrossed in his researches. He ploughed on through file after file, marking here, noting there. Colchester knew better than to talk to him about his work. Occasionally, peering over the rim of his mug of Oxo and shaking a puzzled, rather sheeplike head, Stanton would volunteer some comment on the matter in hand, the handwriting he was trying to decipher, the oddness of some expression. But Stanton kept locked away within himself the heart of his work. He jealously guarded his private territory, the slice of public affairs entrusted to him. The less he exposed of his doings the safer he was. The confidences he respected, the secrets he kept, might not amount to much but they would live and die with him. They reflected and magnified his own importance.

Most people in the office were rather like that. Most had compartments within which they worked. Few had a clear idea of what was happening elsewhere. Colchester had recently realized that he could not accurately describe the work of his colleagues only a few yards down the corridor, past the noticeboard. In theory there were office meetings, papers circulated in a common float. But in practice anyone who wished to keep themselves to themselves could do so. It was called the 'need to know' principle. I don't need. You don't know. Loose talk costs lives.

The telephone rang.

'Mr Colchester?' a male voice enquired. 'I was told to contact you by my office in Cyprus. Are you dealing with the credits for the Bosporus–Izmir railway link?'

Colchester reflected. Was he? He scanned the box of cards that contained the alphabetical index on his desk. He was.

'Yes. Can I help you?'

'I have to pass a message on. My name is Smalls. The message is to cancel the request which Polyform Ltd have submitted for coverage in drachmas. And transfer the facility to Swiss francs. Is that clear?'

'Perfectly, Mr Smalls. I shall note that.'

Smalls rang off. Colchester, slightly mystified, jotted on his pad. Cancel drachmas. That should be easy. Probably nothing had happened anyway. He suspected that Finance had contacted the Treasury or the Bank of England for clearance but had not yet received it. No problem with changing what did not exist.

He was rooting around for the relevant papers when the phone rang again. This time a woman's voice, distant. 'Mr de la Fosse on the line for you, Mr Colchester.'

'I beg your pardon?'

And then a silence. Or rather something like white noise. The impression of connections being made to a far-off planet. Like hearing the distant roar of the sea in a shell close to the ear.

Then a startlingly clear male voice. 'Good morning, Guy.'

'Hello. Do you know me?'

'Quite well, in fact, Guy. Quite well.'

'Did you try to call me last week?'

'It may have been someone working for me, Guy. I would not rule out the possibility.'

A military voice?

'Why did he break off?'

'The moment may not have been right. I could not say.'

25

'But today is different?'

'As you imply, Guy.'

Colchester looked across at Stanton. Still burrowing.

'So how can I help you?'

There was a pause.

'That is an interesting question. But not one, I fear, which we can go into on the open telephone.'

The open telephone?

'I'm sorry. I don't quite follow.'

'Better that we meet. Let us lunch. Where do you lunch?'

Where?

Colchester generally wolfed the sandwiches in his briefcase at his desk, pen in hand. But the speaker did not await a reply.

'Let us lunch today at my club. One o'clock. The Constitutional. Can you be there?'

What about the sandwiches? thought Colchester.

'I said, can you be there?'

A note of authority in the voice reminded Colchester of one of the senior officials in the department.

'Yes,' he said. 'Yes, I suppose I can.'

'Excellent. Then I shall see you there, Guy. Ask for de la Fosse.'

The line went dead. Colchester gently replaced the receiver. For the rest of the morning he tried to concentrate his thoughts on the affairs of Mr Alfred Weatherby MP.

The rain from heaven was dropping on many other places beneath in London that Monday morning in November. Dispassionate in its victims, it sought out not only the commuters of Northumberland Avenue but also the slightly different breed who thronged around an equally bland building off the Tottenham Court Road, part of which was known to its occupants as the cage. But here there was a certain studied wear and tear. A touch of the shabby-genteel. Don't bother with us, it seemed to say. Look the other way. We're up to a bit of no good, but don't mind us. We're all pals together, aren't we?

A somewhat bored young man named Stuart-Smith, wearing a well-made green tweed waistcoat rather as if he was just off to the races, stared gloomily out of the reinforced plate-glass window of the cage – as if, laughably, they needed protection from the sun – and watched the interesting effect of the morning light on the

Post Office Tower, its surfaces glittering against the darkening clouds. He seized his dictaphone and muttered into it the words he had learnt on his training course six long years before:

> The rain it raineth on the just
> And also on the unjust fella:
> But chiefly on the just, because
> The unjust steals the just's umbrella.

How many umbrellas had he stolen since then? Metaphorically speaking, you understand. Well, for a start there was that rather nice girl from the South African Embassy. PNG-ed she was, in the end. (And, if the truth be told, pregnant too.) And then there was Zbigniew what's-'is-name from Poland. The Man in the Iron Mask they called him. Another perfectly good career down the drain. He at least should have known better. And then there had been the regrettable case of Manuel, the gorilla, the killer from Manila . . .

Stuart-Smith sighed, stared at the mountain of papers on his desk, and rewound his tape. He loathed deskwork. When he joined the service no one had told him about it. And yet it was extraordinary just how much of it there was. The entire Warsaw Pact seemed to march through their files. He had a nightmare: he would spend ages reading through every single file they had and find, right at the very end, buried beneath the lot, a succinct signal announcing that Bonn had capitulated two days previously. He shook his well-groomed head, assumed a voice of mock dignity and this time intoned: 'Section RB report for month ended October. Indent following. Sightings: nil. Technicals: nil. Proximity approaches: four. Near encounters: seven. Appraisals: three. Distant relations: twelve. Wolverhampton Wanderers: five. Hamilton Academicals: three.'

He paused, rewound and erased the last section of tape and resumed: 'Loss of memory: one. Walk-ins: nil. Indent again. Liaison with MRO Unit proceeding as planned. Nothing to report. Indent again. Future activities . . .'

Here Stuart-Smith laid down his dictaphone and reflected. This was the really hard part. The justification of his existence. The bit where – under the new thinking – you had to give value for money. What is your value added? he remembered the trainers tried to drum into them. What is your return on capital? How are you satisfying your clients? Are the customers happy? In particular: *is Madam being served?* Stuart-Smith wondered, not for the first time, if it had been like this in the war . . .

The buzzer sounded on his desk, the blue one beside the signed photograph of Gorbachov (courtesy of the Soviet Embassy).

The call to glory.

Pleased to be distracted from his distasteful task, Stuart-Smith stood up at his desk and walked over to the coat stand. He unhooked his green tweed jacket and put it on, revealing the poster which he had once abstracted from Sloane Square tube station, and which he had proudly put on the wall:

ARE YOU LEGAL? DECENT? HONEST AND TRUTHFUL?

With the words of the Advertising Standards Authority giving him their usual inspiration, Stuart-Smith opened the door of his office (one office per officer: no nonsense about open plan here – bad for security) and made his way down to the chief's office (*Chef de Bureau? Bureau de Chef?* he asked himself). He paused outside for a moment, secured the middle button of his jacket, knocked four times for form's sake (Beethoven's Fifth) and went in.

Fergusson, sitting at his desk, was already looking at his watch. He was a thin, lean, tanned man in his fifties. Background Hong Kong and Rhodesia, then a translation from the colonies to the defence of the home front. He had supervised the eastern watches for a decade now. Few things upset Stuart-Smith, but Fergusson could still inspire in him a certain sense of fear. Fergusson's office was understated, but a portrait of Churchill behind the desk and a framed manuscript note from the Queen were just two of his secret trophies.

'Alan, I have to see our lords and masters in five minutes.'

'F Committee?'

'Q Committee.'

'I see.' Stuart-Smith exuded the proper degree of sympathy.

'These wretched objectives,' went on Fergusson. 'We have to submit a joint return after all.'

'But I thought—'

'I know.' Fergusson stood up, buttoning his jacket. 'It transpires that Fitzgerald was unsighted when he saw the committee last week. He sold the pass.'

'And that means . . .'

'And that means we have to seek a further mandate. I'm propos-ing camping on last year's objectives.'

Stuart-Smith thought back through all those very confusing messages they had been getting this year, back through those disagreements among the analysts . . .

'They might say times are changing.'

'Pure sophistry,' replied Fergusson smoothly, striding over to his personal safe. 'Can the leopard change his spots? Or the Ethiop his hue?'

'Or the Warsaw Pact its battle plan?'

'Precisely.' Fergusson pulled out a yellow departmental folder. 'I have five solid quotations from Lenin to back me up, if we get any trouble from the Treasury.'

'And you want me to . . . ?'

'Look at your own objectives again, Alan. You'll see I've recast them a little. Made them more – robust.'

Fergusson handed the folder over, and then sat down again.

Stuart-Smith looked at the sheet of paper pinned to his own typed minute to Fergusson, dated only two days ago, on which he had written: 'Our objective therefore in the next twelve-month period should be to cultivate liaison relationships with likely targets from Central and Eastern European countries . . .' Fergus-son had substituted: 'Our aim must continue to be to combat hostile forces throughout these isles, and work with all like-minded agencies in doing so.'

Stuart-Smith reflected. 'It's simpler.'

'It's better. Here, take it away and get it amended.'

Fergusson ticked his name off the minute, wrote, 'We spoke' beside it, initialled it, dated it and gave it back to Stuart-Smith. He paused and looked up at Stuart-Smith with his pale grey eyes.

'Just remember, Alan, that sometimes the best can be the enemy of the good.'

'Oh, quite.'

Stuart-Smith thought of a further year stretching ahead. More hot pursuit. More eviction notices. More activities 'incompatible with your status, sir, if you understand our meaning'. More, on the other hand of that red-headed cipher clerk at the Soviet Embassy, the one who liked Solzhenitsyn. Enjoy it while it lasts, he told himself.

Because he knew, as did Fergusson, that something was rotten

29

in the state of Stalin. The arguments had been raging freely now for eighteen months. The majority view was that never before in the history of the Soviet Union had the military machine been so finely tuned, so overwhelming, so dangerous, so capable of simply rolling forward out of its barracks one fine morning and obliterating the rest of Europe. According to this view the SS20s were just the first instalment, a downpayment in a final massive effort to annex the western countries as they had once annexed the east. And so they were living through the time of maximum danger, vulnerable, weak, the soft decadent democracies who agreed on nothing, the blind mice squabbling while the cat sharpened its claws. The CIA of course practically wrote this script.

But there was also the minority view, propounded most notably by that guru Featherstone from the Royal College of Defence Studies and secretly shared by one or two unconventional spirits – maybe even by one or two Treasury cut-throats. It went as follows: look at Chacoa; look at the Maya; look at the western Roman Empire in the fifth century AD. There comes a point where all complex societies become *too* complex. Their bureaucracy becomes too bloated. Their military sector grows too big to feed. They drain more and more from their economy in taxes and levies. They are vulnerable to shocks, to crises, to the very wear and tear of history. They use up their reserves. They eat into their operating budget. And – this was the point – sooner or later they collapse. Chacoa, the Mayans, Rome – all societies that collapsed because they became too difficult to run. Because they outgrew their support economy.

Now have a second look at the Soviet Union. The collectivization of agriculture. The central planning of industry. The fixing of countless numbers of prices by the state. The planned allocation and transfer of trade by Comecon. The feeding, clothing, washing, housing, bankrolling of the entire military industrial establishment. In fact, altogether, the most complex society ever known. Just running the Soviet Union for a week made the Strategic Defence Initiative seem like simplicity itself. The supercomputer that could make such a system work had yet to be invented.

And so – some argued – it was all going to collapse. Sooner or later it would go the way of Rome. And then – who knew what was going to happen?

And, speaking of SDI, it was impossible not to make the connection with what was now taking place in the talks between Washington and Moscow in a certain town on the continent . . .

'Would there be any developments in the Geneva Group that we should take into account here?' Stuart-Smith asked innocently.

Fergusson did not reply immediately. He stood up and crossed the room to lock his safe. With his back to Stuart-Smith he said softly, 'I think not, Alan. You know that we have no official awareness at all of the Geneva Group. Any written material from here could well end up with the Americans. That could be . . . suicide . . . at this stage.'

Stuart-Smith nodded slowly.

It was not the least of the ironies in this age of ironies that they had no *locus* (as Fergusson put it) in what was probably the most radical attempt to rethink defence since the end of the war. Probably the most radical and certainly the most secret. And – to those who were not supposed to be party to the discussions in Geneva – absolutely the most unsettling. Because those talks had recently taken on a most disturbing turn, impelled by the prospect of the approaching December deadline.

It was good, of course, that they had their source of information. But that source was not one that they could exactly quote in a Defence White Paper . . .

Stuart-Smith shrugged his shoulders. It was not his job to worry about these things. He was concerned with facts, not theories. The means, not the end. The operations, not the grand design. It was much more satisfying.

Fergusson opened the door, let Stuart-Smith out first, and locked it behind them.

'*Bon courage,*' said Stuart-Smith as Fergusson strode off down the corridor, his jaw clenched, files under his arm, a member of the warrior class going into battle.

# Chapter Four

The dark recesses of a London club. Darkness in light. The palmy
expansive entrance. White stucco on the outside walls. A reception desk lit up, the brass fittings glowing like the sun. A green
carpet stretching away. To either side doorways off. Pools of light
in the distance picking out the rich colours of oil paintings, the
pale shades of watercolours. Healthy, tanned old squires chatting
with bishops and tippling at champagne. The aroma of roast beef,
port, cigars and books. A ginger cat sneaking into the library. Past
all these, through many rooms, Colchester was led. On and on.
Beyond the coffee room, beyond the silence room, to where a few
old gentlemen sipped their claret at separate tables, reading their
newspapers or musing on the slowly turning world. And at the
far end, in a recess among the books, a standard lamp shone
down over a table laid for two, highlighting the silver, making the
redness of the wine glow faintly, and throwing into relief every
line on the thoughtful face of de la Fosse. An English gentleman
in an English gentleman's hiding place.

'Guy!' de la Fosse beamed. He stood, a tall, distinguished fellow
in the prime of life, extended a friendly hand and summoned an
aperitif from a passing waiter in one rapid, complicated movement.

Colchester tried to size de la Fosse up. A mobile, expressive face
beneath short greying hair, equine in its structure, the eyes alert,
darting naturally this way and that, then also, as if at will, ceasing
to move and resting, fixed upon Colchester with acute concentration. A face, in fact, whose every feature looked superbly in
training, ready to assume the attitude demanded by its owner. A
courtier's face, perhaps? At present it registered sympathy, welcome, even a touch of conspiratorial piracy. The strong body too,
clad in a finely cut light-grey suit, inclined to a posture signifying
poised friendliness, a controlled balance of forces.

'You must take a seat. You have arrived just in time. I suppose
you took a taxi?'

'No. A bus,' replied Colchester, experiencing for the first but not the last time the sensation of receiving the ball from an unexpected quarter of the court.

'Ha! Much more sensible.'

'Why?'

'You can't trust taxis any more. Too many go to the wrong place. Too many don't go anywhere.'

In the weeks to come Colchester was to recall this opening observation. But for the moment it meant nothing.

The waiter reappeared and de la Fosse busied himself ordering two regal lunches. He seemed well acquainted with the internal secrets of the club kitchen. Then he turned his amiable gaze to Colchester.

'Tell me about yourself, Guy.'

Colchester decided it was time to return the service.

'No. Perhaps you could tell me about yourself. How do you know who I am? What do you do? And why have you asked me here?'

'How long have you got?'

'What do you mean? I have a meeting at three.'

'What sort of meeting?'

'An important meeting.'

'With whom?'

'My head of department.'

'That sort of meeting. Sounds very important. I shouldn't worry, Guy. We can see to that. Now, enjoy your lunch.'

De la Fosse would only chat urbanely of this and that as they made their way through the meal. Over the devilled kidneys, through the tournedos en croûte and until the end of a bottle of club claret he preserved something like radio silence, emitting only the briefest of signals to placate an increasingly restive Colchester.

After the raspberry pavlova de la Fosse summoned two cigars and asked Colchester whether he would like a brandy.

'A smidgeon, if you like.'

'It takes only a smidgeon to poison a pigeon,' murmured de la Fosse.

'I beg your pardon?'

'Tom Lehrer. American singer.'

Blue cigar clouds billowed across the lunch table and hung, like layers of mist, between them in the alcove. De la Fosse stared keenly at Colchester for a moment through the fog, as if calculating a ranging shot.

'I must apologize for being discreet,' he began.

Colchester watched him in return but said nothing.

'You will understand why in a moment. You work in one branch of government. You understand the complicated nature of official business. The nature of discretion. Well, there are many mansions in the house of the Lord. You work in one. I happen to work in another.'

'You?'

Colchester surveyed the remnants of the munificent lunch. The empty bottle. The two handsome, slowly burning cigars. It had not occurred to him that these riches might have come from the public purse.

De la Fosse stared thoughtfully at the lighted end of his own cigar. Without shifting his gaze he said quietly, 'What, Guy, do you know of the Secret Service?'

Colchester jerked upright in his seat and almost knocked his brandy glass to the ground.

'The what?'

De la Fosse drew on his cigar and exhaled slowly, almost vanishing behind the smoke.

'The word within a word, unable to speak a word,' he murmured to himself. Then he looked direct at Colchester.

'I shall not repeat myself. I think you heard me perfectly well. If you did not . . . then you need not stay, Guy. You can go home in a cloud of unknowing.'

Colchester remained rooted, sitting bolt upright, his heart beating slightly faster. He took a sip of brandy.

De la Fosse let amiability drain from his features, and they assumed, imperceptibly, a hard, resolute cast.

'On the assumption that you stay, I am now going to talk about purely hypothetical circumstances. Imaginary events. Situations that do not exist. I do not see any movement. Good. Now, let us be frank. What *do* you know?'

'Precisely nothing,' said Colchester.

De la Fosse took another puff and nodded, as if this was the correct reply.

'As I would expect. You have no need to know, therefore you do not know.'

Colchester seized on this. 'No need to know. They say that at the department. That's what they tell you if you ask what is happening on the next floor, or in the next office.'

De la Fosse nodded again. Again the right answer.

'Exactly, Guy. It is a universal principle. Everyone works in compartments. You have your compartment. Somewhere else in the ministry someone else is working in another compartment. And the strange thing is the compartments extend beyond your ministry. There are compartments you would never have dreamed existed. Compartments you will never know about. And, just once in a while, a compartment like yours and a compartment like mine bump up against each other. And we do business with one another.'

'What do you mean – business?'

De la Fosse smiled. 'We cannot go quite so quickly, Guy. You are intelligent. You will pick up the threads by and by. For the time being, I think all you need to know is that there exists a demand for the particularly astute and resourceful public servant. The type who can do not just the work that is ordinary, but the work that is extraordinary. Special work. Work demanding a high level of ability. A high level of courage. There are rewards. They are few. But they exist. They could be yours.'

He puffed on his cigar once again.

Colchester was silent. Had he actually been *waiting* for something such as this? A summons to progress into the next phase of the priesthood? Beyond the thickets where you trained in the stoic arts, the love of patience, the discreet skills of marshalling facts, figures, arguments, the silent mastery of difficult problems. And into the sacred grove where the final mysteries lay. Then he thought back to the office. The draft answer waiting for Alfred Weatherby MP. The meeting with Fulbright due at three. Three! He looked at his watch. Ten past three already. Never had he been so late after lunch.

De la Fosse noticed Colchester's agitation. Sympathy crept back into his features.

'I shouldn't worry overmuch about your meeting,' he said quietly. 'We will take care of your absence. I do not think you will be troubled.'

'What makes you so sure?'

'Never mind. We have our contacts within the administration.

Now, I have a simple proposition to put. Then you may go. I want you to consider whether you are interested in performing special duties. I just want you to think it over. Think of it this afternoon, tonight, tomorrow, whenever. Think of it seriously. Think of it when doing your bird watching. Or when writing your piece for *British Birds*.'

'You know about that?'

'A little. I would not have approached you without some spadework, Guy. What is your title? I forget.'

'"The Psychology of the Pheasant",' Colchester mumbled.

'Ah, yes. A most learned monograph, no doubt. I wish it well. Now then, what I want you to do is to contact me if you feel you would like to accept my challenge. But you will understand that, one way or another, I would appreciate it if you would not mention this conversation to anyone else. Will you at least do that?'

Colchester hesitated an instant. 'Well, if you insist.'

'For now, I will give you a telephone number. Use it to re-establish contact. Any time of the day or night. After sufficient mental preparation. And remember, ripeness is all, Guy.'

With another rapid gesture de la Fosse had signed for the meal, left a small plain white card on the table and was standing beside Colchester offering him his hand to shake. He smiled, and into that smile he seemed to Colchester to inject a note of conspiracy. This is my club, it said. Look around. Do you want to join?

'Think seriously about this,' de la Fosse repeated. 'There are very few people whom I would turn to as I have turned to you.'

He then stole off into one of the side rooms of the club, apparently as unemployed that afternoon as any of the country squires who lounged among the potted palms or who tickled the ear of the passing ginger cat in a languid fashion.

Out on the pavement the afternoon clouds were breaking. Already a light or two had been switched on. Colchester breathed the freshening November air deeply. The fumes of brandy dissipated. He felt in his pocket for the sharp outline of the little card and plunged off down the street.

Stanton, returning from the office meeting, noted that Fulbright had let Colchester's absence pass without comment. Stanton resumed his work, mildly curious that Colchester had not opened his briefcase before going off for lunch several hours ago. The sandwiches and fruit he'd brought clearly would not last. Stanton picked up his pen and continued with his record of the Anglo-Italian trade talks.

'The British side undertook to investigate with a view to establishing the bona fides or otherwise of the complaints by the Italian side regarding the counterfeiting of textile imports from Milan. The Italian side noted this assurance. Turning to the question of cement substitutes, both sides agreed that insufficient data had been forthcoming from the Italian customs authorities . . .'

# Chapter Five

The day after his meeting with de la Fosse was a particularly trying one for Colchester.

To start with, the Alfred Weatherby correspondence did not go well. Fulbright rejected his first draft in a summary fashion, complaining it was 'too short'. Colchester thus had to spend the greater part of the morning inflating his draft reply, like a tired old balloon. He added wordy sentiments, inserted unnecessary adjectives and adverbs and puffed up empty excuses. He hoped that Alfred Weatherby would appreciate getting the bureaucratic equivalent of the red carpet treatment.

And, all the time, he could not help thinking about de la Fosse. His knowledge that somewhere out there a shadowy but acute intelligence was present gave a strange perspective to everyday life. All of a sudden an entirely new dimension to bureaucratic existence had been opened up. As well as the normal three dimensions of the office there was now this hidden fourth dimension, an inner reality. Invisible except to those few aware of its presence.

So when Fulbright went painstakingly through his revised draft letter, jabbing his cheap biro here and there and making the style even more sententious than before, Colchester was conscious of a certain sense of detachment. If Fulbright was such hot stuff with a pen why was *he* not chosen for special duties?

He also looked at Stanton with fresh eyes. As ever, Stanton was deep in his work. Could it be that he – Stanton – was in some way in touch with this ulterior universe? Colchester could readily imagine Stanton undertaking wartime duties. In a bombed-out ruined farmhouse somewhere he could picture Stanton, the radio operator, painstakingly tapping out signals in Morse, pausing from his duties only to sip gingerly from his ration of wartime Oxo. In some ways Stanton seemed to represent that spirit of dogged determination, of doing one's duty in the face of adversity. But his duties today were surely not the same. The adversity was more that of an indifferent bureaucracy than an enemy in war. And what were the signals which Stanton tuned in to today? Export statistics, industrial indicators, economic facts and figures. Could Stanton tell the difference? Could he read and understand his own messages? Or was he content simply to tap, tap, tap his way through the baffling undergrowth of life?

And the curious thing was that Stanton could not possibly remember the war. It would have been his father who had seen active service. The father who was said to live a secluded, lunatic existence, locked into an era now past, reliving each day his glorious moments of wartime heroism. Ministered to by a son who dwelt cannily in the peace which his generation had procured.

So Stanton was a mystery. Whether he was part of this other mystery which Colchester had come up against was impossible to say.

Colchester's second difficulty that day was over Molly.

'Nothing like a good long lunch, I always say,' she had observed, when they first passed in the corridor that morning.

Later that day, when standing beside the photocopier, she returned to the theme.

'Understanding of himself not to make a fuss. Unlike him too. One phone call from someone and he's sweet as pie. Did you enjoy yourself?'

'Business lunch, Molly. Enjoy isn't the word for it. Merchant prince of the usual kind.'

'All out to lunch. Very nice. Very sweet.'

Molly paused to collect her batch of papers. She looked at Colchester.

'I'll bet you'll never guess what I'm copying here.'

Colchester glanced without interest at the official forms in her hand.

'Someone's personal report?'

'Almost there. But not just someone's. It's *yours*. And . . .' she made a play of scanning it while shielding it from Colchester, '. . . it's not a very good one, I'm sorry to say. Could do better, it says. Could show more application and attention to detail.'

'Hey!' protested Colchester. 'You're not supposed to read those things!'

'I was doing it just for you. To give you advance warning. Stop you from getting a nasty surprise.'

'Well, thanks for nothing. There are some things I'd rather not know about.'

Colchester stumped back to his office.

Molly paused awhile at the machine, busy with her papers. She sighed. What was the use? She had been half in love and half out of love with Colchester for about six months now. But he was being very difficult.

She was twenty-five. She lived in Tooting Bec. She was a good typist and a good secretary. She had been told she would go far in the Ministry of Exports. But she had little intention of staying there much longer. During the wet months of autumn she had been saving up her pennies for that little New Year's holiday. She'd get a bit of experience in under Fulbright and move on to something better with a good reference. It was only Colchester, really, who provided any interest at the office. He, at least, had remembered her birthday. He had produced a card from somewhere during the course of Friday. It was signed 'love, Guy'. You never knew.

Just now, Colchester was thinking more about what Molly had said than about Molly.

Another bad report! He really could do without these things. It was strange, but they never seemed to get any better. He suspected that someone in the higher management was just copying out the previous year's report, changing the dates but keeping the main observations. Sheer laziness, really.

He'd noticed that once you were set on one track in this business you seemed to keep on it for ever. Try as you might, it was impossible to shake off the trappings of mediocrity. They followed you everywhere: to your meetings, to your coffee breaks, home on the train. What on earth would his father say? But yet not everywhere. Someone, somewhere, had spotted that extra something. That extra spark which meant you were fit for special duties.

Molly put her head round the door and smiled.

'Something else for you to think about. He's had another go at Alfred Weatherby. I'm typing it up. Just look at his scrawl!'

Fulbright had crossed out most of Colchester's redraft. He had substituted some near-illegible scribble which ran all over the page and on to a separate sheet. Colchester recognized the style: the fast, furious jottings of an exasperated Fulbright.

Molly withdrew with a merry giggle. Colchester fiddled around with his paper clips for half an hour or so and brooded on his future, while Stanton brought his day's labours to a close. When Stanton had finally left to catch his train to Wembley Colchester got up, closed the door, and fished from his pocket the small white card with a telephone number on it.

As he lifted the receiver and dialled the number, some rather odd electronic connections shifted into place. Like railway signal points that switched the routes of suburban trains, the lines of communication crossed over and led out to an utterly different world.

For someone who had such traditional habits, de la Fosse lived in a decidedly modernist environment.

To his left was a bank of telephones, to his right a desktop computer with monitor screen. A videophone. Two scramblers. A document faxlink with encoder. Behind him was a safe, the door studded with tiny yellow lights.

He was for all the world like some international currency dealer. But de la Fosse was not just playing the markets.

His office was built into the very heart of a converted Georgian town house on the fringes of the City. A machine for living, carved out of antiquity itself. Set in concrete and steel far beneath the tiles and stucco, beneath the oak and walnut, beyond the view of the antiquarian and the prying senses of the electronic detector.

Here new money and old lived together. The house was built on the fortunes of the tea trade, and had seen the decline of commerce and the old money ebb away, far overseas. The domestic wealth had been taxed from one generation to the next until the house was naked, alone, unsupported by income, an asset shifting to a liability. And today bought up by a new generation plying a modern profession. Instead of a vast network of tea clippers crossing the seas, rounding the Horn, a new breed with a network of communications bearing other cargo, flashing far quicker round the globe.

'Get me Tewkesbury. On the open line.'

'Yes, Mr de la Fosse.'

His secretary put through the connection, setting in train the fibre optics of the communication system.

Tewkesbury was in New York.

41

'Hello, de la Fosse.' His mid-Atlantic voice came through a moment later.

'What's the latest?'

'Hard to say. Spot is down but three month is firming. I'd say the market is digesting the Tripoli communiqué without too much difficulty. Gold is weakening as a consequence.'

'Good. Get out of gold, slowly. Move the reserves into yen, Deutsche Marks and dollars in that order over the next week. Call me when fifty-one per cent has been transferred.'

'As usual, de la Fosse.'

The line went dead.

De la Fosse turned back to the paperwork on his desk. Before him lay a series of jottings on a pad. He had drawn connecting lines between blocks of phrases. Lines of argument. Lines of attack. Lines of retreat.

He stared in silence at his notes for a couple of minutes, as if assembling his thoughts, then picked up his dictaphone. He lifted his eyes, looked into the middle distance, switched on the machine and spoke in a slow voice.

'People often ask me what it is that ails this country of ours. Ladies and gentlemen, I suggest that the answer is not a simple one. If it were, I do not think that generation after generation would have been preoccupied by it. If it were a simple matter of passing better laws I rather think our politicians would have found the answer by now.

'No, ladies and gentlemen, for anyone who has studied the inner workings of our economy – for anyone, that is, who has worked, as I have, in finance – I suggest the cause is more profound.

'Ladies and gentlemen, let me suggest to you that we have failed collectively to make a distinction between capital and current expenditure. We are too prone to consume wealth. We are less keen to save it. We devote billions to current consumption and we neglect to transfer resources to productive investment. Investment so that future generations can produce future consumer goods. Instead we want the world and we want it now . . .'

The light flashed on the daily cipher. De la Fosse let it blink for five seconds before putting down his dictaphone and picking up the receiver. The beams of light glowed a faint crimson down the fibres beneath the house.

'Sheffield here,' came a robotic voice. 'Am I disturbing you?'

De la Fosse pressed switch number fourteen. Then he spoke. 'Surrey here, Sheffield. No, you're not disturbing me. I was working on my party piece. Thanks for calling back. Our friend Colchester has been in touch. He thinks he will and he thinks he won't. He doesn't quite know what he wants to do. But he doesn't like what he's doing now.'

'Sounds to me as if he is in a pre-recruitment phase.'

'I agree. Incubating a marked tendency to come aboard.'

'Congratulations. Tell me, Surrey, do you get a bonus for every new member you introduce?'

De la Fosse smiled. 'It's a living. But it's a team achievement. I'm only the door-to-door salesman. I wouldn't know which door to knock on if I didn't have good support. And Colchester hasn't climbed aboard yet. We'll need a little time. Which, as always, is something we haven't got. But that's my problem. Anyway, keep the lines open at your end.'

'I will. I'll follow this one with interest. I don't think we've ever done anything quite like this before.'

'I don't think anyone has. It won't last long. We know that. But will it last long enough? That's the thing.'

'What happens next?'

'I'm thinking about it. Another direct contact, perhaps. I'll let you know.

'Going off now.'

'Going off.'

De la Fosse released number fourteen. He picked up his dictaphone again but then, seeming to think better of it, put it back down. Instead he got up from behind his desk, a tall, soldierly figure, and strode across to his secretary and bodyguard.

'I'm going into the operations room, Judith.'

'Yes, sir.'

She opened the metal door.

The operations room of UK Centre resembled in some degree the dealing room of a large stockbroking firm: the same workstations, the same banks of screens, the same chattering of telexes and human voices. But UK Centre had no more than twenty staff, constrained in number by the cramped space hollowed out beneath the house thirty feet underground. Despite its underground location, the lighting and air-conditioning systems gave

43

those who worked there as good an office environment as most people inhabiting more conventional quarters.

De la Fosse passed the UK and Northern Europe work-stations. As he did so the operators stiffened slightly in their seats, but went on with what they were doing. He passed Southern Europe and Northern Africa, Eastern Europe and Western Asia and finally, at the other end of the horseshoe, arrived at Eastern Mediterranean, by far the largest station.

Station Chief Turner stood up to greet de la Fosse.

'Spectroscopic analysis confirms it was no petrol dump exploding, sir.'

De la Fosse looked at the graph paper offered by Turner.

'So we know it was a missile?'

'We don't know that for certain yet.'

'But leaving aside spontaneous combustion it is the only reasonable supposition.'

'Yes, sir. The satellite photographs show an unusually elongated crater, as if the strike came in low and hard. And, of course, taking bearings from the angle of debris the flight path goes directly back to Al Tadj.'

De la Fosse leaned over the shoulder of Pearson, the desk officer, and looked at the enlarged map on the screen. A red line joined the village of Zab to the suspected missile silos of Al Tadj, only forty-three kilometres away to the east. The red line indicated the presumed flight path of an unusual missile.

De la Fosse reflected a moment.

'So now they use their own villages for target practice. Vengeance? A vendetta? Another schism between the true believers? Or a mistake? Whatever it is, it confirms we were absolutely right about Al Tadj. They have the capacity . . . They won't know what effect they're having on the enemy. But, by God, they must terrify each other . . .'

# Chapter Six

'What is a country?' asked Colchester, having to raise his voice.

Over in the far corner of the Coach and Horses – a somewhat misnamed pub standing beside a busy roundabout near the centre of Croydon – the night's band were warming up. They were now into the second number of their set. The moaning and whining of their suburban cowboy music was beginning to drown out the clinking of glasses, and a few disconsolate customers had drifted closer to watch the action.

Terry, a rather clerical-looking young man of twenty-five who was sitting on a stool facing Colchester, jerked his thumb in the direction of the loudspeakers.

'That is,' he said.

Colchester looked blankly at him for a moment. Then he got it. 'Not country. A country.'

'A country?'

Terry reflected.

'A country, I would say, is a place where you live.'

'Is that all?'

Now Terry looked blank. 'What more do you want?'

Colchester looked around the spacious pub as if for inspiration. It was divided into several bars, each selling their own special variety of lager and weak beer. People said that London pubs were no good. That wasn't strictly true. They were at least better than suburban pubs. All the same, he and Terry sometimes came here for a drink in the evening. There was really nowhere else. Another consequence of living for the public good: Colchester had decided that if he was going to have to live as his father wished he might as well get used to the terrain.

'If it's just a place you live in what makes it different from a town or a city? Or a village?'

'It isn't different from a town or a city or a village.'

'It is. A country is something more. A country has *power*.'

'So has a town. A borough council can be a proper little dictator-ship. Take it from me.'

Terry worked in nearby Croydon Town Hall. He married people. And he registered their births and deaths. Not a soul could change status in his district without him getting to know about it.

'But a country can ask things of you. It can make you go to war, if it wants to. A town hall can't do that.'

Terry's eyes glinted. He put down his drink. 'Well, you know my views. Make London nuclear free.'

Terry also laboured on the wilder fringes of one of the public sector trade unions, and had already stood for office unsuccessfully three times at his local branch. In his filing cabinet at work, next to the marriage registers, back copies of *Redder Tape* accumulated for distribution to the faithful. A regular topic of their weekly conversation was when, if ever, Colchester was going to join the flock.

The music stumbled to a close with a final drum roll. Some desultory clapping filled the sudden silence.

Colchester took a drink.

'A country can't be the same as a town. It has to be something more.'

'What is it then?'

How could he put it into words?

'People have always disagreed,' Colchester said. 'We went over all the theory at Edinburgh. Is a nation the same as a country? Is a state the same as a nation? Is the citizen answerable to the state? Is the state answerable to the citizen?'

He thought back to those old unread lecture notes sitting gather-ing dust in a box in his flat. Forgotten for so long. Forgotten, that is, until the night before, when, prompted by some impulse, he had tried to follow up a train of thought that had begun when he had first spoken to de la Fosse.

'So what's the answer?' asked Terry.

'They never told us,' Colchester admitted. 'If you say the state is the most important you're halfway on the road to Hitler. If you say the state doesn't matter, what's the difference between sweeping the roads and fighting in an army?'

'Good question. What is the difference?'

'There *has* to be one. Otherwise . . .'

'Otherwise?'

'How could there be many mansions in the house of the Lord?'

As Colchester was speaking the music began again with a crash.

Terry looked puzzled. 'The House of Lords? Where do they come in?'

'Not the House of Lords . . .' said Colchester over the din.

But Terry was off.

'You've put your finger on the real issue there. In this day and age, with all the problems everyone has, for that collection of overpaid old . . .'

'I'm not talking about them,' interrupted Colchester.

'Then what are you talking about?'

'I'm talking about . . . special responsibilities, service for the country, doing your duty. Where exactly do you draw the line?'

'Draw the line?' Terry pondered. 'If it's a question of overtime, then it's all set out in the statutes . . .'

'Not overtime. At least not exactly overtime. At least . . . I don't know.'

Terry looked squarely at Colchester.

'How *is* the job going?' he asked.

Colchester thought for a moment. Then he said, 'Did I ever tell you about the Anglepoise lamp?'

'No.'

'Well, it was shortly after I arrived. I was in a gloomy office. Badly lit. I could hardly see what I was writing. So I decided to do something about it. I rang up the office supplies department. A complete newcomer. I got an old hand at the other end.

'I introduced myself as a new entrant. I said I couldn't see my desk properly to work at. I said what I needed was an Anglepoise lamp. Could they supply one, please?

'There was a sharp intake of breath at the other end.

' "An Anglepoise lamp? An Anglepoise lamp? What grade did you say you were?"

' "I'm a new entrant. An Executive Officer."

' "An Executive Officer? You need to be at least an Assistant Secretary before we can issue you with an Anglepoise lamp."

'I looked down at my papers. It was getting dark. By this time I could hardly see my hand in front of my face.

' "But I'll be blind by the time I get to be an Assistant Secretary."

'I heard a chuckle.

' "Well, in that case, you won't need any Anglepoise lamp!"

'He then put the phone down.'

Terry chuckled.

'But what do you expect from that kind of place?'

Colchester looked thoughtful. 'My father thought there was such a thing as the public good. A mission to improve the country.'

Terry shook his head. 'That was then. This is now. There isn't anything of that kind any more. He was wrong and you're deluding yourself.'

'Perhaps. Perhaps not. I'm still looking, that's all.'

'Well,' continued Terry, 'when you realize you're wasting your time and you want to jump ship, you know where you can find me. Get out quick while you can, I say.'

'I know where I can find you. If I'm desperate. How is the Object Museum going, by the way?'

'Fine. I added an office calculator to it last week. A classic of its kind.'

As well as having a taste for politics Terry collected things. Literally, things. He had once been impressed to discover an antique shop in Kensington that was full of twentieth-century objects, many of them from an epoch that even he could remember. The idea had then struck him that the time would come when future generations would want to collect the sorts of things which were now everyday objects. All that was needed was to store away good samples and he would have a guaranteed nest egg. Hence the idea of the Object Museum. Terry was patiently filling a lock-up garage in Croydon with pristine household objects.

'Would you be in the market for a nearly new Toyota?' Colchester asked. 'A classic of its kind.'

'What, yours?'

'Careful driver. Full of character. Authentic period features. Genuine antique.'

'I'll give you a valuable two-year-old toothbrush for it, if you like.'

'Throw in a packet of razors and it's yours.'

Terry shook his head.

'No. They're quite valuable, those razors of mine. The trouble is there's too much junk about. That's what a country is, if you want to know. It's a big collection of junk waiting for someone to sort it out. At least this one is. It won't last. Mostly junk. It'll all vanish one day without anyone noticing.'

The band played on.

'Which is more, I should say, than *she* will,' Terry continued.

'Who?'

'Girl over at the other bar. Pretending to listen to the music. With the ferret in the leather jacket.'

Colchester glanced over. A couple of newcomers were sitting on bar stools, slightly apart from the crowd around the band. He was nondescript. A fish in his water. A tired tour guide taking a client round the sights. Or a taxi driver having a moment off. She was the client. The passenger. A dark-haired Kensington girl, with SW3 clothes, looking in to see what was going on on the other side of town – and not thinking much of it. In some way she managed to hold herself apart from the man. Apart, in fact, from everyone else. She sipped what looked like a neat whisky, while her companion gripped his glass of thin lager.

'Now there's the genuine article,' said Terry.

'And you should know,' said Colchester.

'That's right. I've an eye for these things. You don't see many of them down this way. Just once in a while you turn one up. Collector's item. That kind of woman makes you feel alive. But then – bing! – she walks off and that's the last you see of her.'

Colchester glanced over again.

'I wonder . . .' he said thoughtfully. 'I wonder what you have to do to win a woman like that.'

'Rob a bank. Cheat. Lie. The usual. We're talking class warfare here. Serious crime.'

'Maybe. There's something real there.'

'A real little madam. Don't look now.'

'What?'

'I can see in that mirror over there. Behind you.'

'What?'

'I don't know. I could swear she was looking at you, just for a moment. I'm serious. She has her eye on you.'

'Why me?'

'Exactly. Why you? Why not me? If a woman like that looked at me in the same way that she just looked at you, I'd be straight over and . . . Oh, there they go.'

Across the room the girl and the man got up, leaving their glasses on the bar – his, curiously, half full – and started to make their way out.

Colchester watched the girl move fastidiously around the rest of the customers, leading the way. Then the doors swung open and they vanished into the night.

'You see what I mean?' said Terry.

# Chapter Seven

The Projects Committee met again. It was Thursday morning. Ranged on one side of the table in the fourth-floor conference room was, as usual, the Deputy Permanent Secretary, Garrick; the Under Secretary in charge of Finance, Hopkins-Joyce; the Chief Economist, Brownlow; the head of Finance, Simpkins; and the twin advisers, Marsh and Barnes, who covered respectively engineering and agriculture. Stitt, an intelligent young man with a gift for shorthand, took the note.

Fulbright's department was not the only one to have projects up that day. Fulbright was third in the queue, immediately after Foxe and his team. Foxe covered the Americas. He was the rising star in the ministry. His youthful flattery of the seniors who made up the committee meant that his projects were rarely rejected. He could be sure to have put the committee on top form. Fulbright disliked Foxe as too clever for his own good.

Fulbright, plus Colchester, Stanton and Johnstone (of the next office along the corridor) sat waiting in the ante-room outside the committee room. The committee was over-running, but that was quite normal. Fulbright could hear the soothing, reasonable voice of Foxe through the door, his measured tones reassuring the doubters and sceptics on the committee about the merits of his own projects, rather like a circus trainer might calm and reassure an assembly of dangerous cats.

Fulbright was nervous. He went again through the file of papers, which Molly had put together for him earlier that morning, marking the odd important document with a yellow tag. What was going to go wrong today?

'Guy, remind me, what *is* the population of Cairo?'

Colchester blinked. 'In excess of four million, sir.'

Fulbright seemed satisfied. He turned to Stanton.

'Those cement substitutes. What do the Americans think about them?'

Stanton stared without blinking. He responded slowly. 'It all depends. It's difficult to be certain, you see. Some people say they should be tarriff-bound in the GATT. Others want an anti-dumping duty.'

Fulbright stared keenly at Stanton for a full five seconds. Stanton stared back.

'I see,' Fulbright eventually conceded.

Fulbright then looked back at his papers. 'What most concerns me,' he went on, 'is the Bank of England's attitude towards Jordan. Are we sure they're on side, William?'

But Johnstone's answer, such as it might have been, was drowned out by the sudden opening of the door and the appearance of Stitt. He summoned Fulbright and his team to come forward, as a smiling Foxe could be heard receiving the congratulations of the chairman on the excellence of his projects.

While Fulbright and the others threaded their way in to the conference room Garrick turned his schoolmasterly gaze from Foxe and surveyed the new arrivals. Garrick was one of the most senior men in the building, the possessor of a good degree from a good university, the bringer of that little shining touch of class to the rusty machinery of government. Foxe and his acolytes withdrew, no doubt in pursuit of fresh triumphs.

'Ah, Fulbright, once more unto the breach, is it not?'

'Yes, Deputy Secretary.'

'Well, it is always a pleasure to see your happy smiling face here. What oriental delights do you tempt us with today?'

Stitt intervened. 'I think you will recollect that the committee agreed at its last meeting to postpone its opinion on four of Mr Fulbright's projects, Deputy Secretary.'

'How very tiresome of us. We must have been in a contrary mood. But now you have come back to show us the error of our ways. That's the spirit we like to see around here.'

Fulbright launched into an introduction to his four projects, speaking more or less from the same notes as at the previous committee. Colchester, as he listened with half an ear, reflected once again on the cyclical nature of the work. Perhaps these projects would get through this time. Or perhaps they would not. It really didn't matter. Or rather, what mattered more was the process itself. The assembling of facts in due and proper form. Their synthesis and consideration by a group of distinguished intellects.

The reasoned case for and against, on either side. The impartiality. The method of approaching a problem was always the same. You put the pros and cons on a sheet of paper and worked out which was the best. This office block was dedicated entirely to pure thought. Pure thought illuminated by fluorescent lighting. He remembered Churchill: *We had arrived at those broad, happy uplands where everything is settled for the greatest good of the greatest number by the commonsense of most after the consultation of all . . .*

'Forgive me, Fulbright. Forgive me for being so obtuse,' Garrick cut in the other's peroration.

'Yes, Deputy Secretary?'

'This is admirable. It does you immense credit that you are sticking consistently to your line. But I wonder if it might not be better to concentrate on the points which the committee thought needed further work last time. You see, we are all such dunces here that if you simply repeat what you said before we might lose the delicate thread of the argument. I know that you have all the details at your fingertips, but with my feeble brain I can easily be misled.'

'As you wish, Deputy Secretary.'

Fulbright instead addressed himself to the specific points of detail on which he had been unable to satisfy the committee. Minor factual questions, relating to matters such as the correct rate of exchange for a particular transaction or the creditworthiness of the company engaged in the export in question.

'This is all going very well, Fulbright,' said Garrick eventually. 'Your quick answers and ready wit are winning friends and influencing people. I think we might move on to your last project. What is it again?'

'Credits for the mining complex, Deputy Secretary. File number 8763. The pink one.'

'Indeed. Now what appears to be the problem here? Tell us all about it.'

Garrick, in common with most of the committee, had even forgotten why they had rejected the project. Stitt broke in again, at the same time placing a rapidly written note in his neat manuscript on the table before Garrick.

'If you remember, Deputy Secretary, it was a simple matter of obtaining the clearance of a number of other Whitehall departments.'

'So, Fulbright, you are going to tell us that you have now done this, are sorry that you did not do it in the first place, and we can all go away happy in the knowledge that circles everywhere have been squared. Is this not so?'

'I hope so, Deputy Secretary. The committee took the view that the Bank of England, the DTI, the LCCI and the FCO needed consulting on this project because of the political sensitivity of the area in question. I can confirm that this consultation has taken place and that there are no objections to the issuing of credits to Benbow Engineering for the leasing of six mechanical excavators for the mining complex at El Mihr.'

Garrick looked up and down the table. He opened his mouth to say the project was agreed. Then Marsh, the engineering adviser, put down his pipe and uttered his first words that morning.

'And what about the MOD?'

Fulbright looked at Marsh, his beard jutting forward even further. Then he turned back to Colchester.

'Yes. What did we do about the MOD?'

Colchester felt the eyes of the seven members of the committee turn to him. They were all keen to get away for lunch. To get this routine piece of business over.

'The, ah, the committee didn't express an opinion on the need to consult the MOD at the last meeting.'

'And did we do so?'

'Well, not as such, sir.'

Helpful Stitt intervened again. 'Mr Colchester is quite right, Deputy Secretary. The committee did not expressly require such clearance. Mr Marsh was, of course, absent from the last meeting.'

'And had I been there I would certainly have advised consulting the MOD,' Marsh put in. He was a stocky weatherbeaten man, dressed in a tropical suit, who had once built roads across Palestine. 'Mechanical diggers have a thousand and one uses. We're not talking COCOM material. But they can be used in military projects. Can we take the risk of not getting something in writing from the MOD?'

Garrick looked at Marsh. Then he looked at Fulbright. Then he looked at his watch. Marsh was being his usual tiresome self. Committees always went best when he was away. But taking risks was not something Garrick was about to start doing at this stage in his career.

'All right, Fulbright,' he said wearily. 'I suppose we had better do as Mr Marsh requests and requires us. You see what happens when you don't get a project through on the nod. The mice get at it.'

Fulbright glared with angry pink eyes at the committee members.

'So we now have to write to the MOD and delay the whole project until the next meeting of the committee? Is that it?'

Garrick took off his spectacles, laid them on the table before him and stared, as if perplexed, at the ceiling. Then he put them back on and peered at Fulbright again. He sighed.

'As you rightly imply, my dear Fulbright. The rules are the rules. We'll see you at the next meeting, like the good fellow you are.'

The committee was over.

It was only as the members broke up, with much stretching of legs and arms and gathering together of errant papers, that Garrick glanced down at the note Stitt had left in front of him. What he read there made him pause briefly in chatting to Hopkins-Joyce. He looked sharply at both Fulbright and Colchester, but neither of them were aware of him doing so. Garrick then handed the note back to Stitt and said in a low voice, 'What a bore. Keep me posted.'

Stitt nodded, tearing into little pieces the message which read: 'The minister is personally keen that there should be no difficulties with this one.'

Outdoors. Colchester felt the November wind and the rain blowing against his face, and his hair becoming damp. It was like taking root. As he stood there in the cold on the edge of the marsh the impressions, noises and urgency of the city gradually drained from him. Little by little, his mind emptied of all official concerns, all memories of the committee two days previously. As these evaporated there returned instead that calming sense of freedom and well-being which being outdoors always brought him.

He thought of a piece of modern music he had once heard of, where the musicians were required to stop thinking before they started playing. Once they found themselves thinking again they had to stop the music until their minds were empty of thought. At which point they could continue to play.

But as he wandered about the marsh, weighed down with his

birdwatcher's tackle, he found that, whether he liked it or not, his mental scenery filled up. A vacuum was always difficult to maintain for long. As one collection of ideas and thoughts drifted away like clouds, another would come in from a different direction.

He spent the morning engaged in ornithological pursuits. He mulled over some ideas for 'The Psychology of the Pheasant'. The pheasant was in most ways a curious bird. Bred in captivity, it now roamed wild in many areas of England. When you encountered one its instinct was to shoot up in the air in an explosion of noise and feathers, then career off on a lightly rising trajectory, whirring loudly as it went. Why this sudden dramatic change of behaviour? Why did a bird that spent most of its life on the ground, rooting around among cornstalks along the margins of fields, transform itself into such a noisy tempting target? Could it be that it was somehow conditioned by virtue of its mixed origins, part wild and part captive? That because millions of its ancestors had perished in sport it too adopted the inbred attitudes of flight, even perhaps aware that this was suicidal? As Colchester weighed up these points he tracked several birds around the edges of the marsh, making notes as they ran in their erratic way through the undergrowth. Soon he would have enough material to start writing that long overdue article for *British Birds*, analysing the timeless conflict between environment and genes.

It was almost noon. He was beginning to feel hungry. He started to tack back through the vegetation to where the old Toyota was parked, and where he had left his sandwiches. The car was over a mile away, and getting to it involved a good deal of scrambling across fences, through patches of wet ferns and churned-up tracks. True to their instincts, several pheasants burst from their cover and launched themselves haplessly into the air as he passed them by.

He eventually arrived at the clearing where the car was parked. Then he froze.

Someone was sitting in the passenger seat.

He kept his distance and circled slowly round the car, unable to see from outside who it could be. What would somebody with special duties do in these circumstances? Colchester thought ruefully that nothing he had learnt so far gave him much clue.

He quietly approached the car on the passenger side, trying to penetrate the layer of dust and mud which blanketed the side windows. And then, to his surprise, the passenger window was slowly wound down. He found himself looking into the eyes of a young woman, with thick black curly hair, whose attractive face held a slight smile. There was something familiar about her. She beckoned to him to sit in the driver's seat.

'My name is Julia. De la Fosse sent me. I've been waiting quite a while and I'm in need of lunch. Let's go and get some.'

It was the girl he had seen the other night in the Coach and Horses. Colchester, commending his soul to God, got in the car.

# Chapter Eight

Colchester drove along the wet track that led from the marsh to the main road. Neither he nor his female passenger exchanged a word for five minutes. Every now and then he glanced with curiosity to his left. He glimpsed a collected, assured young woman, staring straight ahead, her face half hidden by her dark curls, a visitor from another world come to sit in his car. Once his glance happened to meet hers and before she looked away he caught a snapshot of dark brown eyes questioning his, a mouth upturned as if ready to smile, a dark freckle on the tip of her nose. She swept her hair back and turned to contemplate the bleak November countryside. Her country, thought Colchester. The country she wants me to help protect. Is it mine too?

'Where to?' he said finally, when they arrived at the junction.

'Up to the left. Go through the village. Then down to the hotel on the other side. It's about three miles. I've booked a table.'

Her accent was what, thought Colchester. Cut-glass English. Oxford? SW3? And yet a fleeting sense of other resonances too. International. The world beyond. The World Service. Monte Carlo? The Riviera? Aeroplanes taking off, landing somewhere . . .

'You've booked a table?'

'Yes.'

'You follow me down here. You break into my car. You plan my lunch.'

'Yes.'

'Why?'

'It's my job.'

'You don't think you're taking a risk? Here am I, a complete stranger, alone with you.'

'You're not a complete stranger. We have got to know you quite well. And I don't take unnecessary risks.'

'We?'

'I told you. De la Fosse sent me.'

'De la Fosse? How is he? I haven't heard anything else from him.'

'He's fine. Busy.'

'In fact, now I think about it, I was told that I *wouldn't* hear anything for a while. Direct contact can be dangerous, I think de la Fosse said.'

'That's right. We try and avoid it. Except in cases of extreme importance. Well, one has arisen. Keep your eyes on the road. We're almost there.'

When they arrived at the hotel Colchester was surprised to find that not only was a table booked in the restaurant but a meal had been ordered. As he took in his surroundings it seemed to him that the flagstoned floor, the massive table and the rough and ready décor somehow matched his outdoor gear. In the corner a log fire burned. Julia was also dressed for the outdoors; under a heavy overcoat she wore a thick grey jumper and black trousers and boots. And yet, there was also a suggestion of the exotic. Her perfume, perhaps. Or the silver of her bracelets catching the firelight.

They took their places. A handful of other people were scattered around the room. A waiter brought a bottle of wine, displayed it, then retired. Another brought the first course.

'You know,' reflected Colchester, as they began their meal, 'for you people expensive restaurants seem to go with the job.'

Julia smiled.

'They provide good cover. They are natural places to meet and talk for a while. They are not likely to be bugged. They relax people who may be doing difficult things. And if people see you there with someone they usually jump to the wrong conclusion – Mr Cartwright.'

'Mr Cartwright?'

'The name I booked the table under. I'm Mrs Cartwright. Your wife.' She displayed the wedding ring on her left hand. 'But only until we get out of here. So don't get too excited.'

'I see. Have you been . . . married . . . very often before?'

'An official secret. You have no need to know.'

'No, I suppose not. Just natural curiosity.'

The wine waiter came back, opened the bottle and poured. Colchester was startled when during this ceremony Julia reached over the table and stroked his hand, displaying as if for the waiter a visible degree of marital affection. As the waiter withdrew, so did her fingers. For his benefit or mine? thought Colchester.

'You can't blame me for being curious,' Colchester went on, when they were alone again. 'This is all very odd. First I meet de la Fosse. And then I'm kidnapped by a strange woman who says she is married to me. And there's another thing. I've seen you before. You were pretending to enjoy the music the other night, weren't you?'

Julia paused an instant in drinking her wine.

'So you did see us,' she said slowly. 'I've been observing you. When we recruit someone we need to know as much about them as possible. But from your point of view it's best to know as little as possible about us. I mean it. It is the first rule of our line of business. You must stay in a watertight compartment or you might find yourself compromising other people. So don't ask me too many questions because I simply won't answer. If you're going to work for us you must get used to military discipline – and the toughest is in the mind.'

'So what are we here for?'

'Because a serious problem has come up and we need your help.'

'Are you allowed to tell me what it is?'

'I can tell you so much. What you need to know. No more.'

'So let me hear it.'

Julia paused while they finished the first course. Outside the afternoon was already darkening, and the light from the fire and the candles threw her face into relief, catching the moisture on her lips as she sipped at her glass of cold white wine. She looked steadily at Colchester and her eyes were dark and troubled. Then she spoke quietly and evenly, her voice inaudible beyond their table.

'We have a directive from the Cabinet Office to stop the spread of chemical weapons production. CW is governed by the Geneva Protocol of nineteen fifty-three. You knew that, probably. Well, there are parts of the world where international law doesn't run. The Middle East is one. But that's the most dangerous part of the world of all. Because there is no law, we have to take the law into our own hands. When we discover a capacity in the making we do our best to stop it. By whatever means. It's tough, but we've succeeded so far.'

The waiter came back with the main course, which he laid

60

out for both of them. Julia smiled and said, 'No, darling,' when Colchester offered her some bread. The waiter withdrew again.

'So?' said Colchester.

'But,' she continued, 'we have just picked up some new information. Work at one site which we knew about is far more advanced than we thought. I think you know the name of it. It's called El Mihr.'

'El Mihr?' said Colchester with surprise. 'But that's a mining complex. Of course I know all about it. Benbow Engineering are getting export credits to send some machinery over there.'

'It isn't just a mining complex.'

'What do you mean? It's been gone over with a fine-tooth comb. It's a straight mining project. Everyone knows that. We have reports from the local post. And Benbow are reputable.'

'Take my word for it. It isn't just a mining complex. It might look like one, but it isn't. It's a cover operation. And the cover is good. But we know. NSI proves it.'

'NSI?'

'Nocturnal Satellite Imaging. The fact is, the complex at El Mihr is used for mining by day. But there is a corner of the site – shed seven to be exact – where they are brewing up something rather nasty by night. Or rather they will if we don't stop them. And that's where I need your help.'

Colchester slowly sat back.

'Why me?'

'Because we want you to stop Benbow's export credits.'

Colchester pushed forward his plate and stared.

'You can't be serious.'

'Why not?'

'That project is the bane of my life. You know we have a thing called the Projects Committee? Have you heard of that?'

'Go on.'

'Well, the committee is made up of the Seven Wise Men. That's what we call them. In fact, you're lucky if you can get all seven of them together at the same time. Anyway, the committee has already postponed that project twice. Twice. Once is bad enough. That can happen to anyone. But twice is once too often. If that project doesn't go through the week after next my head of department is going to lock himself in his office and shoot himself. And before he does so he'll shoot me.'

Julia picked up Colchester's hand as the waiter cleared the second course away. She raised it to her mouth and gently nibbled the ends of his fingers. When the waiter left she laid down his hand, but it was some moments before she lightened her touch.

'But this really is a matter of life and death,' she said finally. 'You do know what chemical warfare is?'

'I know.'

'It is of vital national interest that El Mihr is not completed. Stopping Benbow will halt the project, at least for the time being. And in the mean time we can find some other solution. But we need that time. You can help us get it.'

'Look, I just can't. What you're asking is impossible.'

'I don't think so. All you have to do is make a mistake. Everyone makes mistakes. You could lose the file. Or you could give the wrong information to the committee.'

Colchester shook his head.

'Why ask me? Haven't you got some other way of doing your work? All you need do is get the MOD or someone to declare it unfit on security grounds and all bets would be off.'

'We can't do that. They will pick up any overt action. The last thing – the very last thing – that we want is for them to know that we know what they're doing at El Mihr. We have to be covert at all costs. We have to be deniable. You can help us.'

Colchester looked deep into Julia's eyes. All he could read there was anxiety.

'You don't understand,' he said finally. 'It isn't a question of what I will do. It's a question of what I can do. Just suppose I'd had enough of my career. Suppose I decided to commit professional suicide. I go out one night and I drop the file in the Thames. Even then, the whole thing has gone too far for me to stop it. I'm only part of the machine. The machine grinds on without me. Someone in the MOD now has to write a two-line reply giving the all-clear to one I sent the day before yesterday. That letter then goes straight before the Seven Wise Men. They will spend all of five seconds considering it before agreeing the project. With or without me. And if the MOD expert who writes the letter falls stone dead while he is doing it another will just step forward and take his place and write the same letter. And so it goes on until the last man drops. I can't change the course of events. Even if I wanted to.'

Julia sat back in her chair and said nothing. She looked silently into the middle distance, as if pondering Colchester's words. The waiter came and brought the coffee and went away, and she seemed to forget this time to make any display of emotion.

'I'm sorry,' said Colchester, after a while. 'That's just the way it is. It's old man river. It just rolls on. No one can do anything about it.'

Julia focused her eyes on Colchester once again.

'There is perhaps one other possibility,' she said slowly, as if thinking out loud. 'Perhaps we could do something ourselves about the Benbow exports. Suppose, like you say, you let the project go through. Benbow get their export credits and get paid for the delivery. No one knows anything. But we can trace the machines. We can make sure no harm is done. It couldn't get back to you. But we might be able to hold up progress for quite a useful time.'

'Well,' said Colchester. 'That would be better. Assuming you could do it so that no one found out.'

'We could do it if we had some of the basic documentation on the order. Maybe some of the Projects Committee papers, the letters from the company, the details of what it is Benbow are sending over. That sort of thing. Not much really. Can you help us there?'

'How help you?'

'Well, you could put together a little collection of material for me. Not much mind. Just what you judge is necessary. You're the boss.'

Colchester's eyes widened. 'But that's improper conduct.'

Julia shrugged her shoulders. 'So is chemical warfare. It's the lesser of two evils.'

'Even so . . .'

'Look,' she implored. 'I'm not asking for the moon. You seem to think we can do anything. We can't. We need help and support. I didn't even know the name of the company until you told me. God knows, the cause is just.'

She leaned forward in her seat. Her eyes were bright. She was deadly serious now. She looked rather beautiful.

'You needn't worry yourself,' she went on. 'We are stopping future warfare. What they want to do at El Mihr is completely illegal. It could end by killing thousands of innocent men, women and children. If we can stop them in any way, we are doing what is right. If you can help us so that no one can find out you have nothing to lose.'

Colchester looked silently at his half empty wine glass.

'And you might have something to gain,' she added.

He looked up.

'To gain?'

Her face reddened slightly.

'In career terms, I mean. We have influence. We know the right people.'

'How would it work?'

'I'll get in touch with you.'

'You personally?'

'Yes. Soon. Will you?'

Colchester studied his fingernails for a few moments.

'You know,' he said finally, 'you might not realize it but watching birds makes you quite attentive to detail. You see things that other people might miss. You see just that little bit further. It's practice, I suppose.'

Julia's expression changed very slightly. A touch of anxiety?

'You, for example,' said Colchester, raising his eyes to hers once again. 'I know a little bit more about you than you might think.'

Julia suddenly looked rather nervous.

'What do you mean?' she asked.

'I mean last week. Out on the marsh. Someone was watching me. It was you, wasn't it?'

'How did you—?'

'I just know the area. I knew someone was there. You weren't part of the habitat. I waited for you to make a move. I have these very small binoculars. I got a glimpse of your profile, that's all. You're . . . easy to remember.'

Julia was confused.

'You didn't mention it to de la Fosse . . .'

'I thought I'd let him raise it first. He didn't. But when I saw you again in the pub I put two and two together. I was curious. I thought I might end up seeing you again . . .'

Julia was still looking tense, almost alarmed.

'When you say you put two and two together . . . What was your conclusion?'

Colchester smiled broadly at her.

'I'll see what I can do to help you,' he said, and drained his

64

glass. She smiled back at him, relieved. And then she breathed out gradually.

The meal was over. The waiter was hovering in the background. As they rose from the table, Julia came round to Colchester and stood in front of him.

'Thank you, darling, that was marvellous,' she said for the benefit of the world in general, a wife delighted with her husband.

Then unexpectedly she came up to him. She put her arms round his neck and kissed him gently. Then she embraced him closely. For an instant Colchester felt the warmth of her body against his. For an instant her breasts pressed against him and her hair brushed his face. And then she released him. The colour was rising in her cheeks. The waiter came forward with her overcoat.

When they got back to the car Colchester asked Julia where he should take her.

'It's better for us not to be seen together too much,' she replied. 'There's a cab rank in town, if you go left down the road. Leave me there, if you don't mind.'

'If you like. Are you still my wife?'

'Sorry,' she said gently. 'I'm just a professional doing my job. Like you. Think of us as officially divorced.'

They drove on in silence for ten minutes, the buildings and shops multiplying as they came into the suburbs. Sure enough, there was a cab rank, as Julia had said.

'But there's no cab here.'

'It doesn't matter. There'll be one along soon. Just leave me here. Oh – one last thing . . .' She turned to face Colchester. 'If you see de la Fosse again, it would help me if you *didn't* say you saw me before.'

Colchester smiled. 'Your secret is safe with me.'

Julia got out of Colchester's car. She said she would be in touch the following week. She asked him to go straight home. Colchester drove off, with the diminishing figure of Julia in his rear-view mirror, asking himself what this stranger was doing in his life. He looked over to the empty seat on his left. He had never had a woman like her sitting in this car before. He knew, to his discomfort, that he was already looking forward to seeing her again.

Julia stood and waited in the cold for five minutes. Cars and buses came and went, but there was no sign of a cab.

Then finally one drew up, with a man already in the back seat.

It crawled along the kerb for a few yards and stopped beside her. The passenger rolled down the window.

'No cabs free at this time of day, dear. Why don't you come along with us?'

Julia looked up and down the street. Then she opened the rear door and climbed in. The driver turned and smiled at her.

'Doing a bit of overtime today, aren't we?'

'You can tell de la Fosse the cat is in the bag. Like we thought, he bought the fall-back.'

The driver grinned more widely. It was the waiter from the hotel. The cab pulled away. She was safe at last.

# Chapter Nine

Mehmet drove his hire car west, following the sinking sun. He had landed at Heathrow that morning, and was now heading through the open plains of Wiltshire, watching the bands of cloud rising to meet him, showers alternating with pale sunlight. There was little traffic about on this late autumn afternoon. Mehmet, feeling that with every mile west he was going further into a lost land on the edge of the world, was ill at ease. The ridged desert spaces of Wiltshire disturbed him.

He knew he was safe as long as he stayed in his car. The car was an extension of his normal universe, a technical cocoon of metal and plastic, a bubble of reality in this strange dark rural world. Mehmet *looked* alien, looked foreign, with his dark features, hooked nose, deep-set eyes and middle-European suit. But to him, a citizen of the world, this distant part of a remote country was the strangest of all.

The Benbow Engineering works were on the outskirts of Wincanton. It was virtually dark when Mehmet pulled up outside the main gates. Streams of workers were already going home, as the early shift finished. Mehmet's appointment was not until the following morning, but he wanted to study his quarry. It was his pride as a military buyer that he knew more about the companies with which he had dealings than they did themselves. After ten minutes he felt he'd seen enough and he headed off into the centre of town, where he knew he could find a brightly lit hotel.

The next morning Mehmet presented himself to the sales director at Benbow, his card signifying his status as an official emissary of El Mihr Mining. The office was small, dingy, temporary, decorated with the bygone calendars of agricultural machinery firms. The sales director was a young bearded man named Wallace. He sat behind a rickety desk and twisted a ball-point pen in his fingers.

'I am making a personal visit because my principals are worried about the delay in delivery of the construction equipment which your company is leasing to us. Please explain what is happening, if you would be so kind.'

Wallace did his best to exude confidence.

'I'm glad you came, Mr Mehmet. Really I am. It is so much easier to talk things over direct than on the telephone. It's all rather strange, I agree.'

'It is more than that. It is unprofessional. It is four weeks since we have heard anything concrete about this order. Perhaps it was a mistake going to a British firm in the first place.'

'But, Mr Mehmet, we are as mystified as you about what is wrong.'

'You mean you have no explanation?'

'Well, we have part of an explanation. You see, before we finally ship the goods we have to clear export credits through the Ministry of Exports in London. It's to cover ourselves in case anything goes wrong. It's not your principals, of course, we are worried about. It's just that there are parts of the world where there are political risks which we need cover against.'

'I understand the system. So what is the problem?'

'The problem is the Ministry of Exports. We should have had clearance two weeks ago, at least. When we gave you our delivery date that was what we were assuming. But since then – nothing. They can sometimes be a bit late in clearing things through. You know what these officials are. But not this late. Frankly, I don't know what is going on.'

'You have had no indication of what the hold-up is, Mr Wallace?'

'No. You never know. It's like getting blood out of a stone. Bureaucrats. Worse than Moscow. You get a postcard – no picture on it – with a stamp to say your application has been received and they will be in touch after such and such a date.'

'Do you think it is perhaps something to do with El Mihr – its location perhaps, or its activities, which is causing difficulties?'

'Could be, I suppose . . . But we've sent equipment to your part of the world before. And a mining project – well, that's routine.'

'So what do you think, Mr Wallace?'

'I think it's most likely that they're short-staffed in the Middle East section, or someone's away with flu, or they're on strike. Or some such. Pretty soon I expect we'll get the all clear. That's why we didn't contact you before now, you see. We thought it would be coming any day.'

'I see. You thought it was better not to tell us anything than to give us some indication of your difficulties?'

Wallace dropped his pen.

'Well, you know how it is. You always have to look on the bright side, don't you?'

'Always look on the bright side? Yes, maybe that is a wise policy from your point of view. Because we shall certainly not place any more orders with your company unless those machines are ready for delivery very soon. I shall telephone you next week. If they are not on their way then you too might have to look on the bright side in future. You might find it useful to find out what the Ministry of Exports is doing with your order, and ask them to do it more quickly. Of course I do not want to tell you your job, but when I say find out I do suggest immediately. Good morning, Mr Wallace.'

Mehmet's irritation persisted as he drove back to his hotel. He did not like the slow ways, the sloppy habits of these comfortable English. And he deeply distrusted the rural types who lived in this part of the world. In this marginal territory on the edge of civilization the sharp lines of concrete and brick were blurred by moss and damp. Wet growth clung to the signs on the edges of the roads. The people in the streets were spattered with mud, the same mud that streaked the side of his car. The dampness was in the air, you felt it when you breathed in. Who could tell what was going on out there, what these people were thinking? Mehmet had to do business here, but he did not like it.

When he arrived at the hotel he went immediately to his room. He had two urgent telephone calls to make.

Wallace also got straight on to the phone after the meeting. Mehmet had been stirred up, just as he had expected. Not surprising, really. Paid all that deposit out and not yet got his goods. Quite a nice fellow, probably, when you got to know him. You could see he was worried. It must be difficult for these Arab types to get used to English ways. Difficult for anyone to get used to dealing with the Ministry of Exports. That stuff about not placing orders was so much toffee. Anyone could see that. Still, he'd see if he could find out just what was supposed to be happening. He looked at his card index and picked up the phone.

Mehmet put down the phone in his hotel room.

He had been speaking to a man called Yassavi, almost two thousand miles away. He was to change his plans. Instead of going on to Paris that afternoon he was to stay in England for a few more days and follow up the El Mihr order. To start with, Yassavi wanted to know more about this Ministry of Exports. What was it? Did it have functions beyond processing export guarantees? Could other agencies have some shadowy role in this business? Where exactly was this Benbow order stuck? Who exactly was working on it?

That was problem number one.

He picked up the telephone again and made his second call. The phone at the other end rang for a long while. Ten seconds. Twenty seconds. Half a minute. Forty seconds. God knows what difficulty the man at the other end was having in getting to the line. Who could guess how many doors needed unbolting, how many combinations needed unscrambling, how many padlocks opening, how many seals breaking, before this special telephone could be used? This was a number you kept for use once or twice in a lifetime. When – for example – you were thinking of going nuclear.

Finally the ringing stopped.

'Yes.' The voice sounded as though it was coming from within a vault.

'The machines are still delayed. I'll get back to you when we have a firm date.'

There was a pause at the other end.

'I'm afraid you have the wrong number.'

The line went dead. Mehmet put down the phone.

The little light on the miniature switchboard in front of Jill came on. It was an outside call coming through to the private office, as all calls to Tim Warwick at the ministry did. As usual, the private office resembled a cross between a dentist's waiting room and a conference chamber. Officials, secretaries, even tea-ladies were circulating noisily all around, holding impromptu meetings, consulting documents, taking part in and adding to the vortex of activity that always circulated around the minister and his decision-taking entourage.

'Mr Warwick's office,' Jill said into the receiver, in her professional private secretary voice.

She heard a faint noise, as if the speaker was calling from far away.

'Mr Warwick, did you say?'

The speaker repeated his name, rather more loudly.

'Just a moment, if you please. I'll have to speak to him.'

She put the caller on hold and pressed the switch which illuminated the instrument on Warwick's desk in the next door office.

'Yes?' Warwick's negligent voice came through a couple of seconds later.

'A Mr Ramses on the line, Minister, who wishes to speak to you. He says you know him.'

Jill could almost hear the smile in Warwick's voice.

'Yes, yes. Put him through. And can you clear my out tray in a few minutes, please?'

Jill switched the caller through and her line went dead. She picked up a file of briefing material. But then something stirred in her memory and she put it down again. She opened the left-hand drawer of her desk and took out a sheet of blue paper with a long list of names on it. Her eyes rested on one near the bottom of the second column. She glanced around the private office and picked up the telephone again. She made sure the input volume was turned down and in the midst of the bustle and brouhaha cautiously switched on the minister's telephone conversation.

'Yes,' she heard Warwick say energetically in her earpiece to his distant interlocutor. 'Yes, you're absolutely right. It's a scandal. I'll see what I can do. But, honestly, Didier, you have no idea what these people are like. I sometimes despair.'

And the voice from another time zone again. 'That's most helpful, Timothy. I'll look forward to hearing from you. Will you be at Alpbach?'

'No,' replied Warwick. 'I really mustn't have any formal connection with you any more. Rules are rules.'

A brief silence.

'We are all missing you, Timothy. Come back soon.'

The line went dead. Immediately afterwards Warwick opened his door and looked around the suddenly hushed private office before fixing on Jill, who glanced up from her papers.

'A word, if you please,' he called out to her. 'In here.'

# Chapter Ten

It was another routine morning at the Ministry of Exports. For once, Colchester was glad. He was beginning to appreciate that with the new functions he had taken up there were times when a quiet life could be a blessing. Even if it was a blessing in disguise. Colchester knew that if he waited until eleven o'clock Stanton would vacate the office on his daily quest for hot water, which he usually found in a gigantic urn on the third floor. He needed to get his hands on the Benbow file before then.

At half-past ten exactly he rang Bert Cooper in the registry.

'Hello, Bert. Guy here. Do you still have the mining projects file down there? Could you do me a favour and bring along parts G to J? I have some letters to write.'

Ten minutes later Bert Cooper wheezed along pushing a trolley laden with files. He was making his round of the building, dropping off a file here and picking one up there. He parked his trolley beside Colchester's desk and heaved off it four, thick, well-used tomes, which he deposited with a thump on the desk.

'That's what you call information technology, mate. Don't need no fax machines when you've got the fastest registry in town. That'll be fifty quid to you. Or you can sign this instead.'

He proffered a scruffy yellow notebook for Colchester to accept responsibility for the volumes. Colchester signed, as he had done a hundred times before. Then Bert Cooper pushed his groaning trolley back out towards the door. But he was stopped by a voice.

'Just a minute, young fellow. Where do you think you're going?'

Bert Cooper turned round to confront Stanton.

'Don't say you've been awake all this time, after all. Have you got something on your mind?'

Stanton pointed to the mass of files on the floor beside his desk.

'You could get rid of these old Anglo-Italian files sometime. And maybe bring me those other ones I asked for yesterday.'

Bert Cooper scratched his head.

'Yes, I think I did hear something about that. Well, I'll do what I can. I've got a lot of other people to see to, you know.'

He left for the next floor. Stanton shook his head and buried himself in his work. Colchester set about gutting the files, removing papers from each. Stanton took no notice.

A quarter of an hour later Stanton picked up his mug and marched silently out of the room, on cue. Colchester tidied the mass of papers he had created on his desk, and sorted it into a neat pile. Then he got up, clutching the bundle, and headed for the photocopier a few yards along the corridor.

He had to wait until the girl in front of him had finished. She was copying what looked like a batch of football pools forms but which were in fact legitimate export statistics. For at least fifteen years the department had been charged with the responsibility of preparing monthly statistics on all exports, and this task – although those who had originated the request had long since forgotten about it – resulted in a regular deluge of photocopying around the building.

Eventually the machine was free. Colchester stacked the thirty folio sheets, which he had abstracted from the files, in the document feeder. He switched on the programme. The machine rumbled into action, and began to spew out a sheet every second – printed side up – on to the tray by its side.

'So there you are! I've been looking for you everywhere. Haven't seen you in such a long while!'

Molly, spotting Colchester at the far end of the corridor, walked up to him, her face beaming. She was bearing in her arms a pile of papers and files of her own. She came and stood beside him.

'Is this where the queue is? It's always nice to get out and about, isn't it? Doing our own copying these days, are we? You know you don't have to. You only have to ask nicely and I might be able to help.'

Molly glanced down at the papers shooting out of the machine.

'Did you say you were looking for me?' asked Colchester.

'Mmm, yes . . . What was it again . . . ? You know I miss having a good chat now and then. You just can't talk to himself. I asked him today when he was going on his holidays, and he wouldn't tell me. He said, "No doubt I will be in a position to say when I have written to the Caravan Club." That's his idea of a holiday, you know. A week in a caravan in Wales. With Madam Fulbright. Are you going to be long?'

'No, just finishing. Why? Do you want the photocopier?'

'Well, if you're sure you don't want it all morning. I've got some things to do. But it's more you, actually. I was looking for you to say that himself has blocked in half an hour to see you. In ten minutes. So you'd better roll along. It's about your annual report.'

Colchester grimaced.

'It would be. He puts those things off until the last moment and then springs them on you with no warning. It's management without tears.'

The photocopier shivered to a halt. Molly again glanced down at the papers in the tray.

'Are those the Benbow papers you're copying there?'

Colchester stiffened.

'Among others. Why?'

'I've been looking for them. Bert said you had them. The file was on your desk but I couldn't see them. Someone's been on to the boss. He wants to see the file before he calls them back on the telephone.'

Colchester picked up his pile of papers.

'I'll tell you what,' said Molly, 'I'll come back to your office and you can put the file back together while I wait.'

'Yes, you'll enjoy that.'

The procession of two went back to Colchester's office, where Stanton had now returned and was sitting wreathed in clouds of steaming Oxo. He grunted at Molly. While Colchester reassembled the files Molly went and sat on his desk and told Stanton that Colchester was just about to have his annual job interview with Fulbright.

Stanton looked up, mildly interested.

'Shall I tell you an old trick for those meetings? What you do is have a great thick pile of papers – say like those you've just been copying – and you take them with you.'

'Where does that get you?' Molly asked on Colchester's behalf.

'Well, you can stuff them down the back of your trousers so that when you get caned you don't feel anything.'

Molly laughed out loud. Colchester finished his file making, and handed over the finished product to her.

'When do I see his greatness?'

Molly looked at her watch.

'You're on.'

Colchester went into Fulbright's office. As was often the case, Fulbright was scribbling on a sheet of paper with a ball-point pen. His handwriting grew more and more dense as he proceeded down the page and he endeavoured to commit ever more convoluted ideas to a diminishing supply of paper. It was not unknown for him to tack extra bits of paper on to the main sheet with a stapler so that he could continue one of his trains of thought. Balloons were another of his specialities, and there floated around his prose a barrage of tethered phrases, some of which occasionally came loose from their moorings and made no obvious sense at all. Molly, whose job it was to type up Fulbright's emanations, would from time to time take choice specimens around the office to show what she was up against. With practice she had more or less come to comprehend Fulbright's thought processes, and now she thought nothing of discarding whole passages which seemed to her meaningless.

'Take a seat, Guy,' said Fulbright, at length, reaching for the report file. 'I expect you know why you're here. I asked Molly to tell you. Well, I suppose you've had plenty of time to think about things. We have these meetings once a year to let you know how you're getting on. I don't know if they're really necessary, but there you are. Now, tell me, is there anything you want to say?'

Colchester collected his thoughts. This was a new one.

'To say? Do you mean of a . . . policy nature?'

'No. No. I mean do you have any complaints?'

'Complaints? No, I don't think I have any complaints . . .'

'Good.' Fulbright noted this down on the file.

'Now,' he went on, 'I've been looking through last year's report, and I see that much of what was said about you then can still stand. I think, if I may say so, that I was right. Do you agree?'

'Well, sir,' said Colchester, 'if you remember we are not allowed to see our own reports.'

'Yes, yes, I know that. But surely you know what the main points were?'

'I can remember some of them, sir.'

'Well, there you are then. I want you to tell me what you think we have said about you this year. It's a good exercise in developing office awareness.'

75

Colchester groaned inwardly. This was worse than he had expected. Fulbright must have picked this trick up from some book on office psychology. Probably a birthday present from Mrs F. He considered a moment. What was it Molly had said?

'My instinct is that this is not a very good report, sir. I would say that, on balance, your judgement is probably that I could do better. In fact, I think it might be that you think that I could show more application and attention to detail. If your remember, sir, you said something broadly similar last year. I think then the gist was that I needed to adopt a more engaged attitude.'

Fulbright beamed.

'This is remarkably perceptive of you, Guy. I think I should give you better marks for foresight and penetration.'

He paused to annotate the report, and went on in a friendlier tone, 'You know, Guy, there is no need to despair. No need to despair at all. I've seen lots of young fellows here in my time. And there have been many worse than you. You might well – eventually – have the makings of a good officer. You need application, that's all. I see no reason why you shouldn't rise up in the service. Work hard and keep your nose clean and you could end up a head of department, like me. It's not a bad life. You get to have a secretary. She makes you tea if you want it. And you deal with some pretty tricky policy issues. Take it from me. I can't think of a better way of passing the time between the ages of twenty-five and sixty. Can you?'

Colchester shook his head. He couldn't, just for the moment.

'My advice to you is to stick at it. Shoulder to the wheel. It may be some years of hard work yet. But that's what you need. Work hard and the whole service is yours.'

Fulbright paused after this little speech. The two of them sitting there made a tableau. Age handing on wisdom to youth.

Fulbright eventually broke the silence.

'Now I think you understand what I am trying to tell you, Guy. Do you have any questions?'

None that you could answer, thought Colchester.

'No, sir.'

'Good. That wasn't so bad, was it?' Fulbright's voice changed register. 'Before you go, do you know what the devil is happening about that Benbow project? I had someone on the phone this morning wanting to know what was going on.'

'The MOD have now written to say they have no objection. And it goes back before the PC next Thursday. I explained all that to someone from Benbow the other day.'

'Good. I wish that fool Marsh would retire before he gets completely senile. I'm going to be quite busy today, you know. Do you think you could do me a favour and give this other fellow a ring? I've written his name and number down somewhere . . . Here we are: a Mr Mehmet, who says he's from El Mihr Mining.'

Colchester sat forward.

'El Mihr Mining?'

'That's right. He's in London. Have a word with him and set his mind at rest. He asked Molly if he could come and see someone here. I said we'd be back in touch. I don't mind you seeing him. In fact, it might be a good idea. You know, we could do without another complaint from a West Country MP.'

'Well, I will if you're sure it's a good idea . . .'

'I am. Just a minute.' Fulbright picked up the telephone. 'Molly? Did you find the Benbow papers? Would you bring them in, if you please.'

Molly was barely five yards away from Fulbright. But she was used to being summoned on the telephone as if she were in a different building. She came straight in and offered Fulbright the files which she had just retrieved from Colchester.

'Here you are,' Fulbright said to Colchester. 'I haven't got time to look through this myself. You'll find all you need in there.' And he handed Colchester the whole lot back again.

Colchester caught Molly's eye and saw her stifle a giggle.

'I'll remember everything you told me,' he said to Fulbright. But Fulbright was already looking at his watch and showing signs of wanting to return to his paperwork. Colchester left, his job interview over for another year. Molly held the door open. She gave a slight curtsey.

Mehmet was watching television in his Bayswater hotel room when the telephone rang. It was three o'clock in the afternoon. He had been trying to piece together a complicated soap opera, which he occasionally saw when he was on missions. He switched off the sound, rolled over on the bed and picked up the receiver.

'Yes?'

'Can I speak to Mr Mehmet, please?'

'You are speaking to him. Who is this?'

'This is the Ministry of Exports here. My name is Colchester. I was asked to have a word with you. You rang Mr Fulbright this morning. About the El Mihr Mining project.'

Mehmet sat up.

'That is correct, Mr Colchester. It is kind of you to contact me. I asked Mr Fulbright if I might come and see the person who is responsible for the project. My principals asked me, while I was in London, to make a progress report. They are concerned about a delay in the delivery of some construction equipment. Perhaps you can help me set their minds at ease?'

'Do you mean that you want to come and see me?'

'If by that you mean that you are the person responsible for the project, the answer is yes. You would be helping me very much if you could spare fifteen minutes or so.'

'I see. Well, Mr Mehmet, would Thursday suit you? Say four o'clock?'

'That would be perfect. I ask for Mr Colchester?'

'Yes. You know where we are?'

'Do not worry, Mr Colchester. I know exactly where you are.'

At half-past seven that evening, briefcase in hand, Colchester made his way down Jermyn Street. It was a great contrast with the fluorescent lights and clinical décor of the Ministry of Exports to walk down this stylish street of subdued lighting and fancy windows. As he passed each window he could see strange and expensive things glittering in the gloom like expensive fish in an aquarium. Brilliantly striped shirts, outlandish brass scientific instruments mounted on tripods, gigantic sponges, mottled cheeses. The scent of hair oil mixed strangely with a whiff of Gorgonzola. The rain fell slightly, and the pavement reflected a pool of colours.

Colchester stopped halfway down the street, outside Willy's Bar. A large blue awning protected the entrance from the rain. He had never been in here before. Through the windows he glimpsed a cheerful, inviting interior. It was all so English. The secret world held back from the elements. He paused a moment before going in. He wanted to see Julia. That much he knew. Was it her alone that he wanted? Or was it something to do with what she stood for? He could not distinguish. But he knew that this really was a threshold. It was one thing being stopped out in the wilds by a stranger. It was another to come here of his own free will.

After a few moments' hesitation he pushed open the door. He paused on the inside, looking around and taking in the scene. There were at least thirty people, in groups or in couples, spread around a large number of chairs and tables. Off the main area ran alcoves with private tables, and a few of these were occupied. The light of candles reflected in the mirrors around the walls. A bar ran down the length of one wall. He could see a piano over in the far corner, but no one was playing it yet. None the less, lazy music was floating in from somewhere. It was the cocktail hour. A relaxing time before dinner.

He walked in to the centre of the large room. No one approached him. No one asked him for his raincoat. In this bar you came and went as you pleased. A few waiters scurried back and forth.

And then he saw Julia.

She had not seen him. She was sitting in an alcove by herself, her legs crossed, reading a magazine. In front of her, on a low table, was a tall glass with an untouched drink. She negligently turned a page and happened to look up. Then she saw Colchester. Her face lit up.

As Colchester made his way over to her, Julia stood up and held her hand out.

'Guy! How very gentlemanly of you not to keep me waiting.'

This was clearly Julia in civilized mode. She was wearing a shortish black skirt and a red jacket, and a pair of golden earrings flashed behind her curly black hair. There was no trace of the wedding ring which Colchester had seen a few days before. Today the girlfriend: no longer the wife.

'Come and take a seat. One never knows when people will turn up, or even if they will at all. It's one of the perils of the job. I always bring something to read.'

'What is it?'

Julia displayed the cover. The journal of the Institute of Strategic Studies.

'I would have expected *Harper's* at least.'

'You have to keep your hand in. It's extraordinary what they can do with anti-ballistic missiles these days.'

'It's good to see you. You're looking very – elegant.'

'I'm going to a dinner party later on. You have to be ready for anything.'

Colchester took off his coat and sat down. He looked again at Julia's left hand.

'I see you're – disengaged this evening.'

She smiled.

'You're getting quite sharp. Let's say I engage and disengage at will. For this evening, until further notice, I am a free woman. You might, incidentally, order some drinks from this fellow as he passes.'

'But you have one already.'

Julia shook her head.

'It's tonic water. If I'm going to be here for an hour or so I have to keep my wits about me. It's considered unprofessional to drink by yourself.'

'What would you like?'

'The gin that this tonic needs.'

Colchester ordered the drinks. The waiter left them a huge bowl of olives.

'So, Guy Colchester,' said Julia. 'We meet again. I wondered when you would turn up. We always give three choices. But it can mean a lot of waiting around.'

'I – thought about seeing you all day.'

Julia looked at Colchester narrowly.

'You have brought me some goodies?'

'As you asked. Do you want them now?'

He reached inside his briefcase and started pulling papers out.

'No, no,' Julia whispered as the waiter came back with their drinks. Then out loud, 'Not just now, darling.'

When the waiter had gone she raised her eyes to heaven and took a sip.

'We'll do this properly, if you don't mind. First thing is, have you put the papers in some form of cover?'

'Yes. A blank folder. They can't be seen from the outside.'

'Good. Size? A4?'

'Yes.'

She fished a copy of the *Financial Times* from out of a large black leather handbag, and placed it front page up on the table, as if to show Colchester an article.

'You can't do this with the tabloids. Now, I want you to open up the paper so you can read the middle pages. That's right. You're looking for a job advert or something. You'll see it takes up quite a lot of space.'

'OK. What next?'

'Now slide the briefcase under your knee. That's it. Slip the papers out and under the newspaper. There's no hurry. Take your time. The trick is to keep the *FT* on top of everything. Have you got the papers out yet?'

'Not quite . . . yes, there they are.'

'Good. Can I have my newspaper back?'

And Julia folded it up, taking with her the bundle of papers which Colchester had slipped beneath. She stowed them all away in her capacious handbag.

'You've done this kind of thing before,' Colchester remarked.

'Once in a while. As you progress through your career you'll pick it up, no doubt. It becomes second nature. Cheers.'

'Cheers. What are you going to do with the information?'

'That would be telling. Something pretty effective, I expect. We usually are. But you needn't worry. It can't be traced back to you. We'll find a way of letting you know what happens, if you like.'

Colchester looked down at his hands.

'Would that be through you?' he asked innocently.

Julia paused. Had she seen it coming?

'I don't think so. You know we're supposed to minimize contact. It's for your own good. You don't want to be seen around town with a girl like me. Whatever would Molly say?'

'What has she got to do with it?'

'She has her eyes on you, you know. When I spend a couple of months studying a potential new recruit I get to know a little bit about them.'

'So what do you know about me.'

'I know that you don't want to see too much of me. I can be a bad influence. If I were you I should try and do without me. Enjoy your drink. I have to go off to dinner soon and then you can dive back in the ocean.'

'The ocean?'

'Where there are plenty of other fish.'

But Colchester had one last card to play.

'There is something else I haven't told you.'

'What's that?'

81

'Did you know that I am supposed to see someone from El Mihr Mining on Thursday?'

'No,' Julia said thoughtfully, the girlfriend look suspended suddenly; in its place a shadow of something serious. 'No. I didn't know that. Why is this?'

'Because a certain Mr Mehmet is in London and he rang up and asked to see someone from the ministry. I imagine he wants to find out just why we have been sitting on his export order for so long.'

Julia reflected soberly.

'Tell him the truth. It's always the best way. Never tell an unnecessary lie. And if you do have to tell a lie make sure it's got as high a truth quotient as possible.'

'But you and I know what is really going on at El Mihr.'

Julia was concentrating, her dark eyes looking far away into the heart of some mystery.

'But does he?' she reasoned. 'The chances are he doesn't. The chances are he really does represent El Mihr Mining. After all, it's a perfectly straight project, or ninety-five per cent of it is. Would a bad man come in through the front door of the ministry and ask to see the boss? You're seeing him in your office, I suppose, not alone on Hampstead Heath. You'll be all right. Anyway, you told me the parable of the workers and the machine. What's the point of nobbling one man? There are thousands of you. He'll know that.'

Colchester was not altogether reassured.

'Well, I hope so. It still seems strange to me. Why should he come so far?'

Julia appeared to be doing some calculations. Then the girlfriend look switched back on.

'Maybe you're right to be concerned,' she said with a smile. 'Just maybe. We could meet again, one more time, that evening, here. You can brief me on what happens. It would set your mind at rest. We're not supposed to keep meeting, but there you are. I'll be free. Will you?'

Colchester tried to keep his voice neutral.

'Same time? Same place?'

Julia was looking hard at him.

'Yes.'

'I'll be here.'

'Good. Now, enjoy your drink. I have to go.'

Colchester gulped down his drink and accompanied Julia on her way out. The pianist was just sitting down at the keyboard. As they left they heard him begin to roll through some scales. The night was only just beginning.

It was still raining. A taxi drew up almost immediately and Julia jumped in. As it pulled away she wound down the window.

'Haven't you got a home to go to, young man?' She smiled and the cab drove off.

Colchester watched the red tail-lights swing out into the stream of traffic and blend into the middle distance. He looked at his watch. Eight-twenty. He had let her escape into the unknown city again. But she would come back to him. One more time. Just one more time. Time only to meet, talk business and go their own ways. Unless – unless – he could find some other way to hold her attention.

His father, Colchester thought, would not approve of any of this. But tonight he did not feel particularly stoical. Tonight he felt he had been given a glimpse of hidden riches. One of those things you found once in a lifetime. It would be up to him whether it just vanished from his life as quickly as it had come.

Now for the walk back in the rain to the station and a late train out to the southern suburbs. He trudged off, but his heart was singing.

Julia, sitting in the back of the cab, closed her eyes and felt the tension begin to ebb from her body. Her heartbeat was returning to normal. She looked at her face carefully in her pocket mirror. You would never guess, she told herself. You would never guess that someone who looks as composed as you do could in reality be so frightened.

The cab threaded its way through the streets of West London. After fifteen minutes it turned off Kensington High Street and penetrated the maze of leafy streets to the south. Julia asked it to pull up in front of a large brilliantly lit house. The door was open, and other guests were already arriving. She got out and walked up the front steps. A large man in a dinner jacket leapt down the stairs and kissed her on the cheek. The cab driver saw the door close behind her, the rectangle of blazing light shrinking in the wet and dark. He made a note in a small book and drove off.

An hour later, at dinner, Julia looked over the candelabra and past the animated heads of the other guests and for the first time established contact with de la Fosse, who was engaged in conversation with an elderly lady to his left. She raised an eyebrow. It was enough. He would see her later on, in the confusion at the end of the meal, and take delivery of her newspaper.

De la Fosse was on good form. He said something quietly to the elderly lady and she turned away to giggle. He then raised his voice slightly to address the youthful-looking man sitting opposite him at the dinner table.

'Well, Tim, when are you going to get that seat in the Cabinet? I keep reading all these flattering articles about you in the papers, inspired by your admirers. You'll have to get a move on, you know, or you'll disappoint your public.'

Tim Warwick gave the well-known Warwick grin.

'I shouldn't place any bets if I were you,' he replied. He lowered his voice. 'Just between you and me,' he went on, as half a dozen people listened in, 'the word is we need two years of reshuffle-free government to consolidate.'

'A long time,' acknowledged de la Fosse. 'So we should get out of equities and into bonds?'

Warwick pretended to look inscrutable.

'You know, I'm glad to be out of the City. You only think of one thing. There's more to life than interest rates.'

'So they tell me,' said de la Fosse.

Further down the table Julia turned back to the dinner guest sitting on her right, who had been speaking for five minutes.

'I can see from what you say that you haven't the slightest idea about the situation in the Middle East . . .'

# Chapter Eleven

'The future, now, Victor. What do you think lies in store for us in the future?'

Stuart-Smith offered another cigar to the elderly Russian, who was clad in an old black jumper and a pair of blue jeans. A Havana, ironically enough. Apparently they weren't so easy to come by in Moscow these days. Whenever he came over to the West Victor insisted on having at least three good smokes. Fergusson had told Stuart-Smith to take care. He was worried about Victor's health.

The old man lit up and blew out grey smoke. He sighed. His face was lined, careworn. *The spy of the sorrowful countenance*, thought Stuart-Smith.

'I fear I cannot foretell the future any more.'

'But you used to be able to.'

'That was because the future was connected to the past. The march of history. Now the link has been broken. We are living in a continuous present. Maybe I will be of no further use to you.'

They were near the end of the briefing session. It was just Stuart-Smith and Victor, and, piece by piece, year by year, they were putting in place the mechanisms whereby Victor and his wife would one day walk out of Moscow for good – he leaving behind his uniquely well-placed position – and walk into a retirement home near a golf course in Sunningdale. The relationship was not without its strains. They wanted to keep Victor in Moscow for as long as possible. Victor wanted to get out of Moscow as soon as possible. But both sides were professional. Each knew what the other wanted.

Victor was the most extraordinary agent that Stuart-Smith had ever come across. He seemed to know everything. It was he who had warned them a couple of years before that certain NATO war games were being viewed with the utmost alarm in Moscow: that in certain circles there was even talk of moving to a real war footing. After this warning they had arranged quietly to abandon their training exercises off the northern coast of Norway. And just at present – for the past few months – they had discovered a new and rather strange convergence of interests. Because Victor, coming at the problem from the other direction, as it were, was in a position to know exactly what was going on in the exclusive negotiations within the Geneva Group.

And so he told them. He told them just where the Soviets and the Americans had got to in the talks. He told them about the personalities, the sticking points, the areas of agreement, the disputed passages (with square brackets around them) for resolution in December, the technical annexes, the timetables, the protocols, the menus, the mood music. And he told them about the infighting in Moscow, the open warfare between the mathematicians and the military, the overload of decisions pushed ever upwards and – above all – he told them about the frank dismay in Moscow that they could be left behind in the next ruinously expensive spiral of the arms race.

'And I am telling you this, Alan,' he would say, 'because it is my belief that in reality we have a similar view of what our American friends are suggesting.'

To which Stuart-Smith would offer no comment.

'Try,' now urged Stuart-Smith.

Victor looked at him.

'You haven't been to Moscow recently, Alan?'

Stuart-Smith shook his head. 'I keep away from the place. I'm wanted there to help the police with their inquiries.'

Victor smiled. 'You have to live there to understand what is going on.'

'Well, you do. What do you see in the future?'

'You know I have no views about these matters. I am too old and cautious to have views. But there is a small futurology unit in the Academy of Sciences . . . They did an interesting paper recently . . .'

'Oh yes?'

'They say the locomotive of history has stopped working. You know they like to use that kind of language, these futurologists. It is safer. They talk about iron laws of history that are snapped. Fallen idols. Toppled statues. Official newspapers thrown down in the street. A clamour of voices. Hungry people. And then reprisals. The thirst for order. A struggle for power . . .'

Victor permitted himself another slight smile.

'They found a phrase from an article written by one of your American friends: *the end of history*.'

'Anything else?'

Victor shrugged his shoulders.

'I cannot tell. The falcon cannot hear the falconer.'

'I'm sorry?'

'An Irish joke.'

'What about the rest of the Warsaw Pact?'

'The Warsaw Pact?'

Victor seemed to have some difficulty in adjusting his horizons.

'You know, I think the day will come soon when the Warsaw Pact will just fall apart. Poor Alan, what will you do then? What will any of us do?'

Stuart-Smith reflected.

'Join you in Sunningdale, I suppose.'

'Ha!'

Stuart-Smith looked at his watch. The old man was obviously going off the rails. He would soon be making no sense at all. And he would have to leave in a few minutes to get back to Heathrow. By the way, where was Harry?

'There *was* just one thing I wanted to mention to you, Alan.'

Stuart-Smith's attention switched back on.

'What is that, Victor?'

'I am a little worried about the problem of *proliferation*.' The old man rolled the word around his mouth as if it was a curse.

Stuart-Smith was surprised.

'Proliferation?'

'The stealing of the secret fire by the sorcerer's apprentice. The diversion of material to nations less civilized than yours and mine. We have our doctrines, Alan. We have our rules. They do not. They want our weapons for their own wars. Unholy wars. We must not let that happen . . .'

'Do you have something specific in mind, Victor?'

Victor paused before replying. 'There are many people in Moscow who are worried about some of our Middle Eastern friends becoming too ambitious. But there is an odd thing. It seems that the line of supply comes from the western side of the curtain. It seems from certain accounts that it could even be your country that is implicated.'

'That is preposterous, Victor.'

'No doubt, Alan. But you know, even in these difficult times, we still have one or two good sources here and there . . .'

The door opened. Harry put his head round it.

'Time's up, gentlemen. The van's waiting.'

Victor rose and gathered his coat around him.

'Thank you for the meal, Alan.'

They left to get in the van. Harry came into the room and began expertly to dispose of the traces of their presence.

Stuart-Smith got back to the cage at seven o'clock that evening. The streets around Tottenham Court Road were choked with homebound traffic. He drove against the tide and turned down the entrance to the underground car park which was one of the hidden ways of access to the bastion. At the deepest level – the fifth – he parked his car and got into the lift, which rose a clear twelve floors without a break. At the entrance to the cage on the seventh floor the armed guard perused his pass, his briefcase and his signature before allowing him to compose the code on the safe door that finally let him into the building. Stuart-Smith made his way down the gangway to the heart of the cage, musing for the hundredth time on the chances of anyone escaping alive from the building if a fire ever broke out. The health and safety people would have had a fit. They had designed the cage to keep the visitors out: but it also pretty effectively kept the animals in.

Fergusson was waiting.

'You got all that?' Stuart-Smith asked, when the two of them were sitting at the conference table in Fergusson's room.

Fergusson gave a sober nod. He pointed to the folder before him.

'Customer dissemination will begin tomorrow morning. For what it's worth.'

'For what it's worth?'

'There is concern in certain quarters that Victor is overbidding his hand. It is feared that his reach may exceed his grasp.'

'Meaning?'

'Meaning his desire to egress may be stronger than his objectivity.'

'You think he's making it all up?'

'It is not for me to judge, Alan. Although I confess I am hard pressed to fill in the evaluation box.'

'You don't believe in him any more, do you?'

'It is not a question of belief, Alan. We are not at Sunday school. It is a question of weighing evidence. Victor has his voice. It is respected. It will be listened to. His comments on the Geneva Group are beyond price. But this new angle of his – the end of the Warsaw Pact – is going a little bit too far. Consider the weight of history. The onward march of the dialectic. The correlation of forces. The offensive posture. None of that has changed. The bear still has his claws. Victor is asking a great deal of us if we're to follow him down this particular path.'

Stuart-Smith shrugged his shoulders. The analysts could worry about that.

'What about this proliferation angle?'

Fergusson turned to a different folder of papers.

'That,' he said, '*is* rather curious. I want you to study these papers here, sent over from L Branch.'

Stuart-Smith flicked casually through the file. Police records. Eye-witness accounts. Coroner's reports. Identification papers. Death of an Arab on a London street.

'The police,' said Fergusson, 'discovered that the deceased was a regular visitor. He was on a shopping expedition. He did his shopping in Brussels, Amsterdam and London. And look at what was on his shopping list.'

Fergusson handed over a fax paper containing a list of components. Stuart-Smith ran his eye down it, stopped at one or two items and let out a low whistle.

'First point, Alan, is to find out how far this thing has gone. And the second point is to find out who is doing the tidying up. You know,' he added thoughtfully, 'if Victor is right about this he might be right about the rest. We could all end up having to look for new jobs.'

# Chapter Twelve

'Feed that to the analysts,' said de la Fosse to his secretary, Judith, throwing back on to her desk a thick document covered with graphs and indices. It might have been the results of a satellite reconnaissance report. It might even have been the rather exotic financial accounts of Elphick and his troops to the east of London, seeking – as always – a little more money from de la Fosse, a little more love and trust. But it was, in fact, merely a company cash flow study. 'I want a position report by tomorrow morning, with recommendations to buy, sell or hold. Now, where was I?'

'Disintermediation, I think.'

'Ah, yes.'

De la Fosse drifted off into a financial reverie for a couple of moments. Then he looked Judith directly in the eyes and said slowly, 'Disintermediation is the scourge that threatens this great industry of ours. Unless we adapt, ladies and gentlemen, I submit to you that our firms will be overwhelmed by the new financial currents that are washing over our globe. Money is like oil. It has to be refined before it can be used by industry. It is our job as intermediaries to process and refine that oil. We have to explore new sources of liquidity and ensure that firms obtain the finance they need at the time, the place and the price which suits them. We are all of us financial engineers now . . .'

De la Fosse paused. Judith laid her pen down to rest on her note pad and looked at her fingernails.

'Yet,' de la Fosse resumed, 'there are forces at work which are turning the world as we know it upside down. Gone are the days when banks alone raised capital for firms. Instead we are living in a world where many firms can raise capital at finer rates than banks themselves. They have become their own bankers. From there it is but a step to one firm acting as banker to another firm. What then of we professionals, caught, one might say, in a real bear squeeze?'

De la Fosse paused again to marshal his thoughts.

'For us there is only one answer. Reintermediation will come only through innovation. We must refine and refine again. We must process and blend. We must distil and crack. We must always offer something new . . .'

The door was open. A female figure stood on the threshold.

'Come in, Julia. I am near the end of this bout of inspiration. Now, Judith, can you suggest any other ideas?'

Judith thought for a moment.

'The parable of the talents, sir?'

De la Fosse shook his head.

'A little hackneyed, I fear. These are merchant bankers I am addressing. Let us keep away from the Bible.'

His eyes glittered briefly. He added, 'It might be a sore area. After all, some of them are still on the Black List.'

'Black List?'

'A little footnote to Biblical matters.'

'Like us?'

'Like us, my child. Now, let me see all that on double-spaced A4. This afternoon. Before the analysts' conference. Take a seat, Julia.'

Judith gathered her materials and left. Julia positioned herself some distance from de la Fosse's desk. On her crossed legs were balanced two green files.

'I love this job,' said de la Fosse to Julia, as the door closed.

'What do you like about it so much?'

'Power without responsibility. The prerogative of the harlot throughout the ages. You know what they call it when you get your cover up and running smoothly?'

'No.'

'Joyriding. And they're absolutely right. It's a free ride at high speed in a stolen car. I've been here for three years now. I can come and go as I please. I can pop in to see whoever I like in London and I can preserve total confidentiality. Operational bliss.'

'Until you crash the car.'

'I won't. We won't. Not yet. Don't you love your cover, Julia?'

Julia shrugged her shoulders.

'It's a job.'

'Tell me.'

'What?'

'Tell me about Colchester. Are you joyriding?'

'We're running. Let's not get ahead of ourselves.'

'So?'

'So he wants to see me again.'

'Aha!'

'But the question is do I want to see him?'

'Of course you do.'

'Do I? There are risks.'

'No investment is risk free.'

'Please. Keep the proverbs for the moneylenders.'

'Institutional investors, thank you, Julia.'

'If you say so. Were the analysts happy with the stuff from him?'

'Not bad, they tell me. Not bad at all. My next meeting with our friend the minister should be worth all the effort I'm putting into it. But we're missing one important detail. We need the date of shipment. Get it for us, and we'll know what to do next. That's why you have to cuddle up to young Guy just once more.'

'All right. But there is something else I should tell you. He's got someone from El Mihr dropping in on Thursday. He wants to know what the men from the ministry are doing to his scheme. Colchester will tell me what happens afterwards.'

De la Fosse thought.

'But this is better than I'd hoped. He's actually drawing them out. And we have a line into him. Stick close, Julia. Stick close.'

'I've said I'll see him one more time. But that's it.'

Julia . . .' De la Fosse's voice was reproachful.

'I'm sorry,' she said. 'The operation has its limits. It's all in here.' She tapped the top file on her knee. Exhibit A. 'We agreed the rules of engagement. You come in at a high level. I come in further down, get what we need and then I get out. I don't hang around like a decoy duck.'

'Why not innovate?'

'Because I'm not one of your institutional investors. I want to keep alive. And I want to keep my job. You know as well as I do this could all collapse at any moment. When it does I don't want to be the one underneath. I go in one more time and then I get out.'

'Very well.' De la Fosse changed tack. 'Colchester. What do you make of him?'

'I can – handle him.'

'Do you like him?'

'I might. But the point doesn't arise.'

'Did we get our assessment right?'

'I – think so.'

De la Fosse looked at Julia and then reached over and took one of the green files from her. He flicked through the pages. He found what he wanted.

' "I have been watching the subject for three weeks now," ' he read out. ' "He could be ideally suited to our purposes. Reliable, predictable, a strong sense of duty, ingrained habits and customs . . . Will probably need pointing in the right direction and told to march . . . Straightforward. Unlikely to create *feedback problems* . . ." '

He closed the file and handed it back.

'The gospel according to Julia. Were we right? Did we get the right man? Is he feedback free?'

She picked up the other file – the master file – and looked at the opening entry in de la Fosse's handwriting. She read the words, which she knew by heart, aloud.

' "The interesting feature of this case is the fact that we are looking for a subject who will not realize he is working for us. It is a difficult but not impossible challenge. In one sense, this is only a matter of carrying to further lengths our existing policy of total integration. If we successfully become the society we live in we can also become its secret service. For someone with little experience it will be difficult to tell the difference. It is not possible to say how stable this relationship will be. There is a good chance that it will be unstable. But in the mean time we could establish a middle-level source and also gain experience for the future . . ." '

'I think so,' she said slowly once again.

'Good,' said de la Fosse in his best courtier's voice. 'Your father would be proud of you.'

Don't bring him into it, thought Julia, as she looked out of the smoked-glass window down on to the traffic of the Gray's Inn Road fifty feet beneath. I'll do it but don't bring him into it. I'll do my performance once again, even though it frightens me, even though I have no head for heights, even though I don't think I like it or am very good at it. I will swing through the air and pick up that young man and we will fly together for a short time and then I will drop him, even though we have no safety net. And if I am lucky I will swing back to safety one more time.

She wondered if she was feeling homesick. But that made no sense; she'd had no home for ten years. She was partly English, but mostly of no fixed abode; a gypsy, wandering from camp site, learning at every new stop to become part of the local culture, to become more English than the English, more French than the French, more Catholic than the Pope. That's what you got with an international school in Paris, a mother dead and buried in the Chilterns and a distant father everybody else thought was a wonderful patriot.

How could you be homesick for a country you no longer belonged to, she wondered? Could you be homesick for a country you have adopted? Or could it be simply that she was looking for certainty – for a land that was peaceful and quiet, that had known boundaries, where warfare and revenge and killing were not essential to survival?

As she looked over the streets of London she thought how much she would give just to live here without fear, with total integration, no longer a stranger in a strange land.

*Your father would be proud of you.*

But could she be proud of him?

94

# Chapter Thirteen

On the following Thursday a weak sun was shining over Northumberland Avenue, and a shaft of pale light created a nimbus round the distinguished head of a well-contented Deputy Secretary Garrick as he surveyed the deferential inhabitants of the conference room on the fourth floor of the Ministry of Exports. The Projects Committee was taking a moment's break. The committee had cantered through its agenda this morning. It was all due to wise chairmanship, Garrick told himself. He was the pilot who steered this motley crew through the reefs of technicality and the shallows of tedium. Who else but he could have got so many sluggish heads to have grasped so many diverse details?

This morning engineering adviser Marsh, for example, sitting over at the far end of the table, had been as good as gold. He had maintained an aloof silence throughout the entire proceedings. Was he brooding on something? Or was he simply off his feed? There was no telling. And no need to tell.

Stitt, the young secretary, looked at Garrick to reconvene the meeting. Garrick decided this was the psychological moment to speed things up.

'I think, dear colleagues,' he said, 'that since we are going so quickly this morning we should try to keep up our momentum. I propose therefore to institute what I call an accelerated procedure for the remaining items on the agenda. This will focus our thoughts and be good for our constitutions.'

'The next project is Mr Fulbright's mining project, number 8763,' said the dutiful Stitt.

Garrick smiled at Fulbright, squeezed between half a dozen other heads of department at the far end of the table from Marsh. Behind him, among a row of officials sitting in attendance with their backs against the wall, was Colchester.

'Gentle Fulbright, you are most welcome to our counsels. I am giving you just one minute to tell us of the merits of mining project

8763 without hesitation, deviation or repetition, starting . . . now!'

Fulbright shuffled his papers. Colchester could see the back of his neck turning red.

'I hardly think I will need a minute, Deputy Secretary. If you remember the will of the committee was that this project was perfectly acceptable subject to final clearance from the MOD.'

Stitt came to his rescue.

'That is so, Deputy Secretary. It was Mr Marsh who stipulated this as a condition of acceptance.'

Marsh took his pipe out of his mouth but said nothing.

Garrick looked from Marsh to Fulbright. He thought of the brief and acerbic conversation he had had with the minister at morning prayers.

'Well, can we now all settle our differences? Mr Fulbright, I take it that you have passed the time profitably since our last meeting in getting the yea of our military chums?'

Fulbright nodded.

'That is correct, Deputy Secretary.'

'And, Mr Marsh, do you not now feel that the time has come to bury the hatchet and let this project get past you?'

Marsh laid down his pipe. He glanced at the papers before him. Then he raised his head, looked ponderously around the committee room and said, 'I am afraid not, Deputy Secretary.'

Stitt, who had been taking the note, laid down his pen and looked with renewed interest at Marsh. Garrick sat back in his chairman's seat, removed his spectacles and massaged his eyebrows. How on earth could he begin to explain this to his political master? Over at the other end of the room Fulbright was emitting a kind of primordial bubbling sound.

Garrick put his spectacles back on and subjected Marsh to a pained appraisal.

'Are we really to run over a minute on this, my dear fellow? And I had thought we were going so well.'

'I am still not happy, Deputy Secretary.'

Garrick's stare deepened in intensity.

'Your reasons? Let us gauge your discontent.'

'I have only recently obtained some new information about this project, Deputy Secretary. I would like to lay this before the committee.'

Garrick could see Fulbright out of the corner of his eye. Fulbright had picked up an official blotter from the table and seemed to be quietly ripping it to shreds.

'New evidence, my dear Marsh?' said Garrick thoughtfully. 'Well, well. A little late in the trial, don't you think?'

'Better late than never, Deputy Secretary.'

'But is it *material* evidence, Mr Marsh?'

Fulbright could contain himself no longer.

'Deputy Secretary, I think we should call a halt to this comedy—'

Garrick raised a hand in silent reproof.

'My dear Fulbright, I must be allowed to fumble my own way forward as chairman. You have my sympathy but I have to be allowed my own methods.' He sighed. 'All right, Mr Marsh, enlighten us. You have the ear of the meeting.'

'Thank you, Deputy Secretary,' said Marsh. 'It is highly material evidence, I believe. I have been conducting some research into the operations of Benbow Engineering. As engineering adviser it is my duty to do so. And I have found a very pertinent fact.'

He paused for effect.

'Benbow Engineering are the subject of proceedings by the Inland Revenue for non payment of three years' advance corporation tax.'

As the committee digested this a hubbub spread around the table. Someone stifled what sounded to Colchester like a snigger. Garrick drew a deep breath and looked down at his hands.

'Well, Mr Marsh, thank you. That is very illuminating. But is it strictly relevant?'

'I think it is, Deputy Secretary. The point is, can we as a government department authorize a company to take a commercial act with its attendant risks at the taxpayers' expense, while at the same time the IR is trying to recover lost revenue?'

Garrick asked himself whether he had underestimated the cunning genius of this fellow. But he continued in his innocent voice, 'I am confused. What do you think we should do, Mr Marsh?'

'I think we should postpone clearance until we have a proper view from the IR.'

Fulbright exploded.

'Deputy Secretary, this is simply absurd. I must protest most forcefully. Mr Marsh attaches new conditions to this straightforward project every time he looks at it. My professional competence is being called into question here . . .'

Garrick waited for Fulbright to subside. He then looked at Marsh. But Marsh simply withdrew into himself and lit his pipe again.

There was a pause.

'Well, Deputy Secretary,' said Marsh finally, 'I have given my professional advice. The secretary will ensure it is on the record. It is of course up to the committee to accept or reject it.'

It was at this point that young Stitt the secretary picked up his pen and caught Garrick's eye.

'I wonder if the following solution would meet the case, Deputy Secretary . . . ?'

At three-thirty that afternoon a cold and rather anxious Mehmet was lingering on the street near the entrance to the Ministry of Exports half an hour before his appointment with Colchester.

Mehmet watched and waited. For what, he could not exactly say. He wanted as usual to get the feel of the place. He wanted to be able to report back to Yassavi: 'This is what the building looks like. It has so many floors. It appears to have so many people working for it. It is innocent.' Or, alternatively: 'It has the feel of something more than it looks. It has windows that are dark. It has guards who look as if they may be armed. The people who work there look fit and trained – more fit and trained than they should do.'

Mehmet could not decide one way or another. The place *looked* innocent. He could detect no suspicious reflecting windows, no dubious forests of aerials and other communications equipment. The people who went in and out of the main entrance, as he walked cautiously to and fro past it, seemed subdued, peacable, unwarlike. But then again perhaps that was what you would expect. This was not a military society. In this country the civil authorities held the reins of power.

Doubtful, but at least feeling reassured that he was not entering a military citadel, Mehmet presented himself at the front desk at four o'clock. A shrivelled old security guard in a blue shirt took a break from his afternoon cup of tea and responded slowly when Mehmet explained the purpose of his visit. He searched for an eternity through a large ring folder full of details of visitors, cards, scribbled amendments and bits of loose paper. Then he shook his head.

'I'm sorry, sir, we don't seem to have a note of your visit. They're supposed to tell us. But then half the time they forget. Just a minute, if you wouldn't mind . . .'

He picked up the telephone on his desk, made a connection through to someone.

'We have a Mr – what was it again, sir? – a Mr Mehmet down here in reception for Mr Colchester. From El Mihr Mining, he says. Is he expected up there? Then I'll send him up with an escort straight away.'

He put the phone down and filled out a pass which he handed to Mehmet.

'There you are, sir, not your fault at all. Perhaps you could just see this gentleman from security.'

This could be it, Mehmet thought, as from around the corner a hefty and intimidating man lumbered. He beckoned to Mehmet to come into an alcove round the corner from the reception desk. Mehmet froze as the man indicated that he should raise his arms in the air. The man looked at him with an air of regret and took from him the briefcase which Mehmet clutched tightly in his left hand.

'If you could just co-operate, sir. This won't take a minute. We have to check everyone who goes in these days. You wouldn't believe the types we have to watch out for.'

Mehmet slowly put his hands in the air and allowed himself to be frisked. Then he opened his case and allowed the large man to ascertain it contained no bombs.

The large man smiled.

'Thank you, sir. Sorry to be a nuisance, but we need to be certain you're not a terrorist. I'm sure you understand.'

Mehmet managed to smile back. 'I do indeed. We have to be careful where I come from too.'

The large man led Mehmet to the lift and took him up to the tenth floor. When they arrived he handed Mehmet over to a young woman with short blonde hair dressed in bright green who was waiting for him. Molly beamed.

'Mr Mehmet? Can you come this way? Thank you, Justin, I'll do the necessary now.'

The lift doors closed, and Justin returned silently to the lower depths.

Molly led Mehmet into a small meeting room near Fulbright's

office. Twenty seconds later the door opened and a rather large fair-haired young man came in, extending an apparently friendly hand. As they shook the two men considered each other rather carefully.

'Mr Mehmet? My name is Colchester. I'm glad to see you. Please take a seat.'

Mehmet did so, trying to formulate impressions, crystallize what it was that vaguely disturbed him. It was not the building. Not the office. Not the other people. It was something to do with Colchester. Colchester did not appear particularly dangerous. Perhaps he really was the minor civil servant he should be. But there was something else. Some consciousness in his eyes? Some tension? Some hidden awareness? As if he was waiting for something. As if he was watching out for something.

'Have you come a long way, Mr Mehmet?'

Mehmet shrugged.

'Halfway across the world. But that is quite normal. I travel often to Europe on behalf of my firm.'

'I'm glad you came to see us personally, Mr Mehmet. We have had some problems, I admit. It is easier to explain these things face to face than on the telephone.'

'The last man who said that to me had some bad news, Mr Colchester. Do you have some bad news for me?'

'We discussed the El Mihr project just this morning, Mr Mehmet. How is progress going there? The mining, I mean.'

'As satisfactorily as possible in the absence of the new heavy-duty machinery.'

'Copper? Bauxite? Ligneous coal?'

'Yes, all of those, of course. But we cannot make further progress unless and until we obtain the machinery we have ordered. We cannot get that from the firm we have chosen because they tell us they cannot get approval from you, So, Mr Colchester, what was the result of your meeting this morning?'

Colchester avoided his eyes.

'Mr Mehmet, we have decided on a slightly unusual procedure. For a number of reasons I am afraid that granting export credits to ship machinery to your country has not been straightforward. However, after much consideration, we have arrived at two decisions.'

'Which are?'

'Firstly, we have given approval to your project.'

Mehmet breathed out, despite himself.

'But?'

'But, secondly, we are going to ask the company in question, Benbow Engineering, to stage deliveries over a period of time. In fact, to divide the order into three. There are six machines in question. The first two can go immediately. The remainder can be released in batches as our investigations continue.'

'Investigations?'

'I am afraid I cannot give you too much detail, Mr Mehmet. These matters are confidential. But we still have a few loose ends to tie up with the company.'

'What do you mean, "loose ends"?'

'Taxation matters. Questions of British law. Nothing that need concern you. But, unfortunately, some details that do concern us.'

Mehmet was silent for a few moments. He just could not understand it.

'So, two now? The rest later?'

'That is it.'

'When?'

'As soon as possible.'

'Who decides?'

'We will, Mr Mehmet.'

Mehmet shook his head. He had many years of experience of meetings and negotiations. He could not understand why they had chosen someone to meet him who lied so badly.

After Mehmet had left Colchester stood for a while at the window looking down at the moving figures in the street ten floors beneath, contemplating the rather odd encounter he had just had. He had never met anyone like Mehmet in his life before. As he stood there Molly came in.

'You can see a lot from that window,' she said.

'Very curious,' replied Colchester, watching the tiny figure of Mehmet emerge into the street below. He saw him join the stream of pedestrians heading up to Trafalgar Square, and then vanish from view.

'Bit of a sharp customer for an engineer, don't you think?' remarked Molly.

Colchester said nothing for a moment.

'Do you know,' he said, still looking out of the window, 'there isn't a trace of copper, bauxite or ligneous coal in that part of the world.'

Molly looked blank.

'Did you tell him?' she asked.

'Tell him what?' asked Colchester.

'About the minister's note, of course. What else?'

Colchester looked at the piece of blue embossed paper which she held in front of her and which had winged its way down to their department from the minister's private office immediately after the Projects Committee that morning. In red ink, which seemed to leap off the page, Timothy Warwick said he would be very grateful if the department could *cease* its campaign to hinder the affairs of British business and *begin* to take seriously its mission to *promote exports*, in which he was now taking a *personal interest*. Fulbright, his office door closed, was composing a memorandum of reply, which might or might not be passed by the private office to the minister, depending on how contrite it was.

'No,' said Colchester. 'I didn't think I'd mention it.'

# Chapter Fourteen

When Colchester got to Willy's Bar that evening Julia had not yet arrived. He ordered himself a gin and tonic and sat and waited.

It seemed to be the hour of the assignation. Throughout the large cocktail lounge men and women were meeting, uniting after the painful daytime hours of forced separation.

Colchester tried to analyse why he was feeling so anxious. There was of course the unusual pressure from the minister's office, of a kind seldom experienced. That was bad enough. And then the conversation with Mehmet had been unsettling. Mehmet's physical presence had brought starkly home to him the reality of what he had got involved in. And it opened up a further line of thought. Could it all be something that was actually far outside his capability? He cast his mind back to his job interview with Fulbright. According to measurement by the office rules, at least, that capability was clearly rather modest. And what other rules were there? His doubts mounted. Doubts about Mehmet and his affairs. Doubts about himself. And, after a while, he started to have doubts about Julia and whether she would turn up at all that evening. Outside hundreds of other people were passing by, on their way to different destinations. Could there be any guarantee that Julia would really make her way back here to see him again?

And underlying everything Colchester knew that he had one further reason to be worried. Because he had done something that day which he should not have done. And which he already regretted.

But when he saw Julia come in, saw the physical reality of the woman he had thought so much about, he fought back his qualms. He drained his glass and told himself it was time to play his next trick.

Julia came up to Colchester, a slight smile on her lips, and held out her hand. As he took it she brushed back her hair and he caught the scent of her skin. Would a kiss have been out of place, he wondered?

'Am I late?' she asked.

'No,' said Colchester, as they sat down. 'I was early. Tell me, do you have far to come?'

Julia shook her head.

'Don't ask. I'm not allowed to tell you.'

'Not even that?'

'Not even that.'

After more drinks had arrived Julia looked over her glass and said, 'But I can tell you that your work has been greatly appreciated. De la Fosse himself asked me to pass on his congratulations.'

'Thank you,' said Colchester. 'I don't think the visitor I had this afternoon will do that yet.'

Julia leaned forward.

'Tell me. Was he a bad man? Did he wear a black hat?'

'No black hat. And,' said Colchester carefully, 'I don't really know if he's a bad man or not. We didn't go into his ethics. He said he was from El Mihr. Maybe he was. Maybe not. He wanted to know what was happening to his machines. I can't blame him for being upset. He wasn't clapping his hands when I told him the latest news.'

'What do you mean – latest news?'

Colchester looked innocently at his glass.

'That the Projects Committee refused to allow all the machines to go at once. They are going to space delivery out, probably over some weeks.'

Julia looked rather disconcerted. She put down her glass.

'But you told me it was all signed and sealed and ready to go. You told me this morning's session was just a rubber stamp job.'

'Yes,' answered Colchester. 'That's what I thought it would be. But then our engineering adviser got hold of some worrying material about Benbow's tax position. He dug his heels in. You see, he doesn't really like my head of department. It's a long-standing feud. It goes back to a time five years ago when they were grounded together in an airport lounge on the way to Egypt. All night. Anyway, the secretary to the committee came up with a compromise. We agree the project, let two machines through now, and the others in two more batches later. Subject to further consideration.'

Julia sat back and considered.

'Well, that could be an intriguing development.'

Colchester could not suppress a grin.

'I thought it might be,' he said.

Julia kept her voice low.

'What do you mean?'

'I did the research on Benbow myself. The taxation material was buried in my file. I just made sure that Marsh had a copy. His reaction was easy to predict.'

She looked at him carefully.

'But not what the result would be?'

Colchester's grin widened.

'I don't know. The secretary, Stitt, is a friend. I told him beforehand what Marsh was likely to do. I suggested the compromise he put forward myself. We agreed it would spare everyone's blushes. He'll go far, will Stitt.'

'But . . .' said Julia, and then bit her tongue.

'I thought it all out by myself,' continued Colchester. 'I thought a bit more about what you said about slowing things down. And eventually I found a way. I assumed you'd be pleased.'

'I am,' said Julia. 'Of course I am. It's just that it comes as a surprise. We planned a one-off operation. We'll need to rethink our schedule —'

'After all, anything that slows down CW output is a good thing, isn't it?'

'Oh, absolutely.'

'Although to be honest I'm surprised that a few mechanical diggers should make that much difference.'

'Well,' said Julia absently, 'it's a question of parameters.'

'You're the expert. Another?'

'Thank you, no, Guy. It's late. I think I'd better be going.'

'Until the next time, then?'

'The next time?'

'Now that the operation is going to take longer, I assume we'll need to keep in contact. We could meet up regularly if you like. I could keep you posted on developments. Perhaps once a week?'

It was only then that the light dawned on Julia. She stood up.

'You did all that,' she said slowly, 'just to get to see more of me?'

Colchester looked at her for a while without saying anything. It seemed to her that he was on the edge of telling her something important. A confession, perhaps? Or a denunciation?

'You can't just walk into my life and then walk out again, you know,' he finally said.

Now it was Julia's turn to look at him in silence. Could she already sense the operation getting away from her? The ground shifting beneath her feet?

'This is what I was afraid of,' she said.

De la Fosse paid careful attention when, half an hour later, Julia chivvied him out of a bankers' dinner at his club and made him walk briskly around a windswept St James's Square with her, while she told him the news. He looked thoughtful when she described how Colchester had engineered matters so that he could keep on seeing her.

'But the point is, what am I to do?'

'You have no choice, Julia. You must innovate.'

'But it's dangerous to keep this contact going. This was supposed to be positively the last time. I've done what I was asked to do. It's too exposed.'

'Julia,' began de la Fosse in an insistent voice. 'You have to finish what you have started. No one can ever predict operations completely. You are at present only halfway across.'

Julia became all at once strangely angry.

'I didn't want to do this in the first place, you know that. I don't like these open-ended commitments. They're all far too risky.'

'Risky for whom?'

'Risky for me. And you know very well how risky it could be for him.'

They had stopped walking. The night was cold but neither of them felt it. Over by de la Fosse's club the torches of celebration were lit. The flames guttered and swept majestically to and fro in the dark.

'Please remember that on this territory you are under my command, Julia,' said de la Fosse in a distant voice. 'If you feel that strongly I will accept your resignation when this operation is over. But you know how important it is. We are all subject to orders.

If you cannot accept them you should go back to your father and see if he can find you another post more suited to your . . . temperament.'

'You and my father,' said Julia bitterly. 'You're all the same . . .'

# Chapter Fifteen

'Resign? Why should you want to resign?'

Fulbright looked up in astonishment from his desk, like a badger surprised at its labours. He had a pile of papers strewn in front of him. Distressingly, many of them had bright red 'Immediate' labels attached. The flow of papers into Fulbright's office with priority markings was never equalled by the outflow, and the long-term consequence of this was that all red labels in the ministry gravitated to his office. Periodically Molly would return boxfuls to office supplies.

Molly now stood defiantly before him, her hands clenched in the pockets of her bright blue skirt. She looked a little like a rather aggressive kingfisher.

'I don't have to give my reasons. I just want to do something different. I've been here too long already.'

Fulbright got up and closed the door of his office, as he had been told to do on his management courses.

'Is it me?' he said. 'Is it something I have done?'

Molly's eyes widened.

'Oh no, it's not you. You don't have anything to do with it.'

Was Fulbright perhaps a little disappointed?

'Then what? You're a good secretary. Your work is . . . exemplary, I think I put that in your last report. You could rise to the top of the secretarial grade.'

'I have to move on,' said Molly. 'I've been here almost two years already. I can't spend my whole life typing up your handwriting. I'm young. I'm ruining my eyesight.'

'Your eyesight?' Fulbright reflected. 'Have you considered wearing spectacles? I'm sure they would make you look more attractive.'

'No, I haven't considered wearing spectacles. I want a complete change of scenery, not a pair of glasses.'

'But what will you do?'

'I don't know yet. There are lots of possibilities. People are always after secretaries. Maybe I'll go to an agency.'

'I find it astonishing that you can contemplate facing the unknown.'

'It's not the Sahara desert, you know. People do find jobs. I might make more money.'

'But what about security?'

'Security? Do you mean secrets? I don't know any.'

'No, I meant your security. A job is for life, you know. You're secure. With a pension.'

Molly wrinkled her nose.

'It seems a long time to wait. And I don't want to do it here. I want to get as far away from here as possible. Can't you understand?'

Then another terrible thought struck Fulbright.

'But what about me? Who will do my typing? You can read my handwriting—'

There was a knock on the door. Stanton walked in. He was engrossed in a file he was carrying which dealt with Finnish import statistics, upon which he had come to consult Fulbright. It was only when he looked up that he noticed Molly and Fulbright deep in discussion. He frowned.

'I'm sorry,' he said. 'I wanted to know if you'd like to go to Helsinki personally for the talks.'

Fulbright scratched his beard.

'Not now, if you wouldn't mind. Molly and I have something important to discuss.'

'Not me,' said Molly. 'I've said what I have to say. You might as well tell him.'

And before Fulbright could stop her Molly turned to Stanton and said, 'I'm putting in my resignation.'

Stanton did not generally react quickly to news. But at this he let the file slip from his fingers.

'Are you serious?'

'Yes.'

'When?'

'I'm giving two weeks' notice, like I have to.'

'What are you going to do?'

'Who knows? Who cares? Just so long as I get away from this place.'

And so saying Molly brushed past Stanton and ran out through the open door and down the corridor. Stanton and Fulbright looked askance at one another.

'I don't know what's going on. I just don't know,' said Fulbright. 'All she'll tell me is she's tired of being here. But she doesn't seem to know what she wants to do next.'

He regarded the papers on his desk in dismay, the enormity of life without a secretary growing more stark by the second.

'Who can I find who will understand my system?'

'Why don't I have a word with her?' said Stanton, picking up his own papers. 'I might be able to talk to her more easily.'

Fulbright was puzzled.

'You? Why you?'

'I might have some idea why she wants to leave.'

'You do? What is it?'

'Maybe I'd better speak to her first.'

In the small meeting room down the corridor used a few days before by Colchester and Mehmet, Molly stood by herself drying her eyes. She did not usually cry easily, but it was not every day that she handed in her resignation. She was just dabbing the last tears away when the door opened and Stanton came in.

'Oh, go away,' Molly said crossly.

'Can I come in?' said Stanton, as if he had not heard.

'I've just said go away. I don't want to be seen.'

'That's OK,' said Stanton mildly, as he came in the room. 'I don't mind.'

'Oh, what's the use,' said Molly with exasperation.

'Now, what's it all about?' asked Stanton.

'I don't want to talk about it.'

'But I do.'

Molly was starting to get angry.

'What business is it of yours? My life is my affair. I don't ask you to butt in. I just want to go away from here.'

'But I want to know what you're going to do next. Have you got some other job lined up?'

'You just want to know because he asked you to ask me.'

'That's not true.'

'Well, you would say that.'

Stanton collected his thoughts. He was not used to scenes.

'It's something to do with Guy, isn't it?' he said.

110

Now it was Molly's turn to be amazed.

'However —?'

'I keep my eyes open. It is, isn't it?'

Molly looked at the ground.

'I don't see that it's any business of yours,' she said. But then she shrugged her shoulders and added rapidly, 'I've seen him with this woman. They were coming out of a bar on Jermyn Street. He was looking at her. I've never seen him look like that before. He was just . . .' She searched her vocabulary for the right expression. 'He was just on another planet.'

'What was she like?'

'A wardrobe mistress. An executive tart. She'll be leading him down the garden path.'

'So you're not interested in Guy any more?'

'What has it got to do with you?'

'I don't want you to leave here.'

'Why not?'

Stanton hesitated.

'I – need you here.'

Molly looked at him and kept on looking at him, while Stanton began to look more and more abashed. Finally she giggled.

'I don't believe it. Say it's not true.'

Half an hour later Stanton broke the good news to Fulbright that Molly had changed her views about leaving the office. After much persuading and reasoning she had finally agreed to stay.

'Then why did she say she wanted to go?' asked a peeved Fulbright.

'It was all a mistake. She got hold of the wrong end of the stick,' replied Stanton.

# Chapter Sixteen

'How did you get into your line of work?' Colchester asked Julia.
'I mean, did de la Fosse take you to his club and blow cigar rings
at you?'

They were in a small busy restaurant in Soho. It was their fourth
meeting. Outside it was a dark evening, wet and chill. But inside
there were candles and Frascati, ricotta, breadsticks, grappa, olive
oil, tomatoes, pasta and bright red tablecloths. Julia kept her hands
on her side of the table. She was dressed in black. She wore
no wedding ring. For Colchester a sense of what? Of something
unspoken? Some subtle change in Julia's attitude? Or was it just
that he was gradually seeing more than her professional per-
sonality?

Julia shook her head. She was cautious tonight, wary, as if
disturbed by something. Colchester told himself, it is almost as if
she's *afraid* of something. But that was ridiculous.

Then Julia smiled at him, and his doubts evaporated.

'Sorry. Off limits,' she said. 'I can't talk about it. Try again. In
any case it wasn't his club. They don't let women in.'

'Well, all right,' he persisted. 'Stick to generalities. You must
have been drawn into the work. It's that I'm interested in. Your
motives. Your emotions.'

Julia reflected.

'Emotions? I try not to have emotions about it. They complicate
things.'

'But something powerful must have drawn you towards it?'

'Must it? How do any of us end up doing what we're doing?
Take your case. Luck. Chance. Circumstance. You're in the right
place at the right time. Or the wrong place at the wrong time.
Your face fits. It doesn't fit. A thousand reasons.'

'A pretty face helps?'

She smiled again. 'It helps. But it's not enough. I don't have a
mission. I have a job to do. That's all.'

Colchester took a drink. He could sense there was something else, unsaid.

'You don't think you're protesting too much?'

'Do you think I am? Perhaps . . .' Julia paused to think this one through. She seemed to have some difficulty finding the right concepts. 'Perhaps you *could* say I am a patriot. Let's say I owe my country something for looking after me. It's not blind affection. It's just a debt, you might call it.'

'It sounds a bit – old-fashioned?'

'Yes. It probably does. I'm just an old-fashioned girl.' Then Julia changed tone. 'What about you?'

'Me?'

'There's something a bit out of place with you. Something I can't put my finger on. You don't really seem suited for your work, I think.'

Colchester looked surprised.

'I thought you knew all about me by now.'

'We never know enough.'

'We?'

'Is this business or pleasure?' he asked cautiously.

'Don't worry. It's not for the file. I'm just curious.'

Colchester considered for a while, then shrugged his shoulders. Why not tell her?

'I suppose you could say I'm doing time,' he said.

'Time?'

'It was my father's idea. He has this belief – certainty, really – in the idea of the public good. He got it from his father. I was born into the heroic age of public service. A child of the New Jerusalem . . .'

'So?'

'So I'm continuing the family tradition. It's a kind of national service. Only there isn't a war on. So it has to be the civil service instead. Less heroic, wouldn't you say?'

'But why? Why do you have to do what he tells you?'

'You said it yourself.'

'What?'

'A debt. I have a debt to pay too.'

'It was a figure of speech.'

Colchester looked rueful.

'Not for me it isn't. I owe him money. Real money. For my

113

education. School fees. University costs. It mounts up. This is his way of getting me to repay.'

'I see . . .' said Julia, digesting this.

Colchester took a long drink of mineral water, as if he had just got something off his chest.

'So I have to do what he tells me,' he went on. 'Does that sound ludicrous?'

Julia smiled. She seemed to be on the point of speaking, but changed her mind. Then she too shrugged her shoulders as if to say, what did it matter?

'Not as much as you might think. I'm in a similar position myself.'

Colchester put down his drink, baffled. 'I'm sorry?'

'My father is – or was – a senior man. Held in high regard in some exclusive circles. When it came to finding something for me to do it seemed natural I should follow the career he chose. Doors were opened. Introductions made. He was very pleased. The only trouble is . . .' Here she also paused to take a drink, '. . . I happen to disagree with something important he once did.'

'What was that?'

Julia shook her head.

'I'm sorry, I really can't tell you. Most people I work with seem to think it was marvellous. The public good, you see.'

'But what do you think?'

A shadow passed across her face.

'I think it was something really rather terrible.'

Colchester continued looking at her. We can never know anyone, he thought. We meet someone and it is just a contact at the margin, an exchange of atoms at the surface. I can never know her properly. She will always carry with her a past, another side, which will always be a mystery to me.

'Do you see why being connected with you is important to me?' asked Colchester. And, even as he said it, he knew it was the wrong thing to say.

'It is?'

Julia sat back.

He felt he was losing her.

'It helps give me some kind of purpose. Continuity. It helps replace something missing.'

*Why* did Julia look away and seem to withdraw into herself?

114

'You shouldn't come to us for any answers,' she said in a smaller voice.

There was a break in the conversation while the waiter brought the main course. It was as if they had crossed some kind of threshold, as if they had entered some new territory where they were strangers, both trying to find new ground rules, new codes of conduct.

'I don't understand it,' said Colchester.

Julia was peering into the depths of the dish of pasta which had been placed before her.

'What don't you understand?' she asked faintly without looking at Colchester, as if her whole attention was focused on a difficult culinary problem.

'Anything. Aren't you supposed to tell me how important our work is, how important I am to you?'

'Is that what you want to hear?'

She avoided looking at him.

Colchester was even more perplexed.

'Well, not if it's not true, of course. I don't want you to perjure yourself. It's just – I thought you would be different.'

'How different?'

'I thought the idea was you would give me some reassurance. I give you the information you need. You give me – something in return, I don't know exactly what.'

'Do you mean love?'

Now Colchester avoided Julia's searching eyes.

'I didn't say that,' he said awkwardly. 'Perhaps ... Perhaps an *image* of something ... An image I can take away and live with.'

'Look,' said Julia earnestly, 'do you have any conception of what you're doing? Do you know the danger we're in just by keeping on seeing each other?'

'But I'm doing it for you.'

'Are you?'

'You know I am. Do you think I enjoy running risks – spiriting papers out of the office?'

'Well, perhaps you do.'

'What do you mean – perhaps I do?'

'I mean, maybe you get something out of it. You do it because you want to. You're free. Everybody in this country is free. Nobody does anything they don't want to. You want to break out. I just happen to be a way of helping you do it.'

'That's simply not true,' said Colchester. 'It's as if you're trying to excuse yourself. Isn't what I'm doing right? Isn't it necessary? Isn't it helping you?'

Julia was about to say something, then stopped and corrected herself. She smiled again.

'Of course it is,' she said. 'You're right. I'm sorry.'

She took his hand.

'We need you. I need you. Honestly.'

'Can I ask you something?' asked Colchester.

'What?'

'What exactly is it you're so frightened of?'

And Julia did not deny it. Instead she looked more serious and vulnerable than ever before.

'It's not something you can do anything about,' she said flatly. Colchester wondered if he had misheard, but she went on, 'You really would be safer not getting involved with me.'

They were near the end of the meal and perhaps both were slightly drunk. The restaurant was emptying. The candles were burning low. Colchester wondered how he could continue to engage Julia's professional interest.

'Do you know,' he said, 'the minister is now personally displeased with my work? He's convinced there's a kind of conspiracy to hold up the El Mihr project.'

Julia's eyes seemed to flicker very quickly.

'Does he? What does he do?'

'He bombards the department every other day with blue notes asking what is happening. Luckily he thinks everyone is incompetent – not just me.'

'Why is he so worried?'

'Who knows? He's in a hurry.'

'A hurry?'

'Rising star. Burning comet. Meteor flashing through the sky. An astronomical figure, really. We're just in his way.'

'Have you ever met him?'

'Me? We live in different worlds. He even uses a separate lift to get to his office. Of course I haven't met him.'

'Well, I have.'

Colchester was amazed.

'What? When?'

'Oh – socially. You see him about on the dinner circuit.'

'Your dinner circuit?'

'One's dinner circuit.'

'I see . . .' Colchester reflected. 'What's he like?'

'As a person? How can I put it . . .' Julia took a mouthful of pudding, while thinking it over. 'My personal opinion is that he is rather a dangerous type you are best keeping away from.'

Colchester looked blankly at her.

'You're joking, aren't you?'

'Yes,' Julia smiled suddenly. 'I'm joking. Can I have another glass of wine, please?'

There was a slight pause in the conversation. Then Colchester remembered. 'There's something else you haven't asked me,' he said.

'What's that?'

'The date of the next delivery to El Mihr . . .'

They stood together outside the restaurant watching the cab coming slowly towards them. It was almost midnight. The pavement, the shop windows, the passing traffic all gleamed with the rain left over from the earlier shower.

Julia turned to Colchester.

'I enjoyed myself. Honestly.'

Colchester suddenly bent forward to kiss her. But she pulled gently back. She smiled.

'Not now . . . We can be seen . . .'

The cab rattled to a halt beside them, and Julia glanced in and nodded to the driver. She turned back to Colchester and put her hand out.

'Good night.'

And then she added three words in a softer voice, 'Maybe try again.'

She got in the cab, the door closed and Colchester stood watching as it pulled off into the night.

He stood there for a full ten minutes before the spell was broken and he realized that he was freezing cold.

# Chapter Seventeen

The El Mihr Mining complex took delivery of the first two mechanical diggers from the United Kingdom the same week. They trundled solemnly along the road from the port like a pair of large yellow prehistoric beasts, a cloud of dust trailing behind them, their imprints heavy on the ill-made surface.

The Middle Eastern representative of Benbow Engineering accompanied his charges on the three-hour journey inland. He sat in the front cabin, grandly supervising the operation, staring out from his vantage point over the dry morning landscape. He liked this part of the world. Wonderful vistas. Breathtaking scenery. People came out of houses strung along the road, staring in wonder at the great machines. On the side of each was emblazoned a small Union Jack, so the world could see where it came from. The man from Benbow smiled as the occasional child waved at them. The machine in front hooted imperiously when they left each village.

They got to El Mihr at noon, as the sun grew hotter and hotter. Inside the cabin the temperature was becoming unbearable for the Englishman. The mining complex was a long way from any habitation, and in the shadow of the spoil heap an administrative centre had been thrown up.

A party of engineers and officials from the mine welcomed the arrival of the convoy with great whoops and cheers. The Benbow representative jumped down from his vehicle and shook hands with the chief engineer. The chief engineer was proud to accept delivery of these fine machines. Were there papers to sign? There were. Would Mr Benbow stay for a celebratory lunch? He would. The machines were taken round the corner to their pen, where willing hands checked their water and fuel levels.

It was not until the middle of his meal that the chief engineer was called away to the telephone and he received the news from Yassavi which did so much to spoil his day. When he returned to the canteen the Benbow man could not help noticing that he was out of sorts. The chief engineer did his best but his heart was not in the rest of the meal. When towards the end of it the Benbow man offered to stay on for a day or two to help work-in the machines the chief engineer shook his head softly.

'No, Mr Benbow, that is a kind offer, but it is not necessary. My men and I are very used to working machinery of all sorts. We will find our own way. I will ask a driver to take you back to the coast. I am sure you are a busy man and you have other work to do. As we do, I am afraid . . .'

Half an hour later the Englishman, still not quite sure what had gone wrong, was sitting in a jeep as it buzzed back along the road to the coast away from El Mihr. He made the journey back in two hours, making five hours travelling in all. His driver dropped him off and then raced back to El Mihr. This time he cut down the journey even further. It took him only an hour and a half of fast driving, so keen was he to get back and see the new machines in action.

The driver was disappointed.

When he got back to El Mihr, he found no activity of any kind in progress. What was wrong? For answer one of the other engineers pointed to the military car parked by the main building. Better not to take too much notice.

And then in the course of the afternoon the news swept through the camp that they were not going to keep the machines at El Mihr at all. There had been an error of some sort in the delivery procedure. The machines had been sent too soon. Or perhaps they had been sent too late. They were really needed elsewhere in the country. Or they were the wrong machines. They would have to go off again quite soon. And in the mean time they were not to be used but instead must pass the afternoon dozing gently in the sun, while, for a reason which no one there could understand, but no one felt inclined to query, an armed guard watched over their inert frames.

It was after nightfall when the mining crew were roused from their supper by the roar of two engines being started up outside. And through the windows of the canteen hut they could see the bizarre sight of the machines once again setting off on their travels, this time with their front headlights piercing the black night like huge eyes. The men went outside and stood in silence as the cavalcade swept out of the camp and rumbled off into the desert. The chief engineer stood slightly apart.

After ten minutes travel away from the mining complex the machines slowed to a halt. The order came from the front to switch off the headlights. They waited in the dark for half an hour, while the drivers' eyes become attuned to the gloom, and they could dimly see the outline of the desert horizon. And then there came to meet them a military four-wheel-drive vehicle. It stopped fifty yards away from the first machine and dimmed its lights. In answer the first machine blinked on its own powerful front lights for two seconds. The small vehicle turned round and the machines rolled up until they were just behind it.

And so it was that the procession travelled on half blind, following the smaller vehicle in front as its lights picked out a way ahead. It was almost four in the morning when they arrived in the forbidden district of Al Tadj. The first driver knew his way by heart round the military complex. He came up to the front gate and switched his headlights off completely. The guard opened the gate and the two machines crawled into the interior of the complex. They had completed a journey of one hundred and sixty kilometres by cover of night, undetected by the spy satellites.

Mehmet had moved to an international hotel quite near the Ministry of Exports. Near enough for him to feel that he could taste the atmosphere of the district, but not so near that he might be recognized by anyone working there. Sometimes, very late at night, he came out of the hotel, cut a tangent through the streets running down to the river from the Strand and stood looking up at the inert mass of the twelve-storey block on Northumberland Avenue. There was always a light on in the entrance area, and he discovered that relays of blue-shirted guards sat and watched television there. Mostly the upper storeys were blank and lifeless, windows like television sets that have been switched off. But just occasionally someone would be working late, and a light would shine out into the night like a beacon.

As he stood and watched on this cold November night Mehmet tried to piece together the interior life of the building. He had been inside it, once. It could have been *that* office, on *that* floor. He had met the young man there who claimed to be responsible for the El Mihr project. But did that young man know more than he would say? And somewhere near there the committee which had attached these conditions to the release of the machines would meet. Why had they done that? What forces were really housed in there? Where was the heart of this building? What was the mechanism that set the organization to work? What strange gods did they serve here?

Mehmet turned back up Northumberland Avenue, amid rows of other, equally lifeless buildings, each of which hid their secrets well. A buyer's life was sometimes lonely. A buyer was someone who operated in the margin between what was available and what was desired. He had to know what was going on on each side of the margin. He had to know prices, availability, where the intermediary he was dealing with got his supplies, who the producer at the end of the chain was, what worked, what didn't work. He had to know who was doing what back home. Who was really placing the orders? Whose word could he trust? Whose word meant nothing unless it was endorsed by someone else?

And the essence of his profession was to acquire knowledge of what was available without revealing what was desired. Many of the items for which Mehmet was looking had no fixed price. Price was a concept as nebulous as justice, or happiness, or peace. It rose and fell as a function of many things. Availability was one. Desire was another.

And of course there were some things that were beyond calculable price. Who could put a price on becoming a nuclear power?' This city of eight million inhabitants had diverted untold wealth towards acquiring such power. Other countries had done the same. They had paid crippling prices to be able to hold a weapon they could never use. They stood off from each other with guns pointed at each other's heads and said: this is cold war. This is peace. This is stability. This is the balance of terror. And they said to everyone else: keep out. Hands off. Don't touch. Finders keepers.

Except that now there was a leak. Just one. And Mehmet knew how to get at it. And Mehmet's country was not taking part in the cold war. It was taking part in a hot war.

And it believed – quite logically, in Mehmet's view – that there was no point at all in having a weapon you did not use.

It was eleven o'clock by the time Mehmet got back to his hotel. He went up to his room, switched on the television, sat on his bed and waited. He watched the re-run of a late-night gardening programme. He could see an impossible expanse of green, and an old man pottering around with armfuls of tiny bedding plants. He switched the light off and felt himself start to doze. After ten minutes he was asleep.

The telephone rang at one o'clock. Mehmet sat up. The blank television set was humming to itself, electrons chasing each others' tails in the magnetic force field.

'Yes,' he said.

'The first two machines have just arrived,' said the voice of Yassavi, almost two thousand miles away.

'In good order?'

'In good order.'

'The next two should be released soon.'

'When?'

'Next week. I must ring in to get the details. They will not tell me in advance.'

There was silence on the line for a moment.

'All this is taking too long. Far too long,' said Yassavi.

'I know,' said Mehmet.

'Try again to accelerate matters, please. I do not know how long we can hold out here. I have certain doubts . . .'

'I will do what I can,' said Mehmet. 'I will speak to our friend. And there is also the question of closing the other account.'

'Very well. But take care. Hasan was careless.'

'I am not Hasan,' said Mehmet.


Timothy Warwick was not sleeping at all well. In his *pied-à-terre* in Westminster, near Vincent Square, the dull comings and goings of the central London night seemed to reverberate through his dreams like some enormous machine performing tasks which he could not understand. Whenever he drifted back to sleep it was to return to the same picture of himself in the Commons the previous night, the almost empty chamber, the irritating insolence of the opposition spokesman ignoring him as he looked through his papers, searching like prosecuting counsel for the incriminating document and then addressing himself to the Speaker as if to say that this young Warwick fellow was scarcely worth bothering about at all. And then the same litany of questions – little questions, trivial questions – none of which he had answers for in his briefing material. And Warwick kept glancing over to the official box behind the Speaker's chair and he could see the dumb look on the faces of his officials there. He could hear his own voice offering to write to the Honourable Member as soon as possible with answers to all his queries, and, for that matter, any others he could think of. And as he sat down he saw the repressed smile on the face of Hartley from the Whips Office, sitting behind him.

It does not matter, Warwick told himself, politics is not about facts. Politics is about willpower. Nobody cares about anything factual. The important thing when you trip over something is to recover and reimpose your will upon the pattern of events. Everyone trips. It is how you recover that matters . . .

And so, after wrestling with the demon of sleep all night long, Warwick finally subdued it at five in the morning and by an effort of will banished his tormentors from his dreams. The distant mechanical sounds of London waking up mixed with the wind and took on a soothing repetitive rhythm as he finally slept, as if part of a system that was not wholly malevolent . . .

When the telephone by his bed rang at six-thirty it crashed into his sleep like an alarm bell going off in some remote official building. He awoke and lay staring in disbelief into the darkness, willing there to be a return to silence. His head throbbed.

But the telephone continued to ring. Warwick coughed to clear his throat (since you could never tell who might be ringing – it could always be the Prime Minister), and answered it.

'Yes,' he said quietly.

'Timothy?' came a voice from afar; a voice he recognized.

'Didier? Is that you?'

Warwick wondered if perhaps this *was* still a dream.

'Listen, Timothy, I have something to tell you. This is important. Are you listening?'

Warwick rubbed his head and tried to force himself to concentrate.

'Yes, I'm listening.'

Didier Ramses sounded, as always, as if he was calling from deep inside some concrete bunker buried far away in the Alps.

'That business we talked about the other day. You remember?'

'Yes,' said Warwick cautiously, trying to piece together that conversation. What instinct was it that told him he would do better to replace the receiver immediately?

'There are still problems. You have not done enough, I'm afraid.'

Warwick sighed.

'Look, Didier, I am doing all I can, I promise —'

'This has become a serious matter, Timothy. My clients expect satisfaction. They cannot wait any longer.'

'Didier, I understand. But you must realize that legally and constitutionally I am not in a position to give an executive order. I have overall political control. But in a case like this the administration is ultimately responsible. I can't just – instruct them.'

Suddenly Didier Ramses' tone changed.

'Timothy,' he said, 'I think we should not misunderstand one another. Your work with us has been valuable in the past. But no one is irreplaceable. Not even you. We have stretched a point to let you pursue your political career, because we believed it would benefit the bank. But now we wonder if it would be better to end our relationship . . .'

Warwick sat up in bed.

'Didier, is that really you speaking like this? This is absurd. You surely can't be threatening *me*?'

'I imagine, Timothy, that if you leave us you will have nowhere left to go. Politics is an expensive profession. You need us more than we need you.'

'Yes I know, but—'

'And I think it would reflect badly on you if it emerges that you have held your directorship with us throughout your period of office. Those deferred benefits waiting for you on our accounts. These things could be very bad. You would be finished in politics and also with us. What would you do then?'

Warwick's headache was getting worse. It was true. Ramses had no need to spell it out.

'Didier,' he said in a pleading voice, 'just why is this delivery so important to you? What's behind it?'

'You are better off not knowing, Timothy. It is of the highest importance to the bank. That is all. Now, can we please expect results?'

Ten long seconds passed.

'You can expect results,' said Warwick in a dull, defeated voice.

The line went dead. Warwick hung up, trying to stop his agile mind from scanning through the many possible dreadful reasons why he should not be told what it was all about. He mustn't think about it. It required a simple act of willpower.

It was a dazed junior Minister for Exports who dragged himself off to the shower to try to clear his head. He knew he had come – just for a moment – within touching distance of slamming down the phone. But thank God he had kept his nerve. He had kept in the game. And he still had a chance – every chance – of winning.

What Warwick did not know was that over in the bowels of a anonymous building off the Tottenham Court Road a stunned technician was at that same moment staring with disbelief at his recording equipment, wondering if he could possibly have heard correctly.

He rewound the tape and switched it back on again.

'Yes,' he heard Warwick's voice, and then, 'Timothy?' from the caller.

The technician stopped the tape. It was working perfectly. The recording would be preserved for at least one hundred years.

He checked his watch. Twenty to seven. The dovecots would flutter today.

# Chapter Eighteen

'Customer satisfaction is a concept I find very difficult to accept,' said Fergusson briskly to his junior, Stuart-Smith, as they went up in the Cabinet Office lift later that morning. They had gained access to the building by an obscure service entrance off Downing Street, picking their way past the bicycles, umbrellas and mopeds that gave the courtyard the feel of a railway platform in a small market town. It seemed to Stuart-Smith that Fergusson was particularly preoccupied today. The meeting that lay ahead was bad news: but was it really that bad?

The building that housed the Cabinet Office had two distinct functions. One was to lodge and service the Cabinet itself, the political masters whose dynasty ruled the house and whose estate was the entire country. The other was to provide shelter for scores of civil servants who worked there co-ordinating Whitehall views on all manner of subjects, and who might have only rare contact with the politicians. Sometimes Stuart-Smith thought the two halves exactly represented the classical description of the dignified and efficient parts of the constitution. It was a strange master and servant relationship: the former for public show, the latter for public benefit. And then he thought perhaps it was after all just another *Upstairs Downstairs* sort of house, where the servants put on the best performance.

'Too imprecise?' he offered, ever helpful.

'No,' said Fergusson. 'I simply don't understand it. What does it mean? It used to be much easier. Us and them. Black and white. Hostile and friendly. You did your job. You sent out the stuff. Then you forgot about it. Now, who knows what next?'

'Market research? Supply and demand? Competitive tendering?'

'Perhaps. Fitzgerald has told me that the Treasury are thinking about payment by results.'

'Why not just call it prostitution?

'Why not indeed? Here we are.'

126

The lift doors sprang open and they were on the third level. Stuart-Smith stood aside to let the senior man pass. The young squire preparing the way for the battle-hardened knight.

'Committee Room C, Alan?'

'D, I think this time, sir.'

Stuart-Smith had long since learnt that to gain merit it was necessary to double-check small facts, such as the exact meeting room, with the secretariat beforehand. Once you were actually in the Cabinet Office it was virtually impossible to tell where you went next. The corridors of power boasted very few signposts. Convention had it that no meetings were put up on the noticeboard. Nor could the guards or attendants be relied on to know what was happening. At any one time half a dozen official committees could be in session, and it was only with experience that those who came fetched up at the right one. Nor were those attending meetings identifiable in any obvious way. When Stuart-Smith first went to one he found himself facing twenty total strangers, whose functions only became partly clearer as the meeting began and one of their number, seemingly no different from the rest, began to chair the proceedings. Stuart-Smith knew the case of his colleague Jenkins, who had turned up late and spent half an hour in a session of what turned out to be a North Sea oil advisory committee before he realized, mumbled his excuses and left.

'Mustn't keep the *shareholders* waiting,' muttered Fergusson, as he opened the door of Room D and they filed in.

The meeting was already in session. The committee room was a spacious chamber with a long table in the middle, decorated in the style known informally as official gothic. To one side windows overlooked a hidden courtyard, but today the heavy curtains were drawn. Around the walls hung portraits of the great and the good of a century and more ago, the proud and peacock-hued guardians of the high summer of Empire. On a rather fine table at one end of the room ticked a rather fine old clock, performing the same office it had no doubt performed during the last war and perhaps even the one before that. It now registered ten-seventeen.

The extra territorial committee was listening to an account from one of the lawyers of a recent case. Much of their work was quasi-judicial in nature. Jesuitical, almost, thought Stuart-Smith.

'So,' concluded Piper, the eager young law officer, 'case law as usual offers no clear jurisprudence. The intention behind the Act is clear. But the interpretation of the law is confused. Regina against Simmonds can be construed in two different ways.'

'But all we want to know is: is it illegal?' asked Hotblack, the chairman, on secondment to the Cabinet Office from the MOD. He was a pugnacious warrior of a man, a general in civilians' clothes well-used to conducting battles in the awkward territory which was policy. 'Can we not just throw him out and take the risk of an appeal?' He raised a welcoming finger to Fergusson and Stuart-Smith, who took their usual seats beneath a portrait of Marlborough. Twenty men were present round the table. No fewer than three secretaries were taking notes.

Piper smiled a legal smile.

'But that is just the point, Mr Chairman . . .'

Piper continued his theology lecture for a further five minutes. Then Hotblack looked at his watch and said to him, 'Very well. Please redraft your note and recirculate in final form. We will come back to it next time. And be so good as to send three side copies to the secretariat.'

He looked across at Fergusson.

'Next item. RB appraisals. Gordon?'

Fergusson leaned forward, thin and tanned, the colonial guardian back on home tour. Stuart-Smith, beside him, sat back and effaced himself. Fergusson straightened the papers in front of him into a precise pile, coughed and addressed his hands spread on the table before him.

'Thank you, Mr Chairman. I think the committee is already sighted on the Victor transcripts. As you all know, Victor is a Moscow source with quite remarkable access. When he tells us something we pay attention, although we can never discount the possibility that he is attempting to muddy the water. He is, after all, a gamekeeper turned poacher.

'But, that said, we believe we do have clear evidence of unwelcome activity. We will put in a paper with all the details by close of play Friday. It seems clear that illegal third-party action of a systematic nature is in train on home territory. We do not yet know all aspects of the operation. But it should be only a matter of time before we are in a position to serve an eviction notice to both sides. We need, of course, to get all our ducks in a row.'

Fergusson took a sip of water from the glass beside his blotting paper.

'There is one further and rather disturbing aspect I would like to draw to the attention of the committee, with your permission, Mr Chairman.'

Hotblack nodded. He and Fergusson had already discussed the agenda – and what should and should not be said in full committee – on the secure line earlier that morning.

'We understand that a direct physical attack has been mounted by one of our protagonists against a Whitehall officer. With some success, it would appear.'

At this Donaldson, a diplomat from the Foreign Office newly returned to London, sat forward. 'Physical attack? Do you mean they've beaten someone up?'

'He means a personal approach,' translated Hotblack. 'Go on, Gordon.'

'It means,' said Fergusson, choosing his words carefully, 'that someone – we cannot specify exactly who at this stage – has someone else – again, we don't know exactly who – on a lead in one of our departments. It doesn't happen very often. The risks are enormous. But we must assume that in at least this case they are judged worthwhile.'

Fergusson let his words sink in. Around the table in this curtained-off room all the major departments of state were represented. Home Office. Defence. Treasury. Foreign Office. The security departments. Law officers. Each with their different cultures, their traditions, even their style of dressing and talking. But all of them united in one atavistic fear – the primitive loathing of having an uninvited guest at the dinner table. There had been too many of these in the past already.

'You are making my flesh creep,' said Wilson of the MOD. He glanced over to Donaldson. 'This is not the moment one would have chosen to be observed.'

Donaldson of the Foreign Office shook his head in sober recognition. 'Couldn't be worse. The NATO review. The strategic policy review. The trilateral talks. You name it. It's all up in the air.'

Browne of the Home Office was also thinking aloud. 'Should we bring the Special Branch in?' he said tentatively. But then he saw Hotblack's frown and dropped his suggestion.

Clever Jackson of the Treasury spoke next. 'Let me try to understand. We are talking about an unknown entity, *two* unknown entities, operating on British territory, one of them for his own reasons finding it necessary to run an agent, presumably because he has access to useful information. That is the first thing. But then there is this second thing – the proliferation problem – where it seems we do not have the full picture, or we are not told the full picture, and yet there is some connection between the two. Is that it?'

There was an awkward pause.

'I think, James,' said Hotblack, the chairman, 'that it will be for another forum to take a decision about what might or might not be construed as a connection between these two matters.'

Jackson raised his hands a foot in the air and let them fall together on to the table.

'All right,' he said, getting the hint. 'Not my scene. But when this goes higher, Treasury ministers must be kept informed.'

'Thank you, James,' said Hotblack. 'They will be. At this meeting I am anxious that we consider only the operational decisions that need taking. He turned to Fergusson. 'Do you recommend orange alert?'

'Yes, as a precaution, I would,' replied Fergusson. 'And in the meantime we will step up our appraisal activity. We will soon find our man. And when we know who he is we will know exactly who and what they are.'

'Right,' said Hotblack. It was his task to sum up the will of the meeting. 'I am not going to put this to ministers – yet. They will not take kindly to another black sheep just now. I want you to move quickly. Find him, whoever he is, and bring him in. Go through each department thoroughly. You will get every assistance. Catch him and make him talk. When I have to go to ministers about it I want all the answers. They will be *concerned*.'

'What is his legal position?' asked Piper, perhaps scenting fresh business.

'His legal position is that we are going to chop his balls off,' replied Hotblack firmly. 'Next item?'

But they had lost interest in the next item.

'Customer satisfaction?' asked Stuart-Smith as he and Fergusson took the lift down.

'Strong customer response, at any rate,' mused Fergusson absently.

'In some ways it's helpful, isn't it, sir,' asked Stuart-Smith. 'We have been looking for a peg on which to hang our cash bid for next year. We may have it now.'

'Yes, I suppose so,' said Fergusson.

'Hotblack seems rather reluctant to go any higher.'

Fergusson gave Stuart-Smith a meaningful glance. 'Once you tell ministers, you know, you might just as well broadcast it to the American Embassy.'

They left by the same service entrance and came out via a dark passage on to Downing Street. They made their way over to the St James's Park exit. Then Fergusson stopped in his tracks.

'Go on back,' he said suddenly to Stuart-Smith. 'I'll catch you up at the office in a few minutes. There's something I must do first.'

Stuart-Smith looked at Fergusson with interest. He *knew* something else had been troubling him.

'Yes sir,' he said, and left. The policeman opened the park gate grille to let Stuart-Smith out. There was a distant flurry of birds in the air above St James's Park.

Fergusson retraced his steps to the Cabinet Office. The others had already left the building. He took the lift back up to the third floor, but this time he walked past Committee Room D. In his office further down the corridor Hotblack was sitting waiting for him. Fergusson shut the door behind him and sat down. The small, book-lined under-secretary's office was private, quiet, a little like a monk's cell: but Fergusson knew that Hotblack had instant access to anyone – absolutely anyone – in the vast empire of government.

'Coffee, Gordon?' asked Hotblack, pouring a cup into his senior officer's delicate chinaware. 'Thank you for coming back.'

The two sat there drinking quietly for a while, Fergusson looking at the Warwick transcript open and upside down on Hotblack's desk. Unlike the widely circulated Victor material, this was the number one copy of a series of one, and Fergusson had had it delivered by hand earlier that morning in a sealed metal box. He had already memorized the contents.

'This could have all the makings of an absolute disaster,' said Hotblack, after a few more minutes' reading and contemplation.

131

'It is bad enough having foreign intelligence agencies running officials in Whitehall. It is something else altogether when ministers themselves are recruited. And in what an area!'

'It at least shows we were right to start the interceptions at Warwick's home.'

Hotblack slowly nodded his head. He remembered only too well the awkwardness they'd had squaring that with the Cabinet Secretary, who'd had to be persuaded to sign the authorization in place of a minister.

'It's really very logical, I suppose,' Hotblack said. 'If you can do it, a minister is a great catch. Good access. No security problems. Cannot possibly be disciplined by simple officials. An embarrassment factor of nuclear proportions.'

'Nothing to do with ideology,' added Fergusson. 'A simple economic transaction.'

'And speaking of nuclear,' continued Hotblack, 'how much do you think he actually knows?'

'I doubt if he has the full picture. He can surely guess it is big, or they wouldn't be pressuring him in this way. But as for going the final mile and concluding that he is knowingly passing on the material – I would shudder to do that.'

Hotblack closed the file. Then he stood and paced back and forth in his small office, between his mahogany desk and his mahogany bookcase. He glanced at the rows of political and military memoirs, many by people he knew personally. Finally he stopped.

'The essential thing is that this must *not* get out,' he said. 'Especially not now. We all know there are just two items on the agenda in Washington. Number one is the December summit with Gorbachov. Number two is the Middle East. We did a good job in accounting for that Greenham Common break-in in the summer. If it turns out, first, that we can't account for the missing material and, second, that a British minister has connived at getting it out of the country – to an enemy of Israel – we will be *compromised* in Washington.'

'And with the Geneva Group going the way it is . . . ?'

'Exactly. With the Geneva Group going the way it is, we need every ounce of capital to sway the final decision. Between now and the seventh of December minds will be made up in Washington. To deploy or not to deploy. We have to *weigh* in that debate. We need *credibility*.'

And this was the dark heart of the matter, the most *neuralgic* issue of them all (as Fergusson put it).

Because what they both knew – but few others did – was quite how far the Americans and Soviets were getting in their extraordinary private talks in Geneva. A year previously in Reykjavik, over a stormy cold weekend in an isolated building on a bare plain at the edge of the North Atlantic, the two sides had been amazingly close. They had come within a hair's breadth, a nuance, a semantic shift, of actually agreeing to eliminate their stocks of nuclear weapons over a period of ten years. When news of this astonishing fact filtered out from the Reykjavik summit on the Sunday evening, every capital in Europe had been stunned. At a stroke, in a matter of a few hours, their entire strategic universe had been turned upside down. They were looking, for the first time since the Second World War, at the serious prospect of a world without nuclear weapons.

And then the real world broke in. The two sides stumbled over what would replace nuclear weapons: the strategic defence system itself, that half-real and half-fabulous invention, that Leonardo da Vinci helicopter which the Americans offered to share with the Soviets – but only when it was built. The two sides left Reykjavik in disagreement and the outcry from the rest of the world ended all public discussion. And that, most people thought, was that.

But ever since then, in secret talks in Geneva, which only a handful of people in the world were aware of, a tiny team of American and Soviet negotiators had been trying – and succeeding – gradually to bridge the gap that remained between them. Their deadline was the next summit, due to be held in Washington in December. There were many differences of view within the American administration. Some thought that the idea of a world without nuclear weapons was crazy. But the word from the top remained clear: 'Go for it.' And go for it was what negotiators Nitze from Washington and Akhromeyev from Moscow were trying their best to do.

This was not something of idle interest in London. The folk memory still lingered of a November day in 1962 when the US administration unilaterally decided to scrap Skybolt – the missile upon which the future British nuclear deterrent was to depend – and only informed the British after the event.

One thing was clear. They could not afford so much as the

thickness of a sheet of paper to show between them and the Americans. They must stick like glue if they were to have any influence over the outcome of the negotiations.

And now this had come up.

'Warwick's bank,' Hotblack said. 'What do *they* get out of it? Why are they doing it?'

'I don't know,' replied Fergusson. 'They must have their own reasons for financing an operation like this, but what they are I cannot say.'

Hotblack sat down again and picked up the transcript from his desk. He looked at Fergusson. 'This is the only copy we have?'

'The only copy. I have sworn the transcriber to secrecy.'

Hotblack handed the document back to Fergusson. 'Take it away. Bury it somewhere at the bottom of a well. I don't want it kept in this building. We will have to work out a disaster strategy. And, in the mean time, the watchword is containment. This *must* be kept quiet. From everyone.'

He added as an afterthought, 'Thank God we found out in time.'

# Chapter Nineteen

'Hello,' said Terry. 'What brings you here? It's not Tuesday.'

Colchester, who was propped up against the bar in the Coach and Horses with a drink in front of him, looked at his watch. He was surprised to see Terry.

'And what brings you here?'

Thursday night was folk night in the Coach and Horses. Over in the little concert area a bearded man stood with one hand over his ear, whining into a microphone. A few hangers-on were listening to his lament. A dog was lying on the floor and barking at the loudest passages.

'Run out of matches,' explained Terry. 'On my way home.' Croydon Town Hall was just round the corner.

'Working late?' asked Colchester.

'Campaign business.'

'From the town hall?'

'*No Cruise in Croydon*. Not bad, eh?'

'So what happens next?'

'Bring-and-buy sale. Clapham Common. Sunday afternoon. Why not come? Also, I kill two birds with one stone.'

'Stuff for the Object Museum?'

'That's right. You never know what you might get. If you find a good quality video player, let me know. An early model.'

'Why not just go out and buy one?'

Terry looked hurt. 'Let's not go too far. Since you're here, how about another drink? And why *are* you here, anyway?'

Colchester glanced over to the door. Was that the outline of a black London cab cruising past? 'Maybe I like the music,' he said.

'Come off it,' said Terry. 'They play this sort of thing when they want to drive people out. When the landlord wants a quiet night. They . . . My God!' he broke off, staring rapt at the mirror behind Colchester's head. He then leaned forward and lowered his voice to a whisper.

'It's that girl again. She's just come in. The one who was in here the other week. By herself. Now she really is something special. I'd sell my soul for a woman like that. What's she doing in a hole like this?'

'Hard to say,' said Colchester, with an embarrassed cough. 'Perhaps she likes the music too. I'll see you later . . .'

'What?'

And to Terry's astonishment Colchester put down his drink, walked away from him, walked round to the other bar, walked up to the girl, bent over and kissed her on the cheek. At the same time he whispered something into her ear. Terry saw her face light up with recognition when she saw Colchester. When he kissed her she seemed slightly surprised. But then she put her arm into his, and they walked out of the pub and into the night. Terry sat staring at the door as it swung to behind them.

'Did you want anything, love?' asked the barmaid.

'A box of matches,' said Terry, after a while. 'And I think I'll have a double scotch.'

'Who's your friend?' said Julia as they walked quickly, arm in arm, down the street.

'An activist. Or maybe I should say a pacifist,' replied Colchester. 'A registrar of births, deaths and marriages, actually,' he added when he saw Julia look sharply at him.

'Well, it won't go on your file if you want me to keep it quiet,' she said.

'Great,' he answered.

They walked on in silence for a few minutes.

'It's very nice but you don't *have* to hold my arm, you know,' said Colchester. 'He can't see us any more.'

'I know,' said Julia. 'But it's cold.'

Colchester didn't pursue the point. Still arm in arm they arrived at the venue he had chosen for the evening.

'*Voilà!*' he said.

Julia looked with misgiving at the illuminated façade of the Star of Croydon.

'Do you bring many girlfriends here?'

'You said you wanted somewhere different,' said Colchester defensively. 'It's quite good, really.'

'I'm not going in there,' decided Julia. 'I can see flock wallpaper.'

'But I've booked a table.'

'They'll get over it. Did you use your name?'

'Well, no . . .'

'You're learning. Look, I'm not hungry. Let's just walk for a while.'

So they continued on their way through the cold dark streets of south London. It was now the turning point of the year, the moment when autumn definitively slips into winter. Occasionally Colchester stole a glance at Julia. He still could not quite believe that she was there, walking beside him, taking his arm, keeping herself warm. *Try again*, she had said.

'You're quiet tonight,' he began.

'I'm thinking about the life I lead in London,' she replied.

'Whatever for?'

Julia hesitated. 'There's something I have to tell you.'

Colchester caught the tone in her voice and his heart beat faster. 'What is it?'

Julia was looking at him as if she was trying to find the answer to some question in his face. It was a look that Colchester felt he would never understand.

'I'm going away,' she said. 'Soon.'

For the first time Colchester felt the cold cut through his overcoat, and he shivered. He released her arm. He immediately knew he could not be happy again.

'Why?' he asked in a quiet voice.

'It's my job. De la Fosse says I must go. I mustn't spend too long in one spot. My face could be recognized.'

'Does that matter?'

'It – could matter rather a lot.'

'I can't see . . .' began Colchester, but then realized it was pointless.

'Where will they send you?' he asked.

Julia shook her head. 'Abroad. A long way off. The other side of the world.'

'You can't tell me?'

Julia took his arm again, but avoided his eyes. 'You don't understand. I'd stay if I could. It's . . . it's de la Fosse . . .'

'De la Fosse . . . What kind of hold has he over you, Julia?'

'He rules my life,' she replied simply, looking up at him. 'He tells me where to go, what to do, who to be. I used to admire him. I was taught to admire him.'

137

'And now?'

'Now . . .' she looked at the ground. 'Now I think I'm beginning to get a little – disillusioned with him.'

Colchester felt his pulse begin to race.

'Why don't you give up your job?' he asked. 'Don't you ever want to stay with someone?'

Julia was looking at him again. Her eyes were almost amused. 'Whoever would you have in mind?'

'Would you?' he insisted. 'Would you give up your job and stay with me?'

Julia's eyes did not leave his face. She shook her head.

'It can't be done,' she said.

'Why not?'

'You have your world. I have mine. They don't mix. Believe me. You don't know very much about me. I'm not the right woman for you.'

A sudden thought came to Colchester. 'You're married, aren't you?'

Julia displayed her left hand and smiled wistfully.

'Only to my job. Believe me, it's sometimes a difficult relationship . . .'

They had been walking in circles for half an hour.

'Why not in here?' said Julia.

The King's Arms Hotel was one of the grandest in this part of the world. It stood large and four-square against the winds by the multi-storey car park, like a castle or a mock gothic railway station. Victorian values in a rickety modern suburb. The exterior proclaimed gloomy airless rooms, plates of Angus beef and schooners of sweet sherry.

'Well, if you like . . .' said Colchester dubiously. 'What is it?' he added, seeing Julia look anxiously over her shoulder. A car passed on the other side of the darkened street.

'Nothing . . . I thought I saw that car earlier.'

'Earlier? But who—?'

'Have you seen Mehmet recently?'

'No. But you don't think . . . ?'

'No – not really. Well, let's see what suburban hospitality has to offer.'

Colchester put his arm round her shoulder.

The supper was not as bad as they had feared. They ate lightly

138

off seafood and sorbets in a virtually empty dining room. Over at the only other occupied table an elderly couple were playing dominoes. He watched as Julia regained her composure. But he continued to have the oddly pleasant sensation of feeling protective towards her.

'Don't go away,' he said, when they were near the end of the meal. 'I can't bear the thought of you going away.'

'I have no choice,' she said.

'But of course you have a choice,' he said, puzzled. 'You're not a conscript. There isn't a war on. Just say you won't go.'

'And live with you and be your love? They won't buy that, I'm afraid. You see I *am* a conscript. You don't understand. You're only a volunteer. It's a very strange world I live in.'

'Leave it.'

'I can't.'

'Why not?'

'I can't. Don't ask me. Don't press me.'

Colchester tried a different tack. 'Have you never fallen in love?'

'I thought I was in love,' she said.

His heart sank. 'You were?'

'In love with this town, with this country. It breaks my heart to have to go away. This is my home. I belong here. You – you take so much for granted. This is just somewhere to live for you. It's more than that for me.'

'What is it for you?'

'It's – a sanctuary.'

'A sanctuary?' Colchester failed again to understand her meaning. How could this town, which seemed so mundane to him, mean so much to her?

'If it wasn't for your job,' he asked slowly, 'could you still see me?'

'If it wasn't for that we wouldn't have met in the first place.'

'You're avoiding the question.'

'I know. Basic interrogation technique.'

'Is this interrogation?'

'It feels like it.'

'But what if—?'

'What if,' cut in Julia with emphasis in her voice. 'What if we agree to meet just one more time. That's all. That would be – what

– in a week or so. After that I will be gone. We will have to forget all about each other. Do you see?'

'But—'

'And what if,' she continued as if thinking out loud, 'we *were* in love. Perhaps just this once we were lovers. I don't know. Maybe we're pretending. Maybe it might be real. *We* don't know. And we haven't got time to find out. All we know for certain is that it's the last time we meet. Can you find somewhere for us? Somewhere we can make love? Will that make you happy?'

Colchester stared at her, wondering if he had properly heard what she had just said.

'Are you sure?' he whispered.

'I'm sure,' she replied.

'It would be wonderful . . .'

'It would be something to remember each other by,' she said, smiling at him.

Colchester found he had developed a strange catch in his voice.

'The Benbow order,' he managed to get out. 'Do you need more on that?'

Julia's smile deepened.

'No, not really,' she said. 'But it's a very good excuse to see each other again . . .'

They watched as out of the cold November night the lights of two black cabs approached. They were heading to them from the centre of London and would have to reverse direction and cross the road before they pulled up.

'How do they know where to come?' asked Colchester.

'I made a special booking earlier today,' answered Julia. She looked closely into the interior of the first cab as it swept past, her eyes narrowing as if she were searching for someone. Reassured, she took Colchester's arm as the headlights picked out the droplets of moisture starting to form in the winter air.

'Quick,' she said. 'A kiss.'

Colchester bent down to her cheek. But Julia turned round and lightly put her mouth to his. For a moment she closed her eyes and he felt her tongue touch his. Then the car lights swung round, were almost upon them. They broke.

'Think of me,' she whispered.

The first cab drew up. Julia opened the door. 'Till next time,' she said in a businesslike voice, her eye on the driver. 'The one behind is for you.' Colchester slammed the door and the vehicle pulled off back to central London.

Colchester, warmed by Julia's kiss, turned into the chill rain, now starting to fall properly, and pulled his collar up. The second cab came up alongside him, the silhouette of the driver only a lighter shade of grey. Colchester stepped back slightly, moving out of the way of the spray thrown up. He did not see the waiting figure move towards him from the shadows behind.

The red lights of Julia's cab had dissolved in the rain when Colchester cast a last look up the road. He could see no one. He pulled open the rear door of the cab and got in, noticing in the dim interior a pair of attentive eyes watching him.

'All right, guv?' the driver said in a low voice.

Just as Colchester was settling into the gloom of the passenger seat there was a whirl of activity. The cab jerked forward as the driver tried to accelerate away, but the door was already open and a dark bulky figure carrying a briefcase had pushed its way into the interior. Colchester had a momentary glimpse by the door light of someone forcing himself in, and then all was dark again. But in that glimpse he recognized the man, and he felt his stomach contract.

Mehmet was sitting beside him in the cab. And Colchester could feel, but not yet see, the hard cylinder which Mehmet was pressing against his ribs.

'Do not move,' said Mehmet.

And then, as the cab picked up speed Mehmet reached forward, wrenched open the perspex panel behind the driver and jammed his briefcase into the space. The driver, eyes terrified in the mirror, tried to stop the cab. But Mehmet poked his gun through the opening and trained it at the back of the driver's head.

'Go on,' he said in a harsh voice.

The driver, limbs trembling, touched the accelerator and the cab continued on its way. One driver. But two passengers.

# Chapter Twenty

'Has that strange man been round to see you yet asking about Guy?'

Stanton had persuaded a reluctant Molly to come and visit his father on his birthday and they were buying a bunch of flowers from a stall near the Embankment. They were on their way across London to Wembley, where Stanton and his father lived, Molly finally swayed by curiosity about Stanton senior. The orange alert signs had been posted just inside the entrance and, like all members of staff, they had been checked on their way out. It was wet and dark, and the flowers in the stall glistened under a naked light like prizes at a fairground.

'No,' replied Stanton. 'What strange man?'

'He was taking notes,' said Molly. ' "Positive vetting," he said. He wanted to know all about Guy's habits. Comings and goings. Girlfriends. Boyfriends. Is he a member of an extremist group? Does he drink too much? Is he in debt? Does he have character defects?'

'What did you say?'

'I told him he doesn't tell me anything and, anyway, I'm not interested. What does it all mean?'

'Positive vetting?' said Stanton reflectively. 'It means our Guy is going up in the world. They only do it when you're in line for something special. Now what could it be?'

'Mind you,' said Molly. 'I did mention that Guy has been seen in the company of strange women. I told him about the good-time girl. But the funny thing was he didn't seem very surprised. Jotted down a few notes. I suppose it isn't a crime. Though it might be a character defect.'

'I've got it!' said Stanton. 'Normington is moving out of private office. There are three candidates to replace him. One is Stitt. That'll be it!'

'What?'

142

'Stitt goes. Guy becomes secretary to the PC. That's a good job. Lots of access. He must have had a good report after all.'

Molly thought back. 'I'd be surprised . . .' she said. She searched among the soaking blooms. 'Anyway, will tulips do?'

'Yes, fine. Father can't tell the difference. I'll have to buy Guy a drink.'

The civil servants who came every morning to the Ministry of Exports generally travelled from distant and cheaper points of the compass to get to central London to do their work. Stanton was one such: his stamping ground was the pebble-dashed villas and brick-encrusted allotments of the North Circular. It was out of the ordinary for somebody living in one part of London to call on someone else at home, and Molly viewed the prospect of meeting Stanton's father with some trepidation.

Mr Stanton was sitting bolt upright on the sofa in the small living room when Molly and Stanton arrived an hour later. The room was over-heated, the furniture old and heavy – much older than Molly herself. Mr Stanton was fit, but well over seventy. He looked hunted, worried, like a man who still had enemies.

'This is Molly from the office,' announced Stanton in a loud voice.

Mr Stanton looked at her briefly. Then he turned to Stanton.

'Did you bring the oil like I asked?'

'Yes, Father. I put it under the stairs on the way in.'

Molly looked mystified. Stanton had done no such thing.

'Oil for the lamp,' Stanton said to her. 'As an emergency supply. In case we get the power cut off again.'

'Do you get lots of power cuts in Wembley?' asked Molly.

'We used to. Once. Forty odd years ago. He never forgets.' Stanton looked almost proudly at the old man, who was now staring intently at Molly.

'She's very young to be from the office,' he finally said to Stanton.

'They're getting younger every year,' Stanton explained.

'Why has she come here?'

'Because it's your birthday, Father. She wanted to.'

Going a bit far, thought Molly. However, since she was here she might as well enjoy herself.

'Happy birthday, Mr Stanton,' she said. 'How old are you today?'

Mr Stanton looked at her keenly. 'How old am I? You'll never believe me if I tell you.'

'Yes I will.'

'Well, I'll tell you. I'm thirty-two.'

'Thirty-two?'

'I said you'd never believe me.'

'It is difficult.' Molly smiled warmly at him. 'You don't look a day over twenty-five.'

Mr Stanton shot a suspicious look at his son. Who was this strange girl with bright blonde hair he had brought in?

Stanton decided to intervene. 'Now, Father, let's all have a drink to celebrate your birthday.'

'Yes, that's right,' said his father. 'I think I've kept a bottle or two hidden away so the bombs can't get them.'

Stanton rummaged around in a cupboard and emerged with a dusty bottle of cognac. He proudly displayed it to Molly.

'Nineteen forty-four. You can see we don't drink this very often.'

'Nineteen forty-four? You mean you have kept this for all these years?' Molly was amazed.

Stanton indicated his father. 'Not me. Him. Things haven't changed for him since then. He hasn't thrown anything away. And he doesn't drink much.'

So they each had a glass of vintage cognac. And it gradually loosened Mr Stanton's tongue.

'I've hardly touched a drop since the night his mother was killed,' he said to Molly. 'A flying bomb, it was. A wet, cold, nasty night. It came in like some horrible great bluebottle. I was home on leave. I'd been in Greece, fighting the Germans. Not hurt a hair of my head. Then I came home. A horrible great bluebottle it was. It seems such a long time ago. But could only have been a couple of years. That's war for you. It makes you forget yourself. You lose track of time.

'But you know where you are when you're at war. You know what you're about. Yes, sir. No, sir. Yes, sir. No, sir. You don't have to think. You don't have any worries. You just do what you're told, my lad, and we'll look after you.

'And we won in the end, didn't we? We beat them all right. We showed them a thing or two. Now it's all over, we know who's top dog all right. That's what I'm always telling young George

144

here. He works for the government. He's a bright lad. He hasn't even had to do his military service. People who work for the government don't have to. He's still fighting on the same side though. Putting the great back into Britain.

'George, I say to him, it's the fighting spirit that counts. Remember Roosevelt. And above all remember Uncle Joe. We have to stick together. Now that we've won the war it's up to the likes of you to win the peace. We did our bit. Now it's up to you. We've got to put this country back on its feet again. We've been knocked about a bit. We've shown we can take it. Now we've got to dish it out a bit too.

'George is in a good position, aren't you, my lad? When you work for the government you're something special. You know things other people don't. The government looks after you. It looks after its own. Always has. And it gives you a sense of discipline. It's like being in the army. Just like being in the army. I was in the army once. In Greece. Didn't hurt a hair on my head. Now it's the same for George.

'When I see him going out in the morning I say to myself, that's the spirit, George. You go out there and fight for Britain. You go and help the old country along. She's in a bit of a tight spot just now and she needs you. Now George there, he won't tell me much about what it is he does and I respect that. It's the need to know principle. But I know whatever it is it's important. It's carrying on where I left off. It's the Big Three. Uncle Sam and Uncle Joe and us. It was just a couple of years ago but it seems like longer. A horrible great bluebottle it was.

'Well, George, it's action this day isn't it? Action this day. That's what the old man used to say. It seems like ages ago but it was only the other week. Now we've got rationing and everything it's up to the likes of you to pull the country through. Do what you can, my lad . . .'

Mr Stanton suddenly stopped for a moment in his train of thought. Then he turned to Molly.

'See here, young lady, you work with George, don't you? You know what it is he does, don't you? Why can't you tell me, just for once? He won't.'

Stanton stood up.

'All right, Father, you've been going on long enough . . .'

But Molly interrupted him. She suddenly comprehended, as

if in a vision, a father and son relationship built on decades of misunderstanding, revolving around the withholding of knowledge. Mr Stanton believed – and Stanton did not dissuade him – that his son was fighting battles even greater than his own. She knew the answer she must give.

'It's all right,' she said. 'No, Mr Stanton, no. I can't tell you, if he can't. It's important, you can be sure of that. National security is at stake. But there are rules, you know. Mum's the word.'

Stanton looked gratefully at Molly. His eyes were glowing.

# Chapter Twenty-one

'Straight on,' said Mehmet briefly to the driver. They continued to trail through the maze of suburban streets, heading back generally towards central London. As they passed slowly along a row of darkened shops Colchester could see the occasional glimmer of a bar or a closing restaurant. A petrol station, lights blazing in the rain like a ship at sea. And then a police car, pulled up by the side of the road. Two youths under questioning. Then the scene was behind them and they were pressing on into the wet, hopeless London night, the rain pattering against the windscreen.

Colchester turned to Mehmet.

'Don't move and don't say anything,' said Mehmet slowly. 'I will have some questions to put – first.'

Colchester sat back, noting in the glare of each passing street-lamp the way Mehmet held both him and the driver in his steady gaze, the head of his pistol swaying between them in the alternating light and dark, like a serpent undecided where to strike. Colchester realized that both he and the driver were allies. They could not communicate, but if one drew Mehmet's attention the other might risk a sudden hit. He looked into the reflection of the driver's eyes. He was shocked when he saw the expression of abject terror there. Would this man be prepared to fight at all?

They were coming up to some traffic lights changing to red. Colchester looked from the driver's eyes, and glanced at the door handle on his left side as the cab slowed down.

'Lock the doors,' ordered Mehmet, and a little red pinpoint of light down beside the handle glowed.

As the cab waited at the lights, a drunken figure lurched out of a bus shelter and staggered up on Colchester's side. Colchester saw a shambling, bearded, bear of a man claw at the cab and tug at the locked door handle. Suddenly the man rapped at the window and pushed his hairy face, complete with bloodshot eyes, against the glass. Colchester saw the anguish and the crazed concentration on the face of the drunk as he peered inside. He heard a muffled voice.

'For the love of Jesus . . .'

The lights changed. The cab moved on. The drunk cursed at the impassive features of the two men as they stared back at him standing in the rain. He ran forward, stooped and then hurled a small stone at the accelerating vehicle.

Inside the cab there was a sharp crack at the rear window. Colchester turned, involuntarily. Mehmet put his arm out and held him at the shoulder.

'I said, do not move . . .'

But Colchester could still see, now fifty yards behind, the drunk stagger back to the pavement. Then the figure was lost in the pouring rain. Colchester could almost have wept.

At that moment the cab radio crackled into life. From the other side of London came the reedy hiss and chatter of slide guitars, then a thin whining voice, carried over the rooftops on the invisible electric wind. It was Elphick, and he was tired.

'Orl right,' he said abruptly through the transmitter in the dashboard. 'She's home for the night. How about you, Paddy? You comin' on down?'

She? thought Colchester. She?

Mehmet leaned forward a little.

'Do not say anything,' he whispered to the driver. The driver raised his right hand just slightly in reply.

There was a period of silence for some ten seconds as they drove on through the night.

'You gone deaf, Paddy?' complained the voice on the transmitter.

Silence for another few seconds.

'Patrick! Wake up my son!'

Further silence.

'Paddy! We wanna go home. What's going on? Are you lonesome tonight or what?'

Coming through the static of the radio Colchester could just hear a garbled conference, and the words "number eleven gone . . ." Then there was a final, more urgent, appeal, the voice cranked up several notches of formality, and the background music was silenced.

'Number eleven, we know you are receiving. Why are you

148

not transmitting? Repeat, why are you not transmitting? Proceed immediately to rendezvous point F and we'll meet and escort you home. Proceed immediately . . .'

'Switch it off,' said Mehmet. The driver obeyed, and Colchester saw his hand was still trembling.

In the renewed silence Colchester tried to work out where they were heading. It was still back towards the centre of London. It was likely, he reasoned, that Mehmet did not know London very well. So far he had given no precise directions. Seemed, in fact, content to let the driver decide where to go. If this were true, and the driver himself knew London well, perhaps the driver could after all take them somewhere for help. Where might rendezvous point F be . . . ?

'Give me your street map,' ordered Mehmet to the driver. 'And head for the centre.'

The driver handed back over his shoulder a large red London atlas, the cabbie's friend and memory-prop. Mehmet opened it and Colchester watched him as he riffled through page after page by the light of passing streetlamps, trying to make sense of this large, strange, foreign city. Mehmet shut the book with a snap and tossed it over to Colchester.

'I want you to show me where we are.'

Colchester looked again at the pistol in Mehmet's hand and then opened the street plan himself.

'And,' added Mehmet, 'do not try to deceive me.'

Colchester peered out into the dark streets flashing past, trying to get his bearings. It was not easy. He thought how much of south London looks the same at night. They could have been travelling across the Gobi desert for all the richness and variety of the landscape. But after a few minutes a familiar red and blue light shone up out of the gloom and as it receded into the distance he was able to catch the name of the Underground station. He turned the pages of the book and then pointed with his finger to Mehmet.

'Here. Tooting Broadway. We're heading up this road. Going north.'

Mehmet took back the atlas and studied it for a few moments, turning a few pages. Then he lifted his head and addressed the driver.

'Turn left here.'

They passed down narrow roads of dingy terraced houses, curtained up against the winter. A hospital to the left. Then another junction.

'Left again.'

Soon they were on Trinity Road, a stretch of fast dual-carriageway, an underpass, a big roundabout, a glimpse of space where the river lay, and then they were over the Thames, on the north side.

'Continue.'

A few minutes later and they were in Fulham, branching on to the New King's Road. Some lights were suspended in the trees, and there were more people about, and more traffic, most of it heading in the opposite direction.

'Go on.'

Now they were bowling down a wet King's Road, just one more black cab taking people home for the night; clubs and bars still emptying, couples sitting in the windows of restaurants, the light outside growing brighter and brighter. Colchester could clearly see Mehmet's profile against the neon of a cinema, could see that Mehmet was dissatisfied, was looking for something different, looking for somewhere else. Mehmet studied the atlas once again.

'Left here.'

They were leaving Chelsea whitewash and stucco for Kensington baroque. A hint of the orient in the all-night supermarkets. Dusky figures scuttling down brightly lit Underground entrances.

'Keep going north.'

'North? The driver queried silently in despair. What did he mean: north?

'Up. This way. To the park.'

The park! At last Colchester understood. Mehmet was looking for a dark, quiet spot somewhere in the centre of the town. He had ignored plenty of likely places on the way. Why? Answer: because he would want somewhere he knew he could easily escape from. Afterwards . . .

They were driving along Exhibition Road, and Colchester knew where they were going. There was a gate at this end of Hyde Park. Sometimes it was closed. He squinted to peer ahead. No barrier visible. Tonight it was open.

An observer might have noticed that of all the traffic that continued to circulate around Hyde Park at this late hour, only one solitary taxi broke off from the flow and cut up into Hyde Park itself, its white lamps eating into the dark. Only one vehicle drove right into the centre of the park, up to the bridge that crosses the Serpentine. And only one vehicle then extinguished its lights, vanishing abruptly into the gloom like a nocturnal animal that has gone to ground.

But tonight there was no observer: even though the following morning the authorities were to make considerable efforts to find one.

'Switch the motor off.'

They sat in the dark and the rain, Mehmet eyeing Colchester, the driver in front rigid, around them the park, a vast, blank wilderness. As his night vision improved Colchester could make out more and more of Mehmet's penetrating stare, but the face was deformed in the shadows so that the hollows of his eyes seemed like eyes themselves, a line on his nose like the nose itself, the left ear a complex living sculpture of grey and black. Mehmet paused, as if for recollection, then murmured ironically, 'Have you come a long way, Mr Colchester?'

Colchester, surprised, sat well back in the shadows, trying to think of a strategy. Mehmet had declared himself. But what about him? What did Mehmet know about him? How much did he want to learn? How much could he – would he – tell Mehmet before . . . Before what?

'I think you are making a terrible mistake,' he replied, in what he hoped was a neutral voice.

'Copper? Bauxite? Ligneous coal, wasn't it, you were interested in, Mr Colchester?'

Mehmet turned his head to look idly out of the window then twisted back to Colchester.

'The girl,' he snapped. 'How did you meet? Where? When? Who is running who? Think carefully.'

'A friend,' said Colchester quickly – too quickly. 'She is just a friend.'

'Are you sure, Mr Colchester? That girl happens to be among my mortal enemies. If you are her friend then logically you are my enemy. Do you really want to be my enemy? From where you are sitting that is an unfortunate option to choose. Are you sure she is your friend?'

Colchester took a deep breath.

'Mr Mehmet, I am not your enemy. I am someone who processes paper – concepts – for a living. She is someone who does the same, that is all. She is – a civil servant, like me.'

'Not exactly the same as you, Mr Colchester.'

'I don't follow you.'

'Of course you do, Mr Colchester. You work for completely different people. She is an enemy. You work for that – Warwick fellow.'

'Warwick? If you think that I—'

'Be quiet, Mr Colchester. Warwick is supposed to be a friend of ours. And yet you are clearly not. I find this strange—'

Warwick a friend? Julia an enemy?

'Mr Mehmet, there is no point in threatening me—'

'I asked you to be quiet. Now – I want to know what they have told you about the El Mihr project. How much do you know?'

Colchester's mind raced. He did his best to empty it of all those doubts, all those matters of hidden knowledge, all those extraneous details which Julia had told him.

'I know,' he said, trying to recall the wording of the document he had himself prepared for the Projects Committee, 'that it is a mining project which has imports substitution benefits for your country, which will generate foreign exchange savings, which in turn will produce a positive cost benefit analysis. This justifies export credits provided by the UK so long as these are tied to the procurement of British goods and services . . .'

His voice trailed away into the silence. Mehmet did not look convinced.

'And is that all?'

'What else do you want?'

Mehmet looked at his watch and seemed to come to a decision.

'Mr Colchester, it is a waste of time trying to talk to you. I am now going to teach you a lesson.'

Colchester watched with stupefaction as Mehmet released the safety catch on the pistol.

'I want,' continued Mehmet, 'to make it quite clear that meddling in the affairs of my country is extremely dangerous. It is not something I think you properly appreciate. But there it is. Perhaps actions will speak louder than words.'

Mehmet raised his pistol.

Across Colchester's face disbelieving amazement changed slowly to dawning horror. Instinctively he pushed back into the seat, fingers clutching at the upholstery.

'It would be best if you just sat right back. Better for both of us. Now, there is just one final thing. Please unlock the doors.'

The little red light down by Colchester's side disappeared as the driver obeyed the instruction.

'Goodbye, Mr Colchester.'

Colchester closed his eyes. So it had come to this. Too soon! It was much too soon! In a war that was not his, for a cause he had not chosen, at a time he had not expected.

The report of the gun was shattering inside the vehicle. Colchester's body convulsed and rolled forward, off the seat and on to the floor of the cab. As he fell Colchester suddenly felt an onrush of wind and rain, and saw Mehmet stumble out on to the pavement, pick himself up and race off.

But how could he see these things? How could he feel the freezing wind and the rain against his face?

Where had the bullet gone?

Slowly, shivering, Colchester picked himself up. Shock had rendered his body weak, his teeth were starting to chatter with the cold. But he could feel no injury, could see no wound.

Then he looked up and saw the gaping hole in the driver's side window, the cracks reaching to the furthest corners. And by the faint yellow side light, lit up by the door swinging open, he saw the large twitching body sprawled over the steering wheel, the horrible huge bite mark in the back of the neck, the blood – ten pints was it? – starting to well up from the main artery, a lava forcing its black and shiny way down the contours of the dying man.

Colchester looked wildly round the cab. Who on earth was he? Then he spotted the little metallic plate low down beside the passenger seat telling the world that Mr Patrick Flynn was licensed to purvey for hire hackney cab number 5014723. Colchester was trying to make sense of this, when Flynn, in his final act, fell forward on to the car horn and the taxi began to blast a high mechanical shriek into the night.

Unable to think or reason Colchester leapt from the vehicle and was soon running away, across the bridge and through the rain-soaked park. The moon was flickering behind a bank of clouds by the tower of the Hilton through the trees, and behind him the slowly diminishing wail was like that of a spirit departing this earth. He ran blindly, as if at any moment a figure might appear from nowhere and complete the night's tally of executions.

It was well past midnight. The folk of Hyde Park Corner and environs were preparing for bed. The last bus had departed. The last cars with diplomatic plates had wheeled and swooped back to Belgravia from dinner parties around the capital. The dull rumble of powerful engines had faded away, leaving the smaller vehicles of waiters, deliverymen and bar staff to catch up.

Without realizing it Colchester, still in shock, had already performed half a circuit of Hyde Park. He felt an overwhelming tiredness creeping over him. He stood as the traffic swirled past and took stock.

He was alive, and a long way from home. In the park, over a mile away, a man was dead. Somewhere else in London, perhaps even watching him as he stood there, his murderer was on the loose. A random killing did not quite fit. He had witnessed, surely, the resolution of some prior conflict. Some chain of cause and effect already bound the murderer and the victim. But what?

For the moment he had the practical difficulty of getting home. Public transport had long since ceased.

It was with a thumping heart that Colchester stepped to the edge of the pavement, raised his arm into the air and shouted out: 'Taxi!'

# Chapter Twenty-two

It was, curiously, the next day that was the worst in Colchester's life.

He rose, exhausted, at six-thirty in his utility flat. Every hour during the night a gunshot had echoed through his dreams, simultaneously killing him and waking him up. He washed and shaved automatically. He practised his mental exercises, desperately trying to concentrate his mind. Supposing, for example, that he had to describe urgently, without a moment's delay, the people he had encountered the previous day. How would it go? It might run: Maggie Hopkins (messenger at the Ministry of Exports): 'Dull of aspect. Bulky. Unexpected movements. Fiftyish. Drinks tea . . .' Stanton: 'Brown colouring. Younger than he looks. Methodical. Drinks Oxo . . .' Molly: 'Blonde. Darting movements. Wears bright clothes. Smokes five cigarettes a day . . .' Fulbright: 'Bearded. Would be distinguished if he were bigger. Reddish complexion. Always wears blue suits . . .' Bert Cooper: 'Moves steadfastly from place to place. Shod for winter. Lives off chewing gum . . .' Mehmet: 'Dark. Dangerous. Armed. Wants to kill me . . .'

It was becoming increasingly difficult to find a seat on any of the crowded morning trains into Waterloo. And, as a consequence, it had become virtually impossible to read a newspaper. More people were wearing earphones, building a wall of noise between themselves and the increasingly difficult world outside.

Colchester simply stood and watched the parallel rails sliding past. As the train shot past the junctions he saw lines separate out, cross over and gradually disappear into the wilderness of pylons, boxes, wires and lumps of concrete that filled the no man's land of south London. The brown belt. Everything faded to brown, a brown horizon where parallel lines finally met and all mysteries were solved or became irrelevant. And then a line would suddenly swing in from the distance like the track of a comet, rush up gleaming to the train and run right beside it. This is me,

Colchester thought, and that line there is Julia. And we are going to our next stop together. One thought clarified itself in his tired mind through the morning journey. He must speak to her immediately.

He got to the Ministry of Exports an hour early. He was surprised to see a larger number than usual of blue-shirted security guards manning the entrance.

'What is this orange alert?' he asked the guard who insisted on rummaging in his briefcase.

The guard shrugged his shoulders.

'Search me. They're doing everyone. They did me when I came in at six. We're all on the look out. A high state of awareness.'

'What are you aware of?'

'Ah, well, that's what we'd all like to know. Terrorists. Bombers. Arsonists. The usual gang.'

'In that case, why are you searching people coming out too?'

'Don't ask me. I'll tell you one thing.'

'What's that?'

'I don't like the look of those sandwiches of yours. How long have you had them for? You should throw them away and buy yourself some fresh fruit.'

Colchester finally got out of the lift on the tenth floor and reached his office. He opened the door, looked inside and heaved a sigh of relief. He was alone. Stanton had not yet arrived.

He threw himself into his chair, picked up the telephone and dialled.

'Yes?' he heard a rather strained female voice reply.

'Julia,' he whispered. 'It's me. Listen. Something terrible has happened—'

'Guy!' she cut in. 'You're all right! Thank God . . .'

Colchester blinked. 'You mean you knew?'

'I heard about the shooting first thing this morning. But no one knew what had happened to you. I thought you'd been hurt . . . I was so worried. Where are you?'

'At the office.'

'Are you all right?'

'I got away. But I wanted to ask you—'

At this point the door opened and Stanton came in to begin his working day. He nodded briefly at Colchester and began laboriously to unpack his briefcase, spreading folders around on his desk and hunting in his drawers.

'Hello?' Julia said down the line.

'I'll have to call you back later,' said Colchester. 'When I've checked that point.'

Colchester cut the connection and dialled the registry.

'Is Bert there? I wanted the card index searching. Not there yet? Get him to call me when he comes in, would you?'

When he put the receiver down, Colchester saw Stanton looking at him with curiosity.

'Morning,' Stanton said. 'You look rough. By the way – you planning to leave us?'

Colchester's face was blank. 'Sorry?'

'Up for a PV job, aren't you?'

'No. Not me.'

'You must be. Why would they PV you, otherwise?'

'They aren't.'

'They are. Someone's going round doing a PV scan on you. Molly told me.'

'Don't believe everything Molly says. They can't PV you without letting you know.'

Stanton shook his head.

'They can do anything without letting you know, if they want to.'

'You're imagining things. Or Molly's imagining things. Or—'

Colchester's telephone rang. He picked it up, assuming it was the registry calling him back. But instead he heard the precise female tones of one of the senior secretaries, a voice he hardly knew.

'Mr Colchester? This is Mr Garrick's office. Mr Garrick has asked if he could see you. Would now be convenient?'

Colchester sat back, astonished, in his seat. He had never so much as set foot in the Deputy Secretary's office.

'Now?' he repeated. 'Are you sure? This instant?'

'Mr Garrick wanted a word with you. As soon as you came in. They told me you'd arrived. I'm afraid you'll have to ask Mr Garrick yourself what it's all about.'

They? Colchester made a face at Stanton. 'Of course. I'll be right up.'

'What's going on?' asked Stanton.

157

Colchester tidied his papers, put his pen in his pocket, got up from his desk and went to the door.

'Garrick wants to see me, of all people.'

'I told you,' said Stanton. 'The call to glory.'

Colchester shrugged his shoulders and left the room. Ten seconds after he did so his telephone rang again. Stanton went over to his desk and picked up the receiver. It was the registry, returning Colchester's call.

'No, Bert, he's just popped out. I'll get him to call you when he gets back. I think our Guy is getting his marching orders just now.'

Colchester walked slowly up the two flights of stairs to the twelfth floor, the top floor of the Ministry of Exports. What conceivable reason could Garrick have to see him, so early in the morning? Why this unheard of reaching down from the twelfth floor, the rarefied penthouse accommodation of the great and the good? How could he have come to the attention of Garrick? *Was* there anything in Stanton's forecast of a change of job? And above all when could he speak to Julia again?

The twelfth floor was unlike any other part of the Ministry of Exports. Here the usual harsh metallic greys and blues of the filing cabinets and desks, lit from above by pale flickering fluorescent lighting, gave way to softer colouring, more subtle shades, indirect lighting. The corridor which stretched the length of the top floor was decorated with prints and photographs. The odd brass fixture gleamed. On the floor actually lay a long, thin, grey carpet. The prints were views of London, cartoons by Spy. The photographs were portraits of luminaries of the Ministry of Exports going back over the years. Faces of permanent secretaries dressed in suits that grew more angular as the years receded. Then faces from beyond the short lifetime of the ministry to its predecessor, a branch of the Board of Trade. Faces going back to the middle of the century, back to the war and beyond, faces which had presided over the era of exchange controls, tariffs, imperial preference, the sterling zone and the rest of the apparatus of the late-colonial period. Portraits rescued from old cellars and hung up in this modern building to contribute – like the rest of the fixtures and fittings – to the impression that here, on the top floor, time stood still. It was, thought Colchester, like a little club up in the sky.

A door opened. The sudden chatter of voices, the clatter of office machines. And then it shut again. Colchester walked silently on the carpet to the far end of the corridor. Here were the offices of the three top officials, the doors framed in walnut. The Permanent Secretary, and the two Deputy Secretaries. He came to Garrick's office. 'J. K. F. Garrick' read the metal nameplate. 'Enter by Room 1222'. The senior officials all had ante-chambers, in which personal assistants sat and kept guard. Colchester knocked, his heart beating rather faster than usual.

He was surprised when the door drew back and revealed Garrick himself standing behind it. Colchester could see no sign of the personal assistant. Garrick looked down at Colchester and Colchester could not decipher the strange message he could see in his eyes.

'Hello, Guy,' said Garrick, beckoning past the ante-room to his office beyond. 'Come on in. I have asked Mary to leave us for a while.'

Garrick quietly shut the walnut door behind Colchester and followed him into his own spacious office. Colchester could see three figures sitting round a small conference table placed in the middle of the room, in front of Garrick's desk. They did not rise as Colchester came in but continued to stare at him silently. Behind Garrick's desk was a portrait of the Queen bearing a blue sash. On the wall beyond the conference table hung an immense canvas, an oil painting, in deep blues and greens, of a naval engagement in the last century, the scene shot through with flecks of gold and purple, the gleams of an imperial twilight.

'I have some gentlemen who wish to talk to you,' said Garrick in an odd, neutral voice. In a flash Colchester thought he could read Garrick's attitude. It was hard to believe but he could swear it was embarrassment.

'Mr Williamson you will know,' went on Garrick, indicating the head of the personnel department at the ministry. Williamson returned Colchester's gaze by batting his eyelids twice.

'My other two visitors perhaps not. Mr Fergusson. Mr Stuart-Smith. From, er, the Ministry of Defence. Sit down, if you would, Guy. Here.'

Garrick installed Colchester at one end of the conference table and then retired to his desk, like one who has put together the elements of a conjuring trick and waits to see how it will work.

'Over to you, Fergusson,' he murmured.

Colchester sat and watched and waited while the older of the two strangers looked him up and down. Colchester again tried to read the signals. Garrick withdrawn, abashed. Williamson to one side, reserved, a witness at an accident. The younger stranger alert, expectant, listening, thinking. He reminded Colchester a little of a youthful doctor in private practice. The older stranger, tanned from the tropics, suddenly powerful, more powerful than Garrick in his own office, a representative of some deeper force, a card-carrying member of – what? Behind Fergusson's head was a painting of explosions at sea, giving him a naval aura.

'Talk to us, Mr Colchester,' said Fergusson abruptly, his gaze unwavering. 'Talk to us about your work.'

Colchester looked across to Garrick for help.

Garrick made as if to wash his hands.

'Do as Mr Fergusson asks, Guy.'

Colchester turned back to Fergusson. 'What aspect of it interests you?'

Fergusson ignored the question. 'Tell us about yourself.'

Where had Colchester heard this before? Again, seeing nothing in the face of either Garrick or Williamson, he collected his thoughts. Then he began his litany. As they knew he was responsible for the collection of material on export markets in certain Middle Eastern countries. The dissemination of information through regional chambers of commerce. The processing of requests for export credits from applicant firms. The presentation of material to the Projects Committee in due and proper form. The insurance of such credits with the overseas finance arm of the Bank of England. The filing of insurance policies. Correspondence with companies who wished to draw on their credits when importing countries were in default. Answering ministerial queries on trade flows and patterns . . .

As he continued to recite the list of his activities Colchester noticed that neither man's attention wandered for one moment. It was as if he was telling them extraordinary facts, bearing news of the highest importance. And yet they must know all this. They must know who he was, what he did. And, gradually, Colchester became aware that they were actually listening to his voice, not to his words. They were trying him out, testing him, getting the feel of his speech patterns, listening to the silences, the pauses, the hesitations.

Colchester finally ground to a halt, having run out of things to say. Fergusson remained impassive. The silence grew between them, and outside the faint hum of traffic became audible.

Fergusson waited a full minute. Then he spoke again, quietly.

'Now tell us what you know about the INF Treaty, Mr Colchester.'

Colchester, baffled, looked once more at Garrick. No reaction. Garrick was in on this. Garrick knew what the next question would be, he was sure of it. What on earth was going on?

'The INF Treaty . . .' Colchester began. 'It stands for Intermediate Nuclear Forces, doesn't it? An agreement between the US and the Soviet Union eliminating a certain category of nuclear weapon. Medium range, I think. Isn't there a destruction programme?

'And the UK?' asked Fergusson.

'I'm sorry?' said Colchester.

'The UK signature on the Basing Nation annexe?'

'I don't follow.'

'Do you not? Basing Nation Number One Destruction Programme, Article 3(b) of Annexe Five?'

'Should I know about it?'

Once again Fergusson ignored his question.

'Report of Soviet inspector Kutzov of the Third Army Technical Corps to Moscow dated the fourteenth of August last, one copy obtained by clandestine means, indicating a shortfall in nuclear fuses unaccounted for by the UK authorities?'

'It means nothing to me.'

'Material abstracted from site, believed to remain in the UK, reprocessed by British affiliate of Austrian communications and armaments company S. G. Zwann?'

Colchester's face remained a blank.

'Reprocessed, repackaged, camouflaged and built into mechanical equipment distributed to suppliers by Manchester firm Peters Anderson, in turn prepared for export by leasers and shippers Benbow Engineering and Co. Ltd. of Wincanton?'

'But —' began Colchester.

'And,' continued Fergusson without a pause, 'licensed, insured, authorized, cushioned, patted on its back and sent on its merry way down the road to hell in the Middle East by our very own Ministry of Exports.'

Colchester looked over to Garrick. Now he could understand

the expression on his face. Garrick had turned a slightly deeper shade of salmon and was avoiding Colchester's eyes; he looked as if he was calculating the distance that lay between this day and his pension, and whether the obstacles on the way had suddenly become insurmountable.

'That is one thing,' went on Fergusson. 'This,' he said, pulling an envelope out of the briefcase he held under the table, 'is another.'

He drew out of the envelope two black and white photographs which he laid on the table. He turned them round so Colchester could see them.

'Tell me what you know about these people.'

Colchester bent over. The first photograph was grainy and dark, obscured by shade that fell across the top half of the picture. It depicted a tall, lean-looking man getting out of a taxi in a London street. The street was busy, the camera angle odd. The expression on the man's face seemed to be one of joy, his face uplifted in the contemplation of a higher vision. The second photograph was over-exposed. A pretty young woman entering a large department store, glancing to her left, transfixed in an attentive attitude, the eyes watchful, cautious, looking for the traps that lay before her.

Colchester's perplexity deepened. 'De la Fosse. And Julia. But you must know them.'

'Why?'

'Because they work for you, don't they?'

This time Colchester saw the younger stranger shoot a glance at Fergusson.

'What makes you say that?' asked Fergusson.

Colchester felt as if he had just trodden on air. 'Because – because they do. Don't they?'

And then he thought: nuclear fuses? INF? Whatever happened to chemical warfare? Whatever happened to El Mihr?

'There's something wrong,' he said. 'It's chemical weapons, isn't it? Isn't that what's going on?'

'Where?'

'El Mihr, of course.'

'I don't know about El Mihr,' said Fergusson. 'What I do know is that the material that goes to El Mihr doesn't stay there. It goes on to a place called Al Tadj. And they have an awful lot of missiles in Al Tadj.'

'Why?'

'To attack someone with, obviously. I'll give you three guesses who, Mr Colchester. Which state is the least popular with its neighbours in that part of the world, do you think?'

'Well . . . Israel, I suppose?'

'And which state do you suppose would do anything to stop its neighbours acquiring a nuclear capacity, including stopping material at source coming from the west?'

'Israel?'

'And,' Fergusson went on, 'I wonder if you can also guess which state thinks it's on to a good thing when it finds it can recruit and run a useful idiot in London, who can keep it in the picture; including, for example, passing it the odd document that comes his way?'

Colchester stared. 'I don't believe it,' he whispered.

But then he knew he did believe it. He knew, as he looked down at the smiling face of de la Fosse and the watchful face of Julia, that it was true. They're planning to send me away soon, she said. Abroad. The other side of the world. She had been right. They *were* from two separate worlds. Had he half guessed all along that she was putting on a show for him? Had he known, deep inside him, that Julia was holding something in reserve? And had he gone on regardless precisely because he had wanted to find out what it was?

As if in a daze he could hear Fergusson say, 'You have gone way out of your depth, Mr Colchester. We are going to need a signed statement, now. With all the details. You had better co-operate, you know. There are legal implications.'

And he heard his own voice, like that of a stranger, say, 'What legal implications?'

And Fergusson said, 'The Official Secrets Act, Mr Colchester. The law of this country. I have discussed this with your minister. He insists we take a firm line. Do you have any conception of the gravity of your offence?'

Offence? thought Colchester. Offence?

'But I didn't know what I was doing,' the distant voice said.

'No doubt the jury will take that into account, Mr Colchester.'

And then Fergusson stood up. He walked deliberately over to a door that Colchester had not noticed before on the other side of Garrick's office. He opened it and stood to one side.

'Wait in here if you would, Mr Colchester. We need to discuss what to do with you.'

Colchester left the table and went to the door. It opened into another small waiting room, which contained a photocopier, a table, two chairs and a metal filing cabinet.

'If you wouldn't mind,' said Fergusson.

Colchester stepped forward. The door closed behind him. He heard the key turn in the lock. He was a prisoner.

'We'll give him five minutes,' said Fergusson, breaking the pained silence in Garrick's office after Colchester's departure. Garrick and Williamson were looking aghast at each other, each trying to work out exactly how bad it was, how far they were going to be held, could be held, might conceivably be held, responsible. How much history was going to need rewriting? Already Garrick had made a mental note to get at the records of the Projects Committee before anyone else could. And Williamson had made a mental note to re-read the jottings of his last, routine meeting with Colchester twelve – or was it eighteen? – months ago. Only Stuart-Smith seemed unperturbed by events, as if this sort of thing happened every day. Callous blighter, thought Garrick in passing.

'Excuse me,' said Fergusson. He reached over Garrick's desk and picked up one of the telephones. He dialled a four-figure number, a connection on the Whitehall exchange.

Hotblack was sitting waiting in the Cabinet Office at the other end.

'He was the one,' said Fergusson. 'He'll sign a confession if we need it. A false flag operation, like we thought.'

Hotblack considered.

'All right, Gordon. You can go ahead now. Don't do anything foolish.'

Fergusson replaced the receiver and then turned and looked at Garrick and Williamson in turn.

'Apart from yourselves and the head of the ET Committee no one else is up to speed on this. It is vital, I repeat, vital, that we maintain security. I hesitate to say so, gentlemen, since you are both senior men, but my department will if necessary apply the Official Secrets Act to you as severely as to our friend next door. Is that clear?'

'I really doubt the need to lecture us,' observed Garrick mildly.

'You may,' said Fergusson. 'You may. But the fact is that I do not want one whisper of this to get out of this room. Above all we must keep ministers out of it. There must not be the slightest suggestion – to them, to the press, and particularly not to the Americans, that material in UK hands has gone astray. If we are careful we can contain this disaster. If we are not it will devour all of us. Is that understood?'

Fergusson saw Garrick and Williamson nod thoughtfully in assent.

'Right,' he said. 'Now, Colchester. What is his ideology? Williamson?'

'Ideology?' repeated Williamson. 'I don't think he has one. At least, no more than anyone else.'

'Well,' said Fergusson, 'he keeps odd company. You can confirm this, Alan?'

Stuart-Smith cleared his throat. 'Indeed, sir. When we did the PV sweep we dug up one suspect character. Name of Molloy. Lives in Croydon. Works in the town hall by day. Union activist. And also a member of CND. Two contacts of his were jailed for disturbing the peace two years ago. Molloy and Colchester meet once a week. We trailed Molloy one night and found he had a lock-up garage in Croydon. We took a look inside. Most peculiar. Full to bursting with household goods. Tables. Chairs. Lampstands. Record players. Shoes. Suits of clothing. All in good condition. Only one of anything. We presume stolen goods. Or supplies – for something.'

Fergusson turned back to Garrick.

'We don't like dark corners,' he said. 'I want to try something on Colchester. I want collateral on him. I want to know more about his reactions. His character. What to expect. Is he bent? Is he sound? Do you have anything here?'

'Why yes,' said Garrick feeling, for the first time that morning, that something might be going right. 'We have his latest personal report, do we not, Williamson?'

Williamson too felt the touch of grace. 'Absolutely, Deputy Secretary.'

He abstracted a folder from a collection before him and handed it over. Garrick rapidly ran with his finger through Fulbright's dense, tight prose, trying to follow the train of argument.

'Here we are,' he said. 'The comments of his line manager. Only the other week. I choose at random: "Guy is a willing worker. He is prepared to be assiduous. But he could still do better. I continue to believe that he could show more application and attention to detail. I see no reason to deviate from the general assessment that I reached last year that he simply needs to adopt a more engaged attitude." '

Garrick handed the file over to Fergusson. He felt renewed confidence. This was a home match, after all.

'Read it for yourself, if you like. I think you will find, as we have, that Colchester belongs to that broad class of officers whose both virtue and vice is their predictability.'

Fergusson in turn handed the file to Stuart-Smith. 'Good,' he said. 'Read it. Quickly. And then it's over to you.'

Colchester was watching the traffic circulate twelve storeys below. Even in this small office he noticed they did things differently. Curtains at the windows instead of blinds. Carpet a deeper pile. Furniture just that little bit darker and heavier. Window catches that looked as if they might work. And, in one corner, unused, discarded, a brand new Anglepoise lamp.

Dully, mechanically, he tugged at the handle of the window. It opened. He pulled at the frame until it had completely swung round, gaping. A gust of icy air hit him in the face and a wave of city noise billowed up from the street. He shook his head, trying to exorcize the feeling he had that he was living through a nightmare. He leaned further out of the window and looked down. There is not one person there, he thought, with whom I would not gladly change places. There can't be anyone in this entire city who just now is not in a better position than me. I would give everything I possess simply to walk out of this building and never come back again. But I am stuck. Stuck with what I have done. Stuck on a railway line heading straight to disaster. And there is no way of leaving it, unless . . .

A hand on his shoulder.

'Don't do it,' an amiable voice said straight into his ear. Turning round he saw that the younger stranger, Stuart-Smith, had come in without him hearing.

'At least,' went on Stuart-Smith, sitting himself on the edge of the table and swinging his legs backwards and forwards, 'Not just yet. I wanted a word first. Shut the window, would you?'

Colchester closed it and fastened the catch. The traffic noise cut off.

Stuart-Smith was silent for a few moments. He looked at Colchester. Then he looked over to the door, which Colchester saw he had closed behind him, and gestured with a nod of his head.

'I personally find old Fergusson pretty hard going at times. It's his generation, you know. It's been downhill all the way since the war. Try and make allowances, would you?'

Colchester looked more closely at Stuart-Smith. Was he hearing things? 'Make allowances?'

'He's only doing his job,' pursued Stuart-Smith diplomatically. 'We all are. Just like you, really. Some civil servants are more civil than others, that's all. Take a seat.'

Colchester did so. Stuart-Smith hopped down from the desk, picked up one of the chairs, placed it over by the far wall and perched himself on it. Then he grinned.

'The girl's a real cracker,' he said appreciatively.

'She said it was a matter of life and death,' said Colchester suddenly. 'I just spaced out the deliveries so I could see more of her.'

Stuart-Smith nodded his understanding. 'Very sensible. I would have done the same thing, if I'd been in your place.'

'You would?'

'Oh yes. Girl like that, worth taking a risk or two for. Even if it went wrong in the end. I think I can understand. Even if *they* don't.'

'What's going to happen now?'

Stuart-Smith pursed his lips. 'That, as they say, rather depends on you.'

'How do you mean?'

Stuart-Smith paused as if marshalling his thoughts. He got up and went over to the filing cabinet, opened it and surveyed the piles of stationery he found within. Then he came back and looked in each of the empty drawers of the desk.

'I thought not,' he muttered.

'What?'

'Not a sniff of an ashtray. Oh well, I'll have to go without. Now there are, really, broadly two scenarios. Scenario one is classic Fergusson stuff. We have you arrested. You are prosecuted under the Official Secrets Act for the unauthorized transmission of official information to a foreign power – that's the sort of language they use, you know. Your defence will no doubt make much of your unwitting involvement. A hapless victim of circumstances. The prosecution will point out that you deliberately contrived to see more of the girl. You just told me that, I'm afraid. The prosecution will pitch for ten years. In the end you'll probably get three or four years. And maximum publicity. It'll be headline stuff. You won't like it.

'The second scenario is rather better. None of us really wants publicity. We want results. We're not too fussy how we get them. There are two things we want to do. The first is to neutralize the leak of material out of the UK. We can do that if we move quickly. The second is to get rid of these foreign bodies who have been running around London recently. That's where we need your help.'

Colchester thought he could see it coming. But all the same, he said, 'How?'

'It goes like this. We have tabs on de la Fosse. But we want the girl too. We need to pick them both up at the same time. What better than for you to arrange to meet her – as usual – and for us then to step in and take over where you leave off? We also get de la Fosse. We stop the shipment. And we arrest the gentleman who is doing the ordering for El Mihr a.k.a. Al Tadj.'

'Mehmet?'

'That's the fellow. He has, incidentally, been following the girl. He knows who she is.'

Colchester knew that already. And he was on the point of telling Stuart-Smith about what had happened, when something odd that Fergusson had said came back to him. *I have discussed this with your minister. He insists we take a firm line.* It reminded him of another odd thing, something that Mehmet had said about Warwick. *He is supposed to be a friend of ours.* He checked himself and asked instead, 'And what happens to them?'

'Oh, I think we'll have a chat with them first and then expel the lot of them. Let them sort themselves out. They're at war with each other. They can go on settling their accounts, as long as it's not on our soil. They'll probably end up cancelling each other out.'

'Why?'

'Well, if Al Tadj is neutralized the Middle East will be pretty hot

168

for a time. They can be quite vindictive, I understand. But they should have thought of that.'

'And what about me?'

'The beauty of this particular scenario is that nothing much happens to you. We might have to change your job, of course. Find you some other little niche away from this place. But otherwise you walk free. You won't see any of us again. You go on with your life in some cosy nook of an office – just like this one – as if nothing had ever happened. You can forget all about us.'

Colchester remembered Julia's words. 'It's the last time we meet. You find somewhere for us. Somewhere we can make love.'

And she had been lying all the time. Now they offered him the truth. Yet was it the truth? There was some aspect to this he still could not understand. Until it became clear he realized he could no longer trust anyone at all any more – except, possibly, himself.

'So,' he said, thoughtfully, 'what it really comes down to is that I hand over Julia in return for keeping myself out of jail?'

'Well,' said Stuart-Smith, 'I suppose that's one way of putting it. It seems a fair exchange to me, considering the mess she has got you in. What do you say?'

Colchester said nothing, was lost in thought. He could see, now, that one way or another he had come to the end of his apprenticeship with the Ministry of Exports. Sooner than he had expected. But he knew it would have happened one day, in any case. The time had come when he had to turn on his axis and head in a totally new direction. For him to decide. But which direction?

There were too many uncertainties. Too many variables. And yet the germ of the idea which had just come to him could allow no error. He did a complicated mental calculation. Perhaps it would work. But there was a very good chance it wouldn't.

'What do you say?' asked Stuart-Smith again.

Colchester looked him straight in the eye.

'All right,' he said in a voice which surprised him by its resolution. 'I need to set the record straight. I'll get in touch and fix a meeting. I'll make it next week, after the next Projects Committee.'

'Good man,' said Stuart-Smith. 'You won't regret it. Now we do need a statement out of you, with details of times, meetings, conversations and everything you gave them . . .'

# Chapter Twenty-three

Colchester picked up the telephone and slowly, methodically, composed the digits of the number which he used to contact de la Fosse and Julia. The only difference was that this time he was not in his own office, waiting for Stanton to go out and for a moment of privacy. This time he was in a makeshift little bunker on the third floor of the Ministry of Exports, a lonely corner by the office supplies department which was always empty at lunchtime. At the other end of the table, propped up against a pile of mail bags and wearing a pair of headphones connected to a dull grey oblong box in front of him, sat Stuart-Smith.

'I have the connection,' said Colchester.

Stuart-Smith nodded. He set the tracer in motion.

Colchester sat and waited. How often had he rung this number? Only three or four times. And yet always that sensation of dialling out to infinity, as if the call had left the London networks completely and was being routed somewhere through outer space. Stuart-Smith had already established that the number was a false one. A false one? Colchester had asked. How can you have a false telephone number? Answer: you can have a number which is simply a junction box, a re-router, a small computer attached to a socket sitting somewhere in an empty house in London, swapping incoming and outgoing telephone lines, a Clapham Junction of the telephone world.

And then, as always, a connection, bright and clear as a morning in spring.

'Hello,' said Julia, direct in his ear.

Colchester's heart bounded within him. Traitress. Liar. Adorable black-hearted schemer.

'It's me,' he said.

'What happened?' she asked. 'Where have you been all morning?'

He thought, they must not know that I spoke to her earlier.

'I couldn't get to a telephone. You know how it is.'

Julia was silent for a brief moment. Then she said, 'So what do you want to do?'

Colchester looked at Stuart-Smith, listening intently.

'Let's just meet next week as we agreed,' he said carefully. 'After the PC. Let's say Thursday. Meet me outside Croydon Town Hall. The main entrance. Three-thirty.'

'Are you sure?' she asked softly.

'I'm sure,' he replied.

'Why there?' She sounded puzzled.

I knew she'd say that, thought Colchester.

'It's near the hotel. Where we had dinner. We could go straight there.'

'But it seems such a strange time.'

'It's the only afternoon I can get away.'

'Can't you think of somewhere better?'

The fool! thought Colchester. The fool! She is going to wreck everything.

'No, I can't think of anywhere better,' he replied.

'Well, I can,' said Julie. 'Hundreds of places.'

'Look,' he said. 'Who is supposed to be arranging this? You or me? Will you be there or won't you?'

A pause. Then back to the softer tone. 'I'll be there, Guy. I'll be there. I'm sorry. Look forward to seeing you.'

'Look forward to seeing you,' said Colchester gently. Then he replaced the receiver. Stuart-Smith was alarmed.

'Careful,' he said. 'Careful. We don't want to frighten her off.'

And over in UK Centre Julia saw de la Fosse frowning at her across her desk. He removed his own earphones.

'How often do I have to tell you, Julia, that the customer is always right. You go where he wants. You do what he wants. He wants to meet you in the dome of St Paul's at five o'clock in the morning? You be there. You can't be fussy. Don't put him off.'

'Don't worry. It's the last time I'll see him,' she said meekly.

'Perhaps just as well. What's this about a hotel?'

'Oh, we'll have tea or something,' she answered vaguely.

De la Fosse narrowed his eyes.

'Or something? Thursday, eh? A red letter day.'

'Why?'

'It's the day I give my big address. It's almost finished. Do you want to hear it?'

'Can I not read it afterwards?'

'Oh, very well . . .'

Julia watched de la Fosse leave to return to his own office. If there is an afterwards, she thought to herself. Because now a decision which had been forming subconsciously inside her for some weeks had been taken. It had been taken when she heard this morning that they had found the body in the park and she thought at first it was Colchester and she thought that she was responsible, that she had killed him . . .

Stuart-Smith and Colchester sat together waiting.

'They'll call me back in a few minutes,' said Stuart-Smith.

Colchester eyed Stuart-Smith. Slightly older than himself. An assuredness. A sense of purpose. Himself in a different life? Someone who had chosen his destiny, found what seemed to him interesting and gone for it.

'Do you enjoy fighting the good fight?' he asked.

'Love every minute of it,' said Stuart-Smith candidly.

'Do they pay you well?'

'A pittance. I mean, hardly, more than you get. But I'd do it for nothing. Just as well, perhaps.'

'What's the attraction?'

'It's what the Sovs call the correlation of forces. You meet people at the turning point. On the cusp. Caught in the crossfire. Like you. Who knows which way they'll jump? It's all a gamble. And the best of it is you're betting with the taxpayer's money, not your own. And I suppose it is just marginally possible that at the end of the day you might be doing something useful. Who knows?'

'What plans for me?'

'We'll think about it. A change of scenery, like I said. We'll have to ease you gently from here. A transfer. Somewhere where your Middle East chums won't think to look.'

'Would a trial have been very embarrassing?'

'The problem is the missing material. If we go public on that, the roof will fall in. A behind-the-scenes operation is better.'

'I see.'

The telephone rang. Stuart-Smith picked it up and listened attentively for a few moments. Then he replaced the receiver.

'They traced the re-router,' he said. 'A warehouse in Wapping. A little black box hidden in the rafters. And there the trail stops. A bunch of wires leading out into the telephone system, branching off in a million directions.'

'So another chance next week?'

'Another chance next week.'

Stanton could barely contain his curiosity when Colchester reappeared in the office that afternoon. Colchester had been told something, that much he could see. But what? He had changed, in some indefinable way. Colchester looked around the office, at the little pile of messages on his desk, and it seemed to Stanton that he was really somewhere else, had already mentally disengaged himself and was travelling down some new path.

'So what's it to be, then?' Stanton finally said. 'Stitt's job, is it?'

Colchester had prepared for this one, with Stuart-Smith's help.

'You were right,' he said. 'It is a PV job. Somewhere else altogether. They want to do a swap with another department. But they're not sure which one yet. Somewhere out of London, it may be.'

'Garrick told you that?'

'He just wanted to sound me out, I think. It all depends on how the PV goes. I've been with the personnel people all morning.'

Stanton gave him a canny look.

'If you want my advice, don't tell them about any strange women. It can set you back.'

Colchester looked sharply at Stanton, but Stanton had already returned his attention to the mountains of files piled in front of him. Colchester began to put his own papers in order, sorting and classifying, his mind a million miles away from his office and his desk.

That evening, for the first time since Stanton and Colchester had shared an office, Colchester went home before Stanton. Stanton sat speculating on which department could possibly want to swap with the Ministry of Exports. On his way out Colchester noticed that the orange alert was over.

I have tonight, thought Colchester as he stood in the crowded early train going home, watching the lights of Waterloo recede in the distance. I have this one night to arrange things. And then it will be too late. The die will be cast. Is even a week enough? I think so. I hope so. Somewhere, locked away in the recesses of his memory, was the faintest trace of the procedure, the barest outline of what he must do. But he might have got it wrong. When he stood there, giving his answer to Stuart-Smith's proposal this morning, he had taken a gigantic risk. It was one thing gambling with the taxpayer's money, like Stuart-Smith. It was another gambling with your own freedom. Because if this went wrong, he would get no second chance.

Was she worth it? he wondered. He did not know. For a woman like that you would rob a bank, cheat and lie. So Terry had said. But would you risk you entire existence? Would even Terry do that? Perhaps no one else would. No one else is lunatic enough to do this, thought Colchester to himself with a certain satisfaction. I am alone in the world. I am detached from every system that has supported me. I am making my way into no man's land.

He knew when he got off the train at Croydon that they would be following him. They would be around him in the crowd at the station. They would follow him for the next week. He could not use the telephone. He could not write a message. And he must act tonight.

It was still early, only just gone six, when Colchester got back to the flat. He quickly prepared a light supper, eggs and bacon and plenty of bread to line the stomach. He might have to drink more than usual tonight, if he was unlucky.

At seven o'clock he left the flat. It was a cold, dank, raw night, the sort of night you were much better off staying indoors. Marvellous, thought Colchester. Just the weather I want. This is bound to tempt him out. He'll probably want to stay at home and read his union rule books.

Colchester pulled the garden gate to and made his way down the deserted street, feeling the damp air, which seemed to have blown in straight off the frozen North Sea. The ignition of a car sounded fifty yards behind him. He didn't even bother to look round. They had no need to hide the fact they were following him. He noticed with some satisfaction that it took three goes before the motor caught. Cold night. Cold engine. Soon they would be getting warm.

Tonight was jazz night in the Coach and Horses. Always a minority interest. The Croydon jazz scene had never struck Colchester as very energetic. As he came in through the swing doors he could hear a saxophonist making that peculiar blaring sort of noise that Colchester always thought sounded as if it came from throttling the instrument. It glided wildly in and out of several minor chords, coming out at the top of a rising crescendo and honking furiously. The percussionist tapped out a misjudged, waltz-like rhythm. The bassist was silent. The clarinettist contented himself with a few intermittent low hoots.

Colchester went up to the bar and ordered a drink. There were even fewer people in than usual this evening. Perhaps the music drove them away. Or perhaps the cold night kept them in. As he turned, with his drink in his hand, to face the band in the other bar, he suddenly thought this must be how Julia felt when she was waiting for him. An evening stretching ahead, waiting for someone who may or may not appear, marking time with sporadic drinks. But Julia was a professional. She drank tonic water. She carried something to read. And I am only an amateur, thought Colchester. I have nothing to read. And I am drinking this really awful lager. The doors opened and two men came in, jackets buttoned up, looking around as if they had not been in here before. They saw Colchester more or less immediately, and went over to the other bar, the one near the music, where they could keep an eye on him. And they are professionals too, thought Colchester. I hope they like jazz.

He tried to analyse his feelings for Julia. I am a patriot, she had said. I owe my country something for looking after me. I am a conscript. And the country she was thinking of all the time was different from his. Her country was at war. His was at peace. In times of war the end justifies any means. He had been a means for her. A means to help her country. But which came first for her: him or her country? And, equally, which came first for him: her or his country? For one important shift had taken place. He now knew both sides of the game. And she only knew one. He had that brief, and quite possibly valueless, advantage.

Amongst the tangle of his emotions towards the end of this dreadful day Colchester felt there were some that were contradictory, that did not quite make sense. Hatred possibly. The desire for revenge, certainly. Fear, yes. Shame, yes. But also a restlessness, an itching, a longing to square the account in some deeper, more permanent way. Despite it all, he knew that he could not just let her go. At least not without one final effort to prove

175

that he had some say in his own life. Perhaps, in the end, even Stuart-Smith would understand.

Colchester was on his third drink by the time Terry came in. Colchester put up a welcoming hand. Over in the other bar one of the men nudged his partner. They knew all about Terry, Stuart-Smith had told Colchester. He was very much on the debit side of the register so far as Colchester's record was concerned. Don't worry. I haven't been subverted yet, Colchester had told Stuart-Smith.

'Slumming tonight then?' said Terry, coming over to Colchester and ordering himself a drink. He made a grimace as the percussionist began to hammer the drums in a solo. Across the room Colchester saw the two men wince.

'I'd have thought you'd be cuddling up to Miss Kensington on a night like this,' went on Terry. 'You are a crafty fox. I see a woman like that and I just shed a silent tear. You jump in feet first. So what's it all about then? How did you get to meet her?'

'I'll tell you later,' said Colchester. 'Just now there's something I want to ask you. Your work. How serious is it for you?'

Terry was puzzled. 'Serious? I don't get your meaning. It pays the bills. But *serious* . . . ?'

Colchester rephrased the question. 'Supposing you had to bend the rules slightly – for a good cause.'

Terry paused. 'Depends on the cause. If it's *political*, for example . . .'

'What I had in mind is more personal. But it is a bit political. Personal politics, you might say.'

'What exactly are you getting at?'

'You said once if I needed to jump ship I should come to you.'

'Yes – but where do you want to jump? Are you in trouble?'

'I think I am, actually. And I need your help. What I want to do is this . . .'

And Colchester poured his thoughts into Terry's ear. The two men, seeing Colchester and Terry in deep conversation, began to regret that they had stationed themselves so near the music. They saw Terry's eyes get wider and wider as he listened to what Colchester proposed. And then a broad grin creased his face as he grasped it. Must have been a good one, they thought, as Terry pounded his fist up and down on the bar in time to the music. Pity we missed it.

# Chapter Twenty-four

After Stuart-Smith left Colchester that afternoon he rejoined Fergusson in the temporary headquarters the latter had made for himself in the innards of the Cabinet Office. Or, to be more exact, Stuart-Smith sat as directed and manned the telephones in Hotblack's secretary's office (who had, like Garrick's secretary that morning, been told to go and do some Christmas shopping), while Fergusson was locked in permanent conference with Hotblack. Although the doors were closed it appeared to Stuart-Smith that Hotblack used the telephones several times in the course of the afternoon. Once he saw the light on the secretary's switchboard glimmer and he knew that the line to the next door neighbours in Number Ten was in use.

Stuart-Smith was used to crises of one type or another, but this was different. For a start there was no mention of activating COBRA – the Cabinet Office briefing room, the traditional cockpit of crisis management, drawing together the different parts of the machinery of government. Nor were legal advisers in on the scene – a strange absence given the notorious intricacies of the Official Secrets Act, and also given what the police had found in Hyde Park early that morning. And – Stuart-Smith had to admit this candidly to himself – neither was he being properly kept in the picture. Colchester was one thing, and his crimes and misdemeanours were bad enough. But there was more, and Stuart-Smith knew it. Fergusson's whole attitude, his conspiring behind closed doors with Hotblack, reminded him of – what, exactly? Of a raising of a drawbridge? Of a withdrawal into an inner fortress within the perimeter of a defence system that has been breached? It seemed to Stuart-Smith that Fergusson and Hotblack had retired into some private world, cut off from official reality, where they and only they made up the rules, in defiance of everyone. Fergusson had even forbidden Stuart-Smith to attend a routine cocktail party at – of all places – the US Embassy that night.

At seven o'clock Fergusson finally emerged from Hotblack's office, closing the door carefully behind him.

'I'm sorry about this, Alan,' he said in a slightly tired voice. 'I'll explain later. It really is important to keep this secure. I want you with me this evening as back up, in case anything goes wrong.'

'Where are we going?'

'You'll see.'

Their first stop was a dark and windy Hyde Park. It seemed deserted, but as their car approached the middle of the park Stuart-Smith saw a cluster of bright lights. The police had roped off the bridge over the Serpentine and pulled to one side the cab that had been driven by Flynn and which was now marooned, a stricken vessel. The body of Flynn reposed in state in an obscure Home Office mortuary in Marylebone.

The plain-clothes officer on duty saluted the senior man, Fergusson. He indicated an invisible route leading along the gravel, out of the illuminated area and off into the dark night.

'You asked us for our analysis, sir. We think the murderer went that way. He was moving fast, probably towards the Underground. No weapon found yet, but forensic traces tally.' He paused. 'This *political*, would you say, sir?'

Fergusson nodded slowly. 'An eye for an eye, a tooth for a tooth. We think we have some idea of the background. Tell me, have you been able to keep this quiet? No press stories?'

'So far. But I don't know for how long—'

'Just a few days . . . You see there are others involved too. We want a *co-ordinated* approach. Get all our ducks in a row—'

'Fine by me. But you know there was a witness?'

Stuart-Smith looked sharply at Fergusson.

'A witness?' asked Fergusson.

The officer pointed away to the left. He indicated a zig-zag path leading erratically into a morass of trodden December mud.

'Someone went off there. Stopping and starting. Back and forth. As if he couldn't make his mind up what to do. He was in the cab too.'

Fergusson frowned. As he had said to Garrick earlier that day, he was not fond of dark corners. 'But you have no way of finding out who?'

'See for yourself. The traces become impossible to distinguish after a while. Whoever it was just went to ground . . .'

The three of them looked out silently into the night. A distant dark mass of trees eclipsed the lights of the buildings which surrounded the park; far off the noise of traffic circulating endlessly.

'They're both out there somewhere,' remarked the officer. 'The man who did it and the man who saw it.'

He turned to look back at Fergusson. 'Strange way of practising politics, isn't it, sir?'

Fergusson nodded sagely. 'Amen to that.'

Their second stop that evening was in Belgravia, in a little street off Belgrave Square which was home to the chancery of one of the less reputable embassies on the London diplomatic list.

Stuart-Smith waited in the car while Fergusson went round to the service entrance, down a tiny cul-de-sac. Stuart-Smith saw him stand there for a few moments, then a door opened and Fergusson vanished into the darkness.

To while away the time Stuart-Smith read a late edition of the *Evening Standard*. The paper was full of background about the forthcoming Washington summit between the superpowers. The battle of the First Ladies. What Raisa had said to Nancy that night in Paris. Who was winning the charm offensive. Who was the brightest star in the Star Wars.

And, in a smaller piece beneath the main article about where Raisa bought her dresses, there was a report from the Washington correspondent on how critics of the American administration – and some within the administration – were seriously worried about rumours of a fabulous breakthrough in the arms talks leading up to the summit. 'The President has been badly advised on this from the outset,' commented one highly placed source. 'It is a dangerous world. We have to be careful we don't add to instability.' The correspondent told his readers that never in the history of an accident-prone US administration had there been such internal warfare in the run up to a major summit. The correspondent did not bother to speculate on whether the same dissent was also rocking Moscow.

After a while Stuart-Smith felt certain he was being observed and, sure enough, a plain black saloon car with two men inside presently appeared and hove to alongside him. One of the men got out of the car and walked slowly round to where Stuart-Smith was sitting. He wound down his side window. It was the Diplomatic Service Protection Squad.

'Good evening, sir. Waiting for somebody, are we?'

For a moment Stuart-Smith toyed with the idea of bluffing his way out, and considered one of the several multipurpose cover stories that he kept tucked away for embarrassing moments. But then he shelved his tale of the lover and the kitchen maid and took out his identity card to show to the officer.

The policeman looked at it dubiously.

'We're delivering the parish magazine,' explained Stuart-Smith.

The policeman shook his head and handed the card back to Stuart-Smith.

'Very well, sir. But if you don't mind me saying so you're choosing a funny place to do it. They have some very odd types in there. But no doubt you know what you're doing.'

As the policeman stood to withdraw Stuart-Smith muttered under his breath, 'I wouldn't bank on it.'

The saloon car moved on.

After a few minutes Fergusson emerged from the pariah embassy. He returned to the car.

'Was Othello at home tonight?' asked Stuart-Smith.

'He was,' replied Fergusson. 'And I'll thank you not to ask the next question. I have a meeting with someone in a couple of hours, that's all.'

They picked up sandwiches from an all-night delicatessen near Trafalgar Square and Stuart-Smith drove slowly down towards the river. At twenty to ten he parked on Victoria Embankment, near Cleopatra's Needle. The lights strung up along the side of the Thames made it seem as usual like the scene of a Ruritanian festivity, but there were few people about on this winter's night.

'Do you know what the black list is, Alan?' asked Fergusson.

Stuart-Smith replied that he did not.

'No,' said Fergusson. 'Nor did I.' He checked his watch.

'Give me half an hour and then if I don't return come and get me,' he then said matter of factly, getting out of the car. Stuart-Smith watched him walk with a deliberate pace along the Embankment, in the direction of Westminster. Clouds scudding across the sky suddenly unveiled the moon. The surreal shapes of the black marble lions lying alongside the public benches glistened briefly. Then the moon went in behind another bank of clouds, and Fergusson had also vanished.

Who or what is he trying to protect? wondered Stuart-Smith.

Near the entrance to Embankment tube station Fergusson mounted the steep flight of steps. He continued climbing until he was out on the footbridge that crossed the Thames parallel to Hungerford railway bridge, and which normally echoed to the footsteps of an army of commuters swarming from Waterloo station over the river to the offices in the north – including Colchester, early that very morning.

Now the footbridge was empty.

It stretched out before Fergusson, over three football pitches in length. Beneath was the sombre moving mass of Thames water, passing remote and silent out to the City and the distant mudflats and estuaries of the east. A train rumbled out of Charing Cross station and, passing Fergusson, picked up speed and clanked out across the bridge, its yellow carriage lights sweeping into the darkness like a liner crossing a midnight sea.

There was still no one on the bridge, but as the train reached the far end of the crossing and moved off into the labyrinth of the south London railway system, its lights momentarily illuminated a distant figure who, like Fergusson, was standing waiting at the far end of the bridge.

Fergusson checked his watch again. It was time. And probably he had now been seen. He began walking.

Fergusson reached the middle of the footbridge first. He waited. Here, suspended above the water, cut off from either bank of the river, was ideal no man's land – the borderline between north and south London, between Middlesex and Surrey. No one could safely attack, or safely defend, this neutral territory.

Fergusson leaned against the parapet, facing the river. He could hear the footsteps coming up behind him, but he did not turn round. Instead he took his hands out of his pockets and spread them before him on the wooden ledge, as if to say that he had nothing to hide.

He sensed, rather than heard, that the man was now directly behind him. He turned slowly round and looked at the stranger standing there, muffled in overcoat and scarf, defending himself against a climate damper and colder than he was used to.

'Good evening, Mr Mehmet,' said Fergusson in a low voice.

181

'Good evening – Mr Fergusson,' came the reply.

Fergusson hesitated a moment. 'Obviously you got my message.'

'My friends contacted me.'

Fergusson looked out over the water.

'I think we need to discuss some terms and conditions. I don't need to tell you that it will be denied that this meeting ever took place. We should both keep that in mind.'

Mehmet did not reply immediately. Then he looked at his watch.

'I can give you ten minutes. Until ten o'clock. That is all. Then I will go.'

Fergusson tried to contain his irritation.

'I am not altogether sure you are in a position to dictate terms. First of all, let me tell you that we found the body of the taxi driver. We know it was a political reprisal. We could have you arrested now as a suspect. You could be shipped out tomorrow – or face charges here. Or . . .'

Strangely Mehmet seemed less worried than Fergusson had expected. 'Or?'

'Or we could arrange matters so that you happened to fall into the hands of some people you are not on very friendly terms with. They would find you a very material witness, I imagine.'

Mehmet also looked out into the night. He seemed to be contemplating some problem a thousand miles away.

'That *is* a consideration,' he admitted. 'So what do you propose?' he asked.

'I propose the following,' replied Fergusson smoothly. 'We will take no action against you, or harm you in any way, provided that you leave the country immediately. There is a flight at midday tomorrow to Geneva. If we see you get on it we will forget about your illegal activities on our territory. We will even forget about the object of your purchasing mission.'

'You know about that?' asked Mehmet.

'Of course,' replied Fergusson.

'Let me think . . .' said Mehmet, still staring out into the darkness. 'It seems to me that there *may* be the makings of a deal here, although it is not necessarily quite as you describe. You know that as a purchaser I always make it my rule to have an accurate assessment of the position of the counterpart in a negotiation.

That enables both sides to arrive at what can be termed the *just price*. Now, in your case . . .' he turned to face Fergusson, 'it seems to me that there are certain unspoken elements in your position which also have to be taken into account.'

'Unspoken elements?'

'Well, for example, the fact that at present the future of your entire deterrence system hangs in the balance. You know as well as I do that if Washington and Moscow can harmonize their positions on strategic defence they will start dismantling their nuclear stocks. Under those circumstances you will come under tremendous pressure from Washington. Why should they continue to pass you something they are giving up themselves? The question would become even more acute if they found out that a British government minister had played a role in creating a nuclear strike capacity in a certain state. A state not exactly beloved of the Israeli lobby, shall we say? I think you will have a very hard time explaining that away in Washington . . .'

Fergusson hoped that the dismay he was feeling did not register in his face. It was as if Mehmet knew exactly what their nightmare was: as if he had been a fly on the wall in Hotblack's inner office. There was one question he needed confirming before everything else.

'How much did you manage to get away with?' he asked quietly.

Mehmet seemed to think about his reply. Then he simply said, 'Enough.'

'Enough?'

'It is a pity that you have stopped the continuation of the Benbow order. It is a great inconvenience. But we are a resourceful people, Mr Fergusson. We can copy and make things ourselves. And the fact that one shipment *did* get through means that we have – in essence – what we want already. You know, once you can make one cruise missile you are well on the way to making others . . .'

Fergusson tried urgently to think through the implications of what Mehmet had said, but Mehmet was still speaking, and he did not have time to think properly.

'. . . And so you see we do, as I say, have a kind of objective coincidence of interest. This is the correct basis for a satisfactory negotiation.'

'What negotiation?'

'Put it this way. We both have an interest in absolute security. You because you have lost something. We because we have won something. We have no desire to publicize what we have achieved. You have no desire to publicize what you have lost. And so I think we have the makings of a deal. What do you think?'

'What kind of deal do you mean?'

'Why, a mutual support agreement. We maintain an absolute silence about your security lapse. And you maintain an absolute silence about what we have achieved. It is as if we had never met – as you have said. Do you not agree?'

Fergusson thought quickly. It was true. There was an alignment of interests. But he also realized that there was perhaps a different way of solving the problem . . .

'You might, of course,' added Mehmet, 'be tempted to consult our enemy and to try to resolve your difficulty that way. So to make our deal work I would need one small assurance that you will not.'

Fergusson heard, across the water, the bells of Big Ben ringing in ten o'clock. Mehmet would be going soon.

'What kind of assurance?'

'The girl,' said Mehmet simply. 'She has – rather important connections. You must let us have her. She would be useful to us. I assume you can get her.'

'Why?'

'Her father was the chief defence planner in Israel until he retired two years ago. He led the team which developed their nuclear weapon. He still lives there. He's quite the hero to them. Using his daughter today has a certain – symmetry to it. But for you it is a very small price to pay, after all. Now, I must go. So we have a deal?'

Fergusson hesitated.

'I will, of course, need to consult . . .'

'What nonsense, Mr Fergusson. You have no choice. Consult who you like. But the important thing is to decide now. Yes or no?'

Fergusson knew he indeed had no choice.

'Yes,' he said. 'Yes, we have a deal. Silence all round. And the girl.'

'Good, I thought we would. Now, good night, Mr Fergusson.'

Fergusson watched Mehmet walk slowly and deliberately away

from him, across the bridge, until he had vanished into the shadows of the south bank, just another figure in the mysterious urban night.

A few minutes later a panic-stricken Stuart-Smith sprinted up the steps on the Embankment side and across what at first looked like an empty bridge. But when he had covered a hundred yards, he saw that there was a figure to one side, leaning out and looking into the water. Stuart-Smith came smartly up to Fergusson, who turned a thoughtful face to his.

'Any luck tonight, sir?'

'No,' said Fergusson after a while. 'Not much. Could you do me a favour? Can you very kindly arrange to activate COBRA first thing tomorrow morning? Round up the usual suspects.'

'To decide something?'

Fergusson reflected.

'Not exactly, Alan. More to ratify something.'

# Chapter Twenty-five

The hall supervisor gave a last, lingering look out from the podium over the rows of empty seats. Like deck chairs on a rainy day they stretched back into the darkness, beyond the circle of light that illuminated the microphones, the flowers and the gleaming carafes of water all in a line.

He always preferred it this way. The conference room empty and silent, waiting to be transformed into a noisy pit. The lights shining on to the bare stage. He could hear the distant rumble from the lunchers as they mixed and became more convivial as the wine circulated. An empty circus waiting for an act, the saw-dust down, the trapeze roped back. How few acts in the end were worthy of the scene!

The hall supervisor ran through the microphone test. The acoustics were good. The crisp ting as his pen struck the water carafe came back to him in a faithful electronic echo from the far end of the room. Then he tested the lights, turning off each in turn, working the spotlight that swept over the podium. Finally he switched all the lights on and looked out over the room as it would never be used during a performance, the brightness reaching out to the furthest seats by the Exit signs.

It was then that he noticed the stranger sitting right at the back of the room.

'Are you late for the lunch or early for the talk, sir?' The voice boomed out of the loudspeakers at the back of the hall.

In answer, the stranger waved an invitation card vaguely in the air. The supervisor could make out a fluttering of white. Then the stranger called out, 'I'm afraid I missed the lunch. Pressure of work. I hoped I could slip in without anyone noticing. Don't tell them, will you?'

'Why don't you come down to the front?' the voice came again through the loudspeakers. But then the side doors opened and with a clattering noise the first of the lunchers came in. Hastily the supervisor turned down the lighting around the hall and the stranger faded back into the shadows.

They trooped in, in twos and threes, chattering, joking, laughing from their meal. Bronzed faces. Well-fed faces. Faces intelligent and humane.

Most of the major banks had someone there. The discount houses. The gilt-edged market makers. The equity market makers. The bond dealers. The forex dealers. The commodity dealers. The euro-market specialists. The corporate financiers. The M and A brigade. The insurers. The assurers. The reinsurers. All the world loving a lunch, and the chance of a bit of off-market dealing besides. In a huddle, rather apart from the rest, came the regulators, the tribunes of the people, appointed by their equals to watch the rule books and henceforth doomed to live outside the tribe. They had all lunched together.

And then, last of all, when everyone else was seated, came a little knot of people who were the real stars of the show. The speaker for the day – a tall, distinguished type, not apparently perturbed by the ordeal before him. The chairman, a retired retail banker, large in girth, who exuded sociability. The girl who kept the water jug full. And finally, chatting together, the lordly president of the Thursday Association and today's guest of honour, a young-looking bespectacled man whose face was familiar to many of those present. Tim Warwick had skipped the lunch, and as he was recognized by those sitting in the hall there rose up a patter of polite applause. Warwick took his seat in the front row. He glanced round and waved to one or two familiar faces from his City days.

There was a further ripple of applause as the chairman took the stage. He looked over at the supervisor down by the side, who nodded to indicate that all was in order.

'Minister, friends and colleagues,' came the voice of the chairman out of the loudspeakers around the hall. 'At our monthly gatherings we invite one of our number to make a presentation on a matter of concern to him. Today we look at ourselves through the eyes of a member of one of our smaller international houses, a man who has spent the last three years in London and who previously worked in some of the more exotic parts of the world . . .'

As de la Fosse sat beside the chairman waiting for the introduction to finish he arranged his notes in front of him. As usual when about to speak in public he felt a rising sense of well-being within him. It amused him to think of the concentrated earning potential packed into the audience, the opportunity cost for those who were going to spend the next half-hour listening to him. He surveyed the clever faces looking up at him, thought how agreeable it was to have a captive audience and mused, not for the first time, on whether he should after all have gone into politics, or perhaps the performing arts.

He waited until the last echo of applause had died away, the last murmured comment. He waited until complete silence enveloped the hall. And then he waited a little bit longer. Slowly he took out a pair of gold-rimmed spectacles, put them on, gripped the lectern in front of him with both hands and said, 'People often ask me what it is that ails this country of ours. Ladies and gentlemen, I suggest that the answer is not a simple one. If it were, I do not think that generation after generation would have been preoccupied by it. If it were a simple matter of passing better laws I rather think our politicians would have found the answer by now.

'No, ladies and gentlemen, for anyone who has studied the inner workings of our economy – for anyone, that is, who has worked, as I have, in finance – the cause is more profound . . .'

De la Fosse listened with satisfaction to the echo of his voice coming back to him and now and then glanced up from his text to the faces before him. There was always the risk of them settling down into an after-lunch stupor. Well, it was his task as orator to stop that from happening. This afternoon he would be devil's advocate. And why not? The content as content was not so important. Form was everything. Style as a type of cover . . .

'We are a nation of critics of films made elsewhere . . .'

The speech rolled on. From time to time the chairman nodded approvingly at de la Fosse. How was it, he wondered, that these cosmopolitan types could put things so well?

'Disintermediation is the scourge that threatens this great industry of ours. Unless we adapt, ladies and gentlemen, I submit to you that our firms will be overwhelmed by the new financial currents that are washing over our globe . . .'

After fifteen minutes de la Fosse felt that he had got into his stride. He knew that he was carrying the audience with him. He took a sip of water and then touched lightly on the accelerator. Joyriding.

'At the end of the day, what is it we are all here for?

'What is the object of this magnificent industry of finance, in which we are all proud to play such parts? This city houses a concentration of capital, expertise and technical capacity unmatched in its time zone. From the Atlantic to the Urals, and beyond – from here to Vladivostock itself – you will not find its like. There is nothing comparable between New York and Tokyo.

'The capital that crosses the foreign exchanges in London exceeds the volume of total world trade. Financial packages amounting to billions of dollars can be assembled here with the ease and speed with which – if you were lucky – your tailor might once have made you a suit. Loans raised in dollars can be swapped into yen. Future market movements can be tamed through present market mechanisms. Nothing that is variable cannot be hedged.

'As soon as anyone can spot a gap in a market, someone else has thought of a new product to exploit it. Risk is passed round and round the globe through continuous day and night trading, broken down, atomized into a million tiny fragments so that it is shared by everyone and no one at the same time . . .'

Warwick sat in the front with his arms crossed, his face assuming a judicious expression of intelligent yet noncommittal interest. He had, of course, recognized the speaker from the social round. De la Fosse was one of those types you saw about the place, being deferential to your hostess, putting in the right word at the right time, taking an appreciative sniff from a glass of brandy, no doubt working hard at whatever it was he did, but not letting it take too great a toll of his energies. And here he was orating like a regular. Clearly another politician-in-waiting lurking in the undergrowth of the City. But then, Warwick asked himself idly, which country's parliament would it be that he would rise to . . . ?

'And yet, and yet, ladies and gentlemen,' continued de la Fosse, 'all this adds up in the real world only to rows upon rows of zeros on a computer screen. We come to our offices, we plug in our machines, we exchange a few billion zeros with the fellow in the office round the corner. The means of exchange was once the promissory note. Then it became cash. Today the means of exchange is nothing more than a quiver of electrons in the memory chips of our computers, as they register the fleeting passage of transactions.

'The danger, I think, is clear. We risk mistaking the shadow for the substance, the appearance for the reality. Our industry is not a glorified casino. It cannot be reduced to a game of three-dimensional Monopoly. The markets are not ends in themselves. They are means to ends. When we forget that we forget our reason for existing.

'For what is that reason?'

Warwick thought he could see it coming. Another revisionist, clearly.

'I submit that what we are here to do is to build. Capital in itself has no value. It merely represents value. It acquires life only when we use it. Our purpose is to use capital to create new productive capacity. That is the unique and sacred trust which we have inherited.

'If you will allow me as a foreigner to say so, this country needs rebuilding. This country – the country which houses the fabulous markets which we serve – is running down. It is spending wealth faster than it creates it. It is a consumer, an importer, a spender, a borrower on credit, a taster of the choicest morsels from the world's storehouses. It recycles billions and puts away virtually nothing. Time-scales are short. Capital return is calculated in terms of months. Cash flow in terms of seconds.

'But, ladies and gentlemen, *ars longa, vita brevis*. Art is long. Capital projects are long. The rebuilding of a country is long. Our purpose is not just to boost current expenditure. Our purpose is to transform raw capital to rebuild factories, cities, countries, civilizations.

'Building a country is one of the hardest tasks known to man. This country is not at war. It has been at peace for over forty years. And yet can we truthfully say that those years of peace have been used profitably? Have we built the foundations of a new society, a healthy economy? Are we, as our forefathers once dreamed, building the New Jerusalem?'

Warwick groaned inwardly. He could read coded language as well as the next man. It was extraordinary how these ideas could pop up in the most unlikely places. Tiresome to have to sit through this. But you got all sorts in the City. Warwick adjusted his expression slightly to register a kind of sympathetic disapproval as de la Fosse reached his peroration.

'The New Jerusalem is not so much a place as an ideal. We can

190

all carry it with us in our hearts as we travel round the world. When I am here in London, I can still see in my mind's eye that city beyond the City, that walled garden of peace somewhere behind the cracked concrete.

'So let us develop the City, certainly. Raise the towers. Sink the foundations. But let us do so with a certain sense of modesty, a certain sense of proportion.

'And let us never forget that while we here are consuming, others elsewhere are trying to build at last. Others elsewhere are struggling to be where we are today.'

There was silence at first. The applause, when it came, was at first puzzled, sporadic. And then a voice at the back cried out. 'Bravo!' It triggered an avalanche of noise which carried right through the hall. It grew in volume. Some people were standing up to clap. The chairman looked bemusedly out over the audience, and at an exhausted de la Fosse gulping thirstily at his water. It was fascinating. But was it finance?

'Thank you for sharing your appreciation so handsomely, ladies and gentlemen,' said the chairman, when the hubbub had subsided. 'Next month we are back to earth. Our subject is "Prudential Control and Pension Funds".'

There was a ripple of laughter. More applause.

De la Fosse stood near the exit as they left to go back to their offices, some pausing to shake his hand on the way out. One or two acquaintances from rival firms exchanged words.

'You'll be drummed out of town if you carry on like that!'

'Oh, come now, Roger,' said de la Fosse. 'It wasn't that bad. We have to get these things off our chest from time to time . . .'

A smiling Warwick came up to de la Fosse, hand outstretched.

'Marvellous!' he said. 'So unusual to hear that point of view in this place.'

'Oh, thank you,' replied de la Fosse with a grin, looking quickly round the hall. He decided there was sufficient confusion all round. He would move *now*. 'Could we just have a quick word, Minister, do you think – over here?'

De la Fosse drew a still smiling Warwick to one side, away from the crowd. It was not an unusual thing for two contacts to have a brief tête-à-tête: it was, after all, what most people who came here did in such circumstances.

'Yes?' said Warwick in a friendly voice.

'Your bank . . .' began de la Fosse in a quiet authoritative voice.

'My ex-bank, you mean.'

'Your bank,' persisted de la Fosse, 'would do anything to get itself off the Arab black list, wouldn't it? Keep smiling and listen carefully to me.'

Warwick stood there grinning, but his eyes had lost their amiability.

'I'm sorry, I don't see what business it is —'

'Unless you can get yourself off the black list you will continue to lose your share of the huge Arab market. But because you once financed Israeli transactions after the Six Day War you are stuck.

'And then along comes the chance to finance a very unusual order for a powerful client. An Arab client. Who can help get you off the black list, if all goes well. He needs discreet assistance. Your bank takes it on. And your bank has the inestimable advantage of keeping a minister for exports secretly in its pay . . .'

Warwick stood transfixed, his eyes glaring. But, as de la Fosse well knew, few can resist hearing their life story told by another, no matter how dangerous it is to them.

'And who are you to talk in this way, Mr de la Fosse?'

De la Fosse ignored him. 'We have official papers from your department which show you have taken a particular interest in the export of mechanical equipment to the El Mihr Mining project – an *unusually* particular interest, wouldn't you say?'

Warwick was now starting to panic. 'It was not unusual. Not unusual in the slightest . . .'

'But it *was* unusual, Minister. And particularly so considering that your bank is on the board of arms supplier S. G. Zwann of Vienna. And that Zwann found a clever way of extracting prohibited material from the UK to export to your client —'

'Who *are* you, Mr de la Fosse? Who *are* you?' Warwick lowered his voice to a whisper. 'Are you police?'

'No,' replied de la Fosse. 'My clients are just people who get worried when their enemies acquire a nuclear strike capacity. Naturally they do what they can to prevent it —'

The expression of shock on Warwick's face was genuine.

'Nuclear strike capacity? Oh dear God . . .'

And then there was a movement behind de la Fosse. A young man – whom the hall supervisor was later to recall was the same young man who had sat alone at the back of the hall – came up and took de la Fosse's arm. It might have seemed a friendly gesture to the crowd thronging about. But de la Fosse knew otherwise.

'It's all right, Minister,' said the young man. 'We'll take over now.'

De la Fosse looked to the exit. A man was standing there, watching; at the back of the hall, someone else.

At the side door, with people still filing out, someone else was casually waiting too. He realized he was trapped.

'My name is Stuart-Smith,' said the stranger in a low voice. 'You know where I come from, I think. And I know where you come from. I'd like to do this with the minimum of disruption. But I'm afraid the party *is* over.'

From the podium the chairman saw de la Fosse turn to salute him and then rather slowly make his way out of the room with the young man beside him. Good of de la Fosse to devote time to the younger generation, he thought. But how odd of the minister to be left standing like that, staring about him as if he had just woken up from some nightmare. The chairman left the podium and went across to Warwick.

'I liked the bit about Jerusalem,' remarked Stuart-Smith to de la Fosse, as they came out of the hall into the darkened lobby where the hats and coats were kept. 'Very appropriate.'

'What now?' said de la Fosse, weighing up and then dismissing the chances of making a break through the remaining people milling around, lingering, chatting as they put their coats on.

'Well,' said Stuart-Smith, 'we have some questions we would like to put to you. Can I introduce you to Mr Fergusson here?'

De la Fosse saw standing in the shadows the senior man he knew would be his interrogator. He shrugged his shoulders.

'Very well,' he said. 'You know, I have very little to say.'

'Perhaps,' said Stuart-Smith. But then someone came up to him and drew him to one side.

'I need a word, sir.'

Stuart-Smith motioned to a man who had been standing behind de la Fosse to come forward and keep an eye on him. The cloak-room attendant looked at her watch and wondered when they were all going to get their coats and leave so she could close for the afternoon.

'Yes, Dick?' said Stuart-Smith when they had moved out of earshot.

'It's just come through on the radio. It's Colchester, sir. At the meet. He's in position. And the girl's on her way.'

'Good,' said Stuart-Smith. 'Take me down there. As fast as you can.'

The chairman reached Warwick through the crowd.

'Is everything all right, Minister?' he asked anxiously.

The boyish face that had suddenly turned white looked into his for a while. Then Warwick shook his head.

'There is nothing the matter. Nothing at all. Nothing the matter at all . . .'

# Chapter Twenty-six

Colchester stood waiting for Julia on the steps of the town hall. It was cold, almost cold enough to snow. Croydon must be the last place on earth to be on such an afternoon, he thought. Who would choose this place for what is going to happen now? Well, I did. Or rather, it chose itself. Behind him the steel and concrete, the civic bustle of the town hall. People were milling about, coming to and from official appointments. He tried to fix the scene in his memory. The last instant of freedom. His last meeting with her.

He saw the black taxi coming round the roundabout towards him, lights glimmering. He stamped his feet to warm them.

And the worst thing was that he still couldn't make his mind up. Julia had deceived him utterly. Why on earth should he place any confidence in her now? Why shouldn't he just do what they told him: give her up and walk away into another life? Surely this was the sensible course: much more sensible than paying attention to the nagging instinct that they had not told him everything . . .

The taxi was at the kerb. Julia sprang out. She was ten yards away. Five yards away. And then she launched herself into his arms, and Croydon in winter seemed a much warmer and better place to be.

They said nothing. As they silently embraced Colchester reminded himself why they were supposed to be here. To meet, to make love and to separate for ever. As he held Julia in his arms he blocked out what was going to happen next and pretended that he didn't know who she really was. What if she had not deceived him, that they were two people on the same side, that everything she had said had been true? They kissed, and he closed his eyes. Five seconds of forgetfulness. When he opened his eyes he saw, beyond them, a man in black standing over by the corner thirty yards away. And beyond him in the car a second man sitting, waiting. He knew other ghosts would also be around them, haunting, invisible. The whole shadow play of her arrest in place . . .

'What is it?' asked Julia, speaking for the first time, feeling the strange tension in his body. She was looking pale, withdrawn, as if she was making some tremendous effort of concentration. It's the deception, thought Colchester suddenly. It's the effort of deception. It's just too much for her.

'Perhaps you shouldn't have come after all,' he said quietly.

'But I wanted to,' she said in a calm voice. 'I wanted to give myself to you.' She noticed for the first time the briefcase which Colchester was holding in his left hand. 'What is that?'

How could he explain? How could he tell her that Stuart-Smith had insisted there be a transfer of material which they could record, that it would be this physical handover of worthless secrets to her which would be the mark of her guilt and the mark of his innocence? He clutched it tightly.

'Something for you,' he said. 'A parting gift. But not yet.'

'I don't think I understand . . .' she began, but then she read the signal in Colchester's eyes, the warning that something was not right. 'What *is* it?' she asked again. 'What is wrong? Aren't we going to the hotel?'

Colchester knew the time had come. He had Julia, here, and they were surrounded by Stuart-Smith's men, poised, hidden, waiting for him to give the signal. And, unlike her, he knew the truth. He had, just briefly, a moment before the operation was triggered. It was the most precious moment of his life. He was in control.

And he wanted her private confession.

'I want you to know that I know – everything about you,' he said slowly, still holding tightly on to the briefcase. 'Please don't show any reaction, for your own good.'

They started walking slowly together away from the town hall. The man on the corner looked anxiously over to the man sitting in the car. He gestured to him to follow. Julia turned to look into Colchester's eyes, seeking desperately for some reassurance. She fought down the old familiar nightmare rising within her, the fear that this time she *had* gone too far.

'You know everything?' she whispered.

'Yes,' he said. 'And I need to know one thing. Why did you choose me?'

She shook her head slightly. It was as if the question was of secondary importance.

'We're at war. We need people like you.'

'People like me?'

'People who are innocent. But it doesn't matter any more.'

'It doesn't matter? How can you say that?'

'But I thought you said you knew? Haven't you worked it out?'

'Worked what out?'

'You mean you haven't? Then what's happening? Oh my God, have you got it all wrong?'

She stood absolutely still. Her face had turned white. She looked ill, tense, haggard. It flashed across Colchester's mind how extraordinary it was that under extreme pressure beauty can turn into ugliness.

'Can't you see?' she insisted. 'I want to defect. I don't want to go away. I want to stay here. I've left de la Fosse for good.'

And Colchester, with a shock, all at once, did see. He saw that something *had* passed between them, some force had pulled them both out of their orbits. She *was* giving herself to him. And now he was under orders to give her to them. And wasn't that best for everyone? Or would it be a terrible mistake?

He glanced back quickly. The ghosts were following, moving in silent formation all around them, to the side, to the front. He took a deep breath.

'It won't work,' he said quietly to her. 'The plan is to evict you anyway. You need help.'

'Help?'

'You'll have to trust me. It's for your own good.'

'What are you talking about?'

'You know we're being watched. They're everywhere. There's one way of escape. Just come with me. Now *run*!'

The man in black, moving slowly, jumped as Colchester suddenly dropped the briefcase, grabbed Julia's hand and led her back in the opposite direction, away from them. The car cruising slowly on the other side of the street came to a halt and another man leapt out.

Colchester and Julia were running now, back the way they had come. Then, with Colchester leading, they turned and rushed up the steps into the town hall itself, pushing through the midst of a wedding party. There was a brief commotion. A single white flower fell to the ground. Then they both vanished into the main entrance.

The element of surprise was one of the few things Colchester had left.

Only seconds later three men tore up the steps after them, threaded through the crowd, careered through the door and found themselves in the huge entrance area. There was a throng of people everywhere. Taxpayers. Ratepayers. People seeking dog licences. TV licences. Car licences. A giant reception and enquiries desk. But no sign anywhere of Colchester or Julia. Over on the other side of the entrance area there were five lifts, three in motion, the lights winking. Two going up. One going down.

'Police,' said Harry to the girl at the reception desk. 'Which way did that couple go?'

The girl looked up and indicated with her hand the mass of people around them.

'Which couple?' she asked.

'How many exits are there to the building?'

The girl considered. 'Four,' she replied.

'And how many rooms are there in here?'

She considered again. 'About two hundred, I think . . .'

Harry turned to the other two. 'Mike, get cars round to cover the exits. Quickly. And Frank, come with me.'

They ran to the lifts and watched the indicator lights of the two lifts that were rising. First one, then the other came to rest for a while.

'Right, Frank. You take the fourth floor. I'll do the sixth.'

Outside in one of the cars another of the men was radioing the news back to Stuart-Smith in the heart of the City.

'But where are we going?' asked Julia as the lift doors closed on them and they began their ascent.

'We have to get married,' said Colchester, leaning against the wall of the lift for breath.

'We have to – what?'

'We have to get married. I'm sorry the engagement is going to be rather short. About two minutes, in fact. But there it is.'

'But you can't just do it like that.'

'Well,' said Colchester, still panting, 'you can. You only need

198

three days' special notice. It's been given. Only one person needs to give notice. I've done it. And you can use false names. I have. Of course,' he added, 'it helps if you know a bent registrar. I do. Let's get out of here.'

The lift doors opened on the sixth floor. They came out into the empty corridor and Colchester immediately pressed the button to call another lift.

'Come *on*,' he grunted. He could see from the indicators that two other lifts were coming up after them. One was coming down from higher up the building.

'But *why* do we have to get married?' asked Julia.

Colchester looked at her. One lift had already stopped at the fourth floor.

'Legal security. It's all we've got,' he said. 'Work it out for yourself. It's divide and rule. Separately we're vulnerable. To-gether we're stronger. You are in big trouble. They won't just let bygones be bygones, you know. They want you out of the country. And Mehmet is still on the loose. He's after you.'

'But what about you?'

'I think I want someone else on my side. And, on the whole, I'd rather it was someone I loved . . .'

'You're mad. You should have forgotten about me when I told you to.'

'It's too late for that now.'

A light went out on the panel. A few seconds later the lift doors slowly opened. But it was the one going straight back down. Colchester pressed the button and kept the doors open.

Then another light went out. This time it was the lift coming up from below. Following them.

'Well?' demanded Colchester.

Julia looked from the open door of the lift to Colchester. And then from Colchester back to the open door of the lift.

'If I go through with it there's no guarantee it means anything, you realize that.'

'I do realize that.'

'It's under duress.'

'That's true.'

'And I don't really know you all that well.'

'Also true.'

'I'll probably be a terrible wife . . .'

'We must go. *Now!*'

He took her hand again and she squeezed with him into the lift going down.

'What names did you use?' she asked.

'Mr and Mrs Cartwright,' he said. 'What else? Witnesses. I hope he's found witnesses . . .'

The doors shut behind them.

Two seconds later Harry jumped out of his lift on to a deserted sixth floor. Planning and Development, the sign said. Offices to the left. Offices to the right. He looked back at the panel. All five lifts were in action. He had lost them. But it could only be for a moment.

Stuart-Smith's car, with Dick at the wheel and a baleful Fergusson sitting stiff and silent in the back seat, was already racing across the river. They'd been given the news. Stuart-Smith had a brief vision of the Thames, an open space between the rearing metallic buildings, a streak of sky and a flash of light on the water far below. Then the bridge was behind them and they were on the south bank, the *Rive Gauche*, *Côté* Surrey, as Stuart-Smith sometimes called it. Into the land of the warehouse, the corrugated iron roof, the furniture discount store.

Hell and damnation, thought Stuart-Smith, as Dick weaved the wrong way round a bollard, causing two cars to grind to a halt and jam on their horns. This is absurd. How can he possibly think they can get away? There is nowhere in London they can hide. We can turn this town upside down if we have to. We can X-ray the entire city. We can find and turn out experienced agents who have spent years in the field, once we have a lead. An amateur will survive for hours. Minutes. Seconds.

Stuart-Smith knew the next step to take. The procedure was straightforward. Crank up the machine. Seal off the ports and the airports. Send men to the railway stations. Yet Fergusson was reluctant to let him take it. The alert would spread far and wide. Explanations would be needed. Stories invented. Pretty soon it would filter through the entire administration that something rather peculiar was going on. Ministers would hear about it. Smithson from the US Embassy would be on the phone . . .

'This is *absurd*,' he said out loud, as Dick accelerated down Streatham High Road.

Then Stuart-Smith had a stroke of inspiration. He reached forward for the car radio.

'Mike, did you say they went *into* the town hall?'

'Yes, sir,' came Mike's voice from the car still outside the town hall. 'We're going through the place now, floor by floor. The exits are covered. They can't get out.'

'I know where they are,' said Stuart-Smith. 'Find out where someone called Molloy works. Terry Molloy. Then tell the others. That's where you'll find them.'

Mike left the car, sprang up the steps, pushed through the crowd around the entrance and went up to the girl at the reception desk.

'Police,' he said.

'Again?' she said.

'Where does a Mr Terry Molloy work?'

The girl looked through her lists.

'Mr Molloy? Third floor. Conference room 302. But you won't disturb him just now, will you?'

'Why not?'

'He'll be doing a wedding at the moment . . .'

Mike went back near the entrance and called Harry and Frank on their portable radios.

'Meet me on the third floor. Outside room 302. They've gone to ground in there.' He raced to the lift.

The three men stood outside the closed door of the conference room on the third floor. By this time a little crowd had gathered, curious to see what was going on. Secretaries, clerks, tea ladies.

'There's no other way out,' said Frank. 'I've been all over this floor. Windows on the other side. Straight drop down. Exits covered. They can't get out.'

Mike took his portable radio and switched through to Stuart-Smith, speeding ever nearer through the back streets of south London.

'We've located Molloy's office,' he said quietly. 'Should we go in?'

Stuart-Smith saw West Croydon station flash past him. He took the microphone.

'Yes. Go in. And hold them until I arrive.'

'Right,' said Mike. He nodded to Harry and Frank, and the two men framed the doorway. Mike stepped back, raised his right foot, jabbed it viciously forward and shattered the lock. A fraction of a second later Harry turned round, pulled back and burst the door open with his shoulder. He fell into the interior of the conference room, followed closely by the other two leaping over him and taking up positions just inside the door.

'Police! Nobody move!' shouted Harry.

A woman screamed.

Harry looked swiftly round the room. A handful of people were sitting on benches, staring at them, numb with horror. A young man stood by a large leather-topped desk, turning pale, recoiling, a big official book slipping from his hands to the floor. A couple stood in front of him, he in a dark suit, she a blonde in a powder-blue two-piece. She let out another scream at the sight of Harry advancing purposefully towards them.

'We need to talk to you, Molloy,' said Harry, waving a card.

The astonishment on the face of the young man presiding over the wedding became even greater.

'But I'm not Terry,' he said.

'What do you mean?' said Harry.

'Terry asked if we could swap rooms for the afternoon. Just for once. He said he had a couple who wanted a small room. He's in mine.'

Harry faltered. 'And where's that?'

'Ground floor. Behind the lifts. So they can slip in and out easily—'

But the three men were already backing hurriedly out of the room, leaving a circle of faces at the door looking in at the distressing spectacle of the bride starting to melt into tears.

In a different, smaller, meaner room Terry looked dubiously across the desk at the couple standing before him. He had done a few rushed weddings in his time but he had never before seen such tension in the participants. Colchester had said it was urgent. But *why* was it so urgent?

'I now pronounce you man and wife,' he said.

Colchester and Julia looked anxiously at each other.

'It is customary to kiss the bride,' remarked Terry.

But Julia had a question. 'How *legal* is all this?' she asked.

Before Terry could reply the door to the junior registrar's dusty office opened suddenly. Colchester turned and saw a rather dishevelled young man standing there. It was Stuart-Smith, looking as if he had just run the half-mile. Colchester gripped Julia's hand.

'It's over, Colchester,' Stuart-Smith panted, catching his breath.

'Let me do the talking,' whispered Colchester to Julia.

Stuart-Smith rested his body against the door jamb and looked around the room, taking in the occupants.

'You,' he said, pointing at Terry. 'And you and you,' he added, jabbing a finger at an elderly couple sitting on official metal-framed chairs by the wall. 'You're all under arrest.'

The nice old couple – who had acted as witnesses and who were counting out the five pound notes which Colchester had given them – began to cluck in alarm.

When the room had finally been cleared of everyone except Colchester and Julia, Stuart-Smith surveyed the pair of them for a few moments, while he regained his composure. He shook his head as if saddened by this lapse in conduct. Colchester opened his mouth but Stuart-Smith signalled silence, went to the door and looked outside. Then an older, taller, grimmer figure of authority came quietly in, and Colchester recognized Fergusson from his interview the week before in Garrick's office.

Fergusson said nothing, but went and sat, upright and impassive, on a seat by the door. Stuart-Smith looked at him, nodded and then turned back to Colchester and Julia.

'We would like to know what you think you're playing at,' he said in a level voice. 'This was a most *unnecessary* interlude.'

Colchester looked Stuart-Smith straight in the eye. His heart was beating furiously. He now had his very last card to play, and everything depended upon it. Unless he managed to pull this one off he might have been better jumping from the twelfth floor in the first place . . .

He raised Julia's hand slightly. She wore a wedding ring.

'My wife wants *political asylum*,' he said, slowly and deliberately.

He could scarcely recognize his own voice. He thought, I have said it. The words are out. I cannot go back now.

There was a pained silence in the room.

Stuart-Smith, trying to work it all out, turned his bewildered gaze from Colchester to Julia. His eyes rested briefly on her face, anxious but still beautiful. Then he glanced back to Fergusson. He turned back again.

'Your *wife*?' he said. 'But we're throwing her out. She's an illegal. She's PNG. Persona non grata!'

'She's legal now,' replied Colchester. 'Legitimate. On our side. She doesn't need to leave. I can look after her.'

'But – we don't hand out political asylum just like that.'

'Why not?' asked Colchester. He dropped his voice. 'If you want me to co-operate she goes with me. Either she stays – or you can have your show trial.'

'But what about our *agreement*?'

'I'm changing it slightly. Julia wants to stay with us. She wants to be on our side. On your side. With me.'

And Stuart-Smith saw how Colchester had worked it out. In a way he had to admire his nerve. He had tricked them all, when they had assumed he was under their control. It was a pity, in a way, that of course it *couldn't* work out . . .

'You have, unilaterally, changed everything,' he said quietly. 'And so, I'm afraid, all our bets are off.'

Colchester still did not see.

'But you wanted her. You've got her. With me, that's all. I don't see your problem.'

Stuart-Smith looked back briefly to where Fergusson was sitting. He saw Fergusson very slightly shake his head, as he knew he would. He turned again to Colchester.

'I don't really think we can do as you want,' he said in his most urbane voice. 'You have put yourself in a very difficult position. You can't deceive us in this way and hope to get away with it, you know. We shall now be forced to seek a prosecution in the courts under the Official Secrets Act. We shall cite your liaison with a foreign intelligence officer. And I expect you will receive a fairly severe prison sentence. I had another look at your file: your father really won't like it . . .'

Colchester tightened his grip on Julia's hand. It felt icy cold.

'But we are *married*. Don't you see?'

Stuart-Smith looked archly at him. 'Forgive me if my memory of the law is a little faulty, but I always thought a marriage had to be consummated before it was really valid. Well, by tonight you will be in the cells and she will be out of the country. This little legal fiction won't really matter that much by tomorrow.'

Colchester looked at Julia.

So that was that. They had called his bluff. He had failed. Failed in his job. Failed in this trial of strength with Stuart-Smith. Failed his father. And failed Julia when she needed help. It had probably been hopeless from the outset. The very suggestion that he could manipulate these people . . .

'It seemed like a good idea,' he said quietly.

She looked into his eyes. 'Maybe it was,' she answered softly.

Then he felt Stuart-Smith calmly detach Julia's hand from his. Colchester closed his eyes as he had to let her go.

*It's not something you can do anything about,* he remembered her once saying.

And he heard the door open as one of Stuart-Smith's men came in. Fergusson stood up and straightened his tie. He didn't look at Colchester. The meeting was over. The game was over. His life was over. Everything was over.

'Can we please get going?' asked Stuart-Smith. 'There are two cars waiting outside. Ladies first.'

Stuart-Smith escorted a dazed-looking Julia to the door. But then she turned back on the threshold and said in a dangerous voice, 'He knows all about Warwick, you know.'

And Colchester saw Stuart-Smith falter just slightly. He saw the rapid, involuntary exchange of glances between him and Fergusson. And he remembered the odd thing they had said to him, which had lodged in his memory: *your minister insists we take a firm line.*

'Mehmet did say Warwick was a friend of his,' he said speculatively to Fergusson.

'I told you,' said Julia. 'He knows all about it.'

Fergusson took a step in Colchester's direction.

'When did he say that?' he asked Colchester in a low voice, coming right up to him.

Colchester looked him in the eyes, then glanced over at Julia.

'Just before he murdered the taxi driver,' he replied.

This clearly surprised Fergusson. '*You* were there? It was *you* there that night?'

'I was there,' said Colchester.

'Did Mehmet say anything else?'

All at once Colchester felt fear, straight fear. He could see something in Fergusson's eyes, a tell-me look, a commanding look, and he knew he had touched some raw nerve. But it was far beyond him. Part of him wanted so much just to give in, to do what they told him, to obey . . .

'Yes. He told me – *everything*,' he replied in the most level voice he could summon up.

'You're lying,' said Fergusson. 'And I think you're a very bad liar. What did he say in specific terms?'

'In specific terms?' repeated Colchester, seeing the fascinated attention on Julia's face as she stared at him, wondering what he would do next. It would only take a few wrong words now and he would throw it all away.

'I think if you're still planning on a prosecution,' he said carefully, 'I would want to talk it over with my defence lawyer – before we go into too much detail.'

Fergusson glared at Colchester, as if he was an unexpected obstacle in the way of all his progress.

'Do you have any *idea* what trouble you're causing us?' he said furiously.

'No,' said Colchester, standing his ground. 'Perhaps I don't. But I do seem to have a certain nuisance value, don't I?'

Fergusson continued to glare at Colchester for a full ten seconds, as if brooding on a dreadful punishment. Finally he said, 'You won't have a defence lawyer.'

'Why not?'

'Because there will be no prosecution.'

Fergusson, still angry, turned on his heel to face Julia. 'You. What is it *you* want, exactly?'

And Julia, removing herself completely from Stuart-Smith's grasp, answered, 'Asylum. Protection. A safe haven. Immunity.'

She looked across at Colchester with a smile deep in her dark eyes. 'For both of us.'

Fergusson and Stuart-Smith exchanged anguished glances. What in God's name could they do now? The deal with Mehmet had just fallen apart . . .

They had a real disaster on their hands.

# Chapter Twenty-seven

Mehmet, nomad-like, changed hotel every night now.

This evening he was over by Tower Bridge, in a large business complex near the river filled with traders from the City. A convention of futures dealers seemed to have taken over the public restaurants and ballrooms, perhaps celebrating Christmas early, and up from the wells and courtyards below there came the low boom of jungle music. In his air-conditioned and double-glazed room up on the top floor Mehmet could look out over the Thames and see the lights of the odd small boat scud over the water towards the empty docklands. The illuminated bridge dominated the skyline, a childish perplexing construction picked out in brilliant blues and pinks. Far below, near the entrance to the hotel, he could see a perpetual stream of taxis dropping off and picking up. The television in his room was switched on as usual, tuned to the news channel which kept Mehmet in touch with the world outside.

There was no moon in London tonight. Which meant that it would also be a moonless night far away at Al Tadj. The spy satellites would be out, of course, dark and inquisitive, but starlight was too feeble an illumination for them. They would be able to work unseen.

And Mehmet knew there was plenty of work to do.

Attaching the nuclear fuses to the nuclear warheads would not be straightforward. Different technologies. Different systems. A mixture of the imported and the homegrown. Testing impossible. No margin of error allowed. And for maximum political impact the first strike had to be accurate. The first strike had to demonstrate clearly what the second strike could do. And then would come the time for the demands, the negotiating, the arm-twisting. But this time they would be negotiating from a position of strength. The first strike might even be the last. Already the theologians were working out the rudiments of a proper doctrine. A completely new doctrine, unlike that of any existing nuclear power. The first offensive nuclear posture in history. A fitting way to end the holy war.

Mehmet checked his watch. It was time.

He turned down the lights in the room and opened the curtains. The illuminations of Tower Bridge shone in. He turned the television volume off. Mehmet picked up the telephone and went to stand by the window, carefully surveying the moving cars beneath. He dialled the number he had been given.

'Yes?' came Fergusson's precise voice a few seconds later.

'The handover arrangements, Mr Fergusson,' said Mehmet. 'I want to go through the handover arrangements.'

A slight hesitation at the other end?

'Which particular aspect do you wish to discuss, Mr Mehmet?'

'It has to be on neutral territory, I have decided. There is a flight tomorrow morning to Athens. I want the girl on it. With you. You can leave the plane in Rome. I will be on the same flight. I will take your seat.'

A pause.

'That sounds reasonable, Mr Mehmet. But there is one other aspect of this we need to discuss.'

Mehmet did not like the tone in Fergusson's voice at all. 'I hope you are not going to create extra conditions, Mr Fergusson. You are not in a very good position—'

'No, no, I assure you,' said Fergusson, calmly. 'There is no question of conditions. It's more that I want to put an alternative proposition to you.'

'You do have the girl, don't you?' demanded Mehmet suspiciously.

'We *have* her, certainly. She is under our jurisdiction. I can assure you she is neutralized. But a complication has come up.'

'I do not understand you.'

'A technical problem. A legal problem. A small matter of British law.'

Mehmet tried to remember exactly where he had heard that before. It had been Colchester, when he had invented that ridiculous stream of lies . . .

'I am not going to argue, Mr Fergusson. Unless she is on the plane I am going to ensure that the name of your Mr Warwick is known to every news agency in Washington—'

'Listen, Mr Mehmet, please hear me out. I have a better idea.

208

Take someone else. Take the girl's superior. Take de la Fosse. He will serve your purpose just as well.'

De la Fosse?

Mehmet considered rapidly. He was well aware who de la Fosse was. In some ways he *was* perhaps as good a catch. More seniority. More access. More responsibility – including responsibility for much which Mehmet would like to avenge. But then again, perhaps there were drawbacks too . . . De la Fosse was, for a start, rather more dangerous, perhaps rather more of a liability . . .

'I am not authorized to be flexible on this point,' replied Mehmet eventually.

'I quite understand,' said Fergusson. 'I was not expecting you to respond immediately. What I hoped was that you – and I mean you collectively – might perhaps consider this offer, and let me have your response. In your own time, of course.'

Mehmet was silent. Finally he said, 'I will call you back in one hour.' He put the phone down.

Fergusson turned to Stuart-Smith, listening in on the other line.

'What do you think, Alan?' he asked. 'Will he buy it?'

Stuart-Smith considered, and then shook his head. 'I'm not sure he will, sir, in the end.'

'I'm not sure either. They have the big one. Why haggle on the details? I think he could create further problems for us. Have they traced the call?'

Stuart-Smith picked up the receiver, had a brief word with one of the engineers in the basement, and nodded his head.

'Yes, sir. Hotel near the Tower.'

'Good. Have him picked up. We'll have to deal with this by more traditional means.'

In his hotel room Mehmet had a further idea. He scanned his pocket notebook. Then he picked up the telephone and dialled a different number.

In the Ministry of Exports the telephone sitting on what had been Colchester's desk rang out. It was by now quite late and there were not many people left in the office. None the less, after a while the phone was answered. Mehmet heard the voice of a complete stranger.

'Mr Colchester's phone . . .'

'Can I speak to him, please?'

'He's been . . . away . . . for a few days. Can I help?'

'Are you dealing with his work?'

'Dealing with his work? Well, I suppose in a manner of speaking I am. But there's a fair old backlog —'

'And you are . . . ?'

'Mr Stanton.'

'Do you know anything about the El Mihr project, Mr Stanton? Are you handling that?'

Mehmet could hear Stanton riffling through a pile of papers. And then, as he had half expected, he heard Stanton say, 'El Mihr . . . El Mihr . . . There was some problem there . . . Now what was it . . . ? Hello?'

'Hello?'

'I know there's *something* going on. There's a query with a red label here. But all the papers are locked away in the registry overnight. I'd have to dig them out and call you back tomorrow. Can you give me your name?'

A silence from Mehmet.

'Could you give me your name?'

Mehmet replaced the receiver.

Mehmet glanced out of the hotel window at the black vehicles circulating beneath. Nothing out of the ordinary. He checked his watch again. On the silent television screen the advertising break was coming to a close just before the seven o'clock news.

He dialled a third, longer, number, keeping one eye trained on the cars far below. As usual with this very special line it took an eternity before the phone at the other end was picked up. Twenty seconds . . . Thirty seconds . . . Connections along an electronic nervous system, filtered, blocked, checked, fed down the line to which only one person in the whole world had access . . .

'Yes?' came the voice that Mehmet knew, the voice of a man he had never met, who lived far away in the mountains behind the vaults of steel.

'I will be returning home soon,' said Mehmet. 'Please prepare suitable documentation.'

'We propose to deduct an appropriate proportion for non delivery,' said the distant man. 'For us it is the goodwill factor, the client relationship, which matters . . .'

Mehmet knew exactly what he meant.

'We shall be suitably grateful.'

'Our board will be pleased.'

Mehmet had one question.

'Your minister. How reliable is he?'

'Do not worry,' said the distant man. 'You can rely on his complete discretion—'

'I assume I can.'

Mehmet put the phone down.

He had only one more call to make, to consult Yassavi about de la Fosse. Before he did so he glanced out of the window and noticed a car trying to make its way through the mêlée of taxis below. He dialled the international number, the one that connected him to Yassavi almost two thousand miles away. As his fingers ran through the digits he was vaguely aware that the news had started on the television. He could see a kaleidoscope of jumbled images, silently assembling themselves into a story.

But then something diverted his attention. Or rather, something that should have happened just did not happen. This time the phone did not even ring. There was simply no connection at all.

Mehmet tried again, just to make certain he had dialled correctly. But he could only hear the same sound. The same sound – of what? Of *nothing*. An electronic connection out into infinity. As if he had dialled a number that did not exist, that never had existed, or that never would exist again . . .

As Mehmet stood listening, transfixed, to the sound of emptiness where there should have been something, he realized that he had also been watching the bright images on the television screen coalesce and sharpen, and then turn into a brilliant map of an area of the world he was very familiar with. His heart caught and began to beat more rapidly. And as he concentrated on the picture he had the uncanny sensation of time coming to a standstill.

Across the silent glowing map a bright red arrow was snaking. It rose from one spot and careered erratically around. Then its movement turned into a kind of parabola, turning round on itself. Finally it bent round completely and began to point back – back, impossibly, to the very spot it had just left. And then the screen cleared completely and all he could see was white, like a sheet held up to the screen. For a moment the entire darkened hotel room turned white too.

As the white screen turned to yellow he put down the telephone receiver and scrambled to find the remote control for the sound. Where was it? Where was it? He seized it from the desk. His hands were shaking as he pressed the button. Suddenly the rage and the chaos of destruction blasted into the room. He caught the words '. . . scenes of incredible pandemonium . . . explosion of terrific force of what seems to have been a missile at a site in the desert called Al Tadj —'

And then the telephone rang.

Automatically he picked up the receiver. Against the roaring of the television he heard an urgent thin voice, as if from another world, pleading to talk to Mr Oulmane.

Oulmane? Oulmane? The name seemed familiar, but Mehmet in his state of shock could not immediately place it. He was about to replace the receiver when he remembered. *He* was Oulmane.

'What?' he shouted into the receiver over the noise. On the screen his world was falling apart.

'Reception! Two men. Just arrived. Looking for your colleague Mr Mehmet. Taking the lift . . .'

Mehmet's eyes could not leave the screen. The scene had now changed. It was some city. New York. The UN? Delegates were coming down steps . . . angry, arms waving, shouting, seizing the microphones —

'Hello? Hello? Mr Oulmane?'

Mehmet stared back at the phone, uncomprehending. He forced himself to concentrate.

'Keep the money,' he said, and replaced the receiver.

So they *had* traced the call . . .

He scanned desperately around the room, looking for the things he must take with him. The papers over there . . . But, despite himself his eyes were drawn back to the television screen. A shouting man, face exultant. 'Proves everything we always knew . . .' he heard him say. Mehmet thought, am I the only one left?

He pressed the button on the remote control. The noise of chaos switched off. Then, forcing himself to move, he went over to the door and opened it slightly. There was nobody outside in the corridor. But over by the lifts a light came on. It would be them.

He quietly closed the door. He felt drained, exhausted. Was it all over? Should he just give himself up? He thought through the options. The embassy would be closed. Maybe for good. So, was his whole mission, his whole purpose, now at an end?

He came to one last decision. There was the fire escape in the bathroom. He could take it and get down to the next floor. And then? Then lose himself in the office parties and people beneath. And then? And then?

As he moved quickly to the bathroom he focused on the only issue which now made sense.

*Someone* must pay.

# Chapter Twenty-eight

Tim Warwick turned on his heel, his hand on the door of the private office to face his private secretary, Jill.

'I should be back in half an hour. Carry on working on the speech. I want to see a new draft by four-thirty.'

Jill lifted an innocent face to his. 'Certainly, Minister.'

The door closed. Jill let drop the stack of blue draft paper on to her desk. She looked idly over it and then picked up her telephone. She dialled a four-figure number on the central government exchange.

'He's on his way,' she said.

Warwick passed down the carpeted corridor on the top floor. He saw Garrick, the Deputy Secretary, coming out of his office. Warwick avoided meeting his eyes. Instead he nodded to the security guard standing by the open lift door. He entered and the doors shut behind him.

Going down.

One of the receptionists held the main door open for him when he emerged on the ground floor. Another offered him an umbrella. It was, as usual, raining outside.

Warwick ignored the offered umbrella and simply walked nimbly through the rain to the open door of the official Rover that was waiting for him.

The woman driver in a bottle-green uniform turned slightly to salute Warwick.

'Number Ten, sir?'

'Number Ten.'

The officials who stood chattering in the reception area watching Warwick depart noticed one odd thing. He didn't seem to have taken any ministerial papers with him.

It took only five minutes to reach Downing Street from Northumberland Avenue. The driver used a system of back streets that cut off the jams caused by the pre-Christmas traffic building up round Trafalgar Square. Whitehall itself was neutral, unseasonal, merely a wide and wet boulevard lined with monolithic dark buildings with yellow lights shining. Servants' quarters. Warwick sat upright on the back seat of the car, looking neither to left nor right, just focusing his gaze on the back of the driver's head.

One or two journalists were prowling round Downing Street in the rain. A photographer chanced a random shot of Warwick as he jumped out of his car and the glossy black door of Number Ten opened to greet him. There was a glimpse of the interior. Then it shut behind him.

It was the last known photograph of Timothy Warwick, Minister for Exports.

'The Prime Minister has asked me to see you,' said a tall, rather austere man in a dark suit, who came forward to greet Warwick. It was Quentin Clark, the secretary to the Cabinet. It did not demand much of Warwick's finely tuned political sense to realize how incongruous it was to be received in this place by an official, no matter how elevated. Warwick followed Clark down a corridor into his office. It was surprisingly plain, functional, almost modern, as if Clark, at the pinnacle of the Civil Service, had deliberately banished all memories of the colonial past from his working environment. There was however a fine view of a rain-soaked St James's Park beyond.

'Take a seat, Minister,' said Clark. He seemed slightly nervous, like one who has been asked to perform an unfamiliar task.

'Why will the Prime Minister not see me?' enquired Warwick.

'Because it would not be appropriate,' replied Clark.

'Not appropriate?'

'Let me explain, Minister . . .'

Clark put his hands together. He examined the signet ring on the little finger of his left hand. Among all the delicate operations which a cabinet secretary might be called upon to perform he could think of none more distasteful.

'We have been informed that the story of your involvement in the leak of material to the former Al Tadj missile site will break in the press this afternoon. Your banking contacts. The link with S. G. Zwann. Everything.'

Warwick said nothing for a few moments. Then he asked in a quiet voice, 'How did it get out?'

'The editor tells us the story comes from one Mr Mehmet. He

thinks it is an act of revenge. In the circumstances it is hard to blame him. The problem now for the government is one of damage limitation. We have to try to contain the incident, to distance ourselves from it. There is too much at stake to let this story fester.'

Warwick looked out of the window. Was it all over now?

'So, does the Prime Minister want – my resignation?'

Clark followed his gaze. Outside a troop of the Household Cavalry were returning to barracks through the rain, mud-spattered and mournful, the horses steaming.

'*That* has just been announced to the press,' he said softly. 'A few minutes ago. What the Prime Minister wants now is your signature on this particular letter of resignation. It explains the facts of the matter, how you were acting alone, your motives, your sincere regret, your agreement to co-operate with the authorities, your wish to be of no further embarrassment to the government.'

Warwick took the sheet of expensive, stiff, blue-crested note-paper headed 'Minister for Exports' that Clark handed him. He read it. After a minute he placed it back on Clark's desk.

'This reads like a suicide note,' he said in a far-away voice. 'Political suicide.'

Clark did not say anything.

'Why should I sign it?' asked Warwick.

'There is a train from Victoria that leaves at one-fifteen,' replied Clark. 'It arrives at Dover an hour later. It connects with a boat that will get you to Calais in an hour and a half. From there you can hire a car under an assumed name. By the time this is released you will have disappeared in France. You will have begun a holi-day and can no longer be traced. It is the best offer we can make to you in the circumstances.'

'But how can I just vanish . . . ?'

Clark sighed, and then opened a desk drawer.

'Here is a ticket and reservation for the train. I have, exception-ally, authorized a direct transfer of your severance pay as minister to your bank account. On your way to the station I suggest you call in to your bank and draw whatever you think you will need. If you are to catch the train you will have to move rather quickly. Now, Minister, can I please have your signature?'

Warwick took up the pen that Clark offered him. He read the document again and shook his head. At this supreme moment he could think of only one detail that troubled him. It was uncanny how, even here, they had contrived to imitate his style.

'Who drafted this?' he asked.

'Your private secretary,' replied Clark. 'Who else?'

Warwick hesitated for a few seconds. He then sighed, shrugged and added a final sentence in manuscript before putting his elegant signature at the foot of the document.

'This meeting has, of course, not taken place,' said Clark. 'We shall let it be known that you wrote the letter this morning and came round to deliver it to a deeply shocked Prime Minister.'

Warwick stood, a curiously gaunt figure now.

'Can I at least *see* the Prime Minister?'

'Clark looked sorrowful. 'The Prime Minister is very, very busy, just at the moment . . .'

Clark glanced at the blue paper, at the words which Warwick, ever the optimist, had added: 'I hope to be able to serve in a future administration, as best I can.'

'I will make sure the Prime Minister sees this, 'he said. 'Now, Mr Warwick, it would be best if you left by the rear entrance, by the Cabinet Office, to prevent further press speculation . . .'

When Clark got back to his office five minutes later both Fergusson and Hotblack from the Cabinet Office were in there waiting for him.

Clark closed the door and shuddered.

'I hope I never have to do that again as long as I live. It feels like sending someone to the gallows.'

Fergusson nodded sympathetically. Then he pursed his lips.

'We needed a name, Quentin. We all agreed that. Someone to draw the fire. To channel the blame. He *is* guilty, after all.'

'I know,' said Clark. 'But it still seems inhuman to send him out in the open like that. If Mehmet thinks Warwick deceived them he'll become a sitting target.'

'A moving target, Quentin. He has a head start of a few hours. When his resignation letter is released Mehmet won't know where he is. And he will soon be on the continent. There is quite a good chance that Mehmet won't ever find him.'

'This must never happen again,' said Clark. 'Never again.'

'It won't,' said Fergusson. 'You have my word on that.'

Clark looked at Fergusson for a few moments without speaking, then turned to Hotblack. 'So what news from the Geneva Group?'

217

'*Good* news, Quentin. Good news.'

Clark nodded, as if in gratitude for small mercies, then checked his watch. He went over to the television sitting in one corner of his office and switched it on.

'Well, let's see how all this is playing in Washington . . .'

The news reporter, standing in front of a White House glittering in the winter sunlight, came into focus.

'. . . As the summit between the superpowers begins here in Washington, hopes are rapidly fading of a dramatic agreement on nuclear arms control. Members of the powerful Senate Armed Services Committee have let it be known that the explosion at the now infamous Al Tadj nuclear missile site in the Middle East has reduced chances of US ratification of a non nuclear pact to near zero . . .'

The screen cut to footage of American and Soviet negotiators emerging exhausted into the blinding glare of television lights. Familiar faces looking stricken and drained.

'A year ago at Reykjavik,' recounted the voice-over, 'President Reagan and General Secretary Gorbachov came within touching distance of an agreement phasing out their nuclear weapons over a ten-year period. "I still feel we can find a deal," were the parting words of President Reagan to Gorbachov as the two delegations separated on the steps of the Hofdi House after many hours of gruelling negotiations.'

The picture cut to a reporter who had been present at Reykjavik.

'We read their body language as they came out, and it said, "Close, but no cigar."'

The picture then cut to a still photograph in black and white of a large formal mid-European house.

'It now emerges that over the past year here in Geneva, in this private house belonging to a wealthy Swedish businessman, US and Soviet negotiators have been working in secret to narrow their differences. It now seems a breakthrough was reached in recent weeks on the key point of sharing research and development in the President's Strategic Defence Initiative – the Star Wars programme as it is generally known. Sam Jefferson of the Washington Institute for the Study of Conflict explains.'

An academic in a tweed jacket filled the screen.

'You have to remember that the point of disagreement between Washington and Moscow at Reykjavik was the unilateral development of SDI by the US. Gorbachov could not just go back to Moscow and tell his side that they had agreed to cut nuclear weapons over ten years while the Americans went ahead with their plans to build a large-scale space defence system. The reason was that if SDI was a success that *could* in theory give a future US government a vital strategic advantage.'

'So what negotiators Nitze and Akhromeyev did was build on President Reagan's offer to share SDI with the Soviets once it was working. They agreed to collaborate jointly, from day one, on a shared strategic defence system, to be put in place, piece by piece, by both sides.

'That agreement in principle unlocked the other half of the negotiation – the possibility of deep cuts in nuclear stockpiles on both sides, leading to the eventual phasing out of all nuclear weapons . . .'

The screen cut back to the reporter standing in front of the White House.

'But the Al Tadj explosion has now destroyed that dream. A US administration already deeply divided over the wisdom of abolishing nuclear weapons has been thrown into turmoil over fresh evidence that nuclear proliferation is growing all the time. White House sources are now saying that the political climate for a bold new move at this summit is getting chillier by the minute . . .'

Clark turned the set off. They could read the rest in the telegrams.

The three men sat in silence for a few moments, while the rain fell outside. Around them the machinery of government continued to hum. There was only one question left.

'But who actually *did* it, Gordon?' asked Clark. 'Was it de la Fosse's people?'

Fergusson shook his head.

'He told us they didn't. Of course, in the world's eyes they will take the blame – or the credit, depending on your point of view. He told us they would have loved to blow the place up. But they could never get that close. It took someone on the inside actually to prime one of the missiles.'

'Then who? Who could have had someone on the inside?'

'We don't know for certain,' said Fergusson. 'But think – who profits from the crime? The timing was perfect. Absolutely perfect.

We know how much resistance there was in Washington to the work of the Geneva Group. The administration completely at odds. A complete defence industry thrown into turmoil. Forty years' work overturned. There were powerful interests at stake. Very powerful and effective *agencies*. The strike stopped the negotiations dead in their tracks. It all fits.'

Clark pondered. 'Let's go with that hypothesis, Gordon. I like it. Try and have it checked out some time. No particular hurry, of course.'

He thought a little further. 'Of course, there is another way of looking at things. There is the mirror image, as it were. We know there are people in Moscow just as worried by the turn of events as people in Washington. Now that is a fascinating thought. Resistance to Gorbachov. Is that within the bounds of the possible . . . ?'

# Postscript

It was two weeks later.

Stanton was, as usual, sitting at his desk writing in laborious longhand with a mug of Oxo at his elbow.

The new arrival, Scott, a fresh-faced youth from university who had replaced Colchester, had at first wondered, as Colchester once had, what drove Stanton to fill his days with the placid continuous production of prose. Notes, memoranda, minutes and annotations would emanate slowly from Stanton's pen to fill the files and consume the department's stationery.

But after a few days Scott got used to Stanton and, like Colchester, gave up trying to talk to him about his work. Even the sensational news that Timothy Warwick had left the department caused Stanton to break off for only half an hour to speculate with Scott about who his successor would be. Soon Stanton was back to work, plodding on endlessly through the wastes of export policy, writing, if anything, more than ever before.

Had Scott, or Fulbright (still head of department) or anyone else at the Ministry of Exports actually persisted in breaking down Stanton's defences they might have learnt something surprising.

Because as well as his official work Stanton had also cultivated the long-standing habit of writing lengthy letters at the office; letters which recounted in detail what had been going on there in the past month, which described who did what, why they did it, how much money was at stake, which country was involved, and which contained all the other sundry routine details which made his intelligence so reliable and interesting.

Now, this afternoon, Stanton was putting the finishing touches to a particularly full report on as many of the facts surrounding the El Mihr/Ad Tadj order, the abrupt departure of Warwick from office, and before him the vanishing of Colchester, as he could obtain from the files and office gossip. It came to ten pages of neat manuscript, written in a hand which varied little from line to line and which promised nothing of interest to the casual reader. When Scott's attention was diverted Stanton slowly and deliberately put the manuscript in one of the official brown envelopes which lay on his desk.

That night, before catching the tube back home to Wembley and his father, Stanton made a small detour. Instead of walking up to Trafalgar Square he cut through a canyon of buildings by Great Scotland Yard to emerge into Whitehall. Surrounded by thousands of home-going office workers swarming through the dark on this December evening just before Christmas, his figure, clutching an old plastic bag, blended completely into the background.

He crossed Whitehall and then – along with a stream of other people – passed through the Admiralty on to Horse Guards Parade beyond (also known as Civil Servants' Car Park, on account of the hundreds of vehicles kept there).

Soon Stanton was in St James's Park, a dark figure moving along with dozens of other dark figures from lamplight to lamplight through the raw, dank, vegetation-smelling open space.

Down by the lake the birds were settling down for the night. The ducks, the pelicans, the geese were huddling together for warmth against what would be the longest night of the year. Some were on islands in the middle of the lake. Others were grouped on the muddy shore, surrounded by ragged heaps of old feathers.

On the bridge that crossed the lake stood a man well muffled against the cold. He peered into the gloom, scanning the birds with an impressive pair of wide-lensed binoculars. Occasionally he jotted notes in a pocket book. Bird watchers were often to be seen in the park, following the doings of the exotic species there. It was not extraordinary for one of these mild eccentrics to continue his researches as evening fell.

And so no one who passed by paid Colchester the slightest attention.

'It's him,' whispered Colchester into the small radio in his inner pocket. 'I can see him now.'

Through his night-vision binoculars he looked out over the lake to the far shore, where the faint shapes of the silent birds were moving restlessly to and fro. On the path along the side of the lake he could also – just – make out the progress of a silhouette he recognized, his watcher's faculties straining.

Colchester stared closely at the figure through the binoculars. He held his breath. He was not sure. He could not quite see. And then the light from a lamp was just sufficient for him to make out the outline of Stanton's freely swinging arms.

'He's got rid of the bag,' he whispered excitedly into the microphone. 'It's in the rubbish bin beside the path, between the lights. It must be there.'

'Got you,' responded a male voice.

The rest would now be up to his new colleague Stuart-Smith.

Colchester watched the dim figure of Stanton slowly move off and eventually disappear out of sight. Then he turned the binoculars back to the lake, back to the colonies of birds sleeping there. He surveyed them for a few moments longer.

The radio in his inner pocket came to life again.

'It's getting rather cold,' said a female voice. 'Is it time to close down yet?'

Colchester raised his binoculars and looked over to the opposite shore of the lake. Another muffled figure stood there in the dark, a hundred yards off, the outline just recognizably feminine. He could see that the figure was also holding a pair of binoculars, which were trained in his direction. The two surveyed each other for a while in the gloom across the park.

'First, tell me what you can see,' he said quietly.

'Well,' came the voice over the radio, 'I think the man standing on the bridge is not quite what he seems.'

'What do you think he's going to do next?'

There was a pause.

'I think he's going to go off with the woman somewhere. Somewhere warm. Somewhere where they have a fire lit . . .'

The strange new life he had begun with Julia – Mr and Mrs Cartwright, recently moved out of London to Sunningdale in search of a bit of peace and quiet – had so far been neither particularly peaceful nor quiet. After forty-eight hours' intensive agonizing Stuart-Smith had finally come up with what turned out to be an obvious career move for the disgraced Colchester. To move him in. To put Colchester finally into that extremely obscure part of the government service which dealt with security matters and where – Stuart-Smith had added – Colchester's rather peculiar talents might not go wasted. It was, reasoned Stuart-Smith to Fergusson, better having him in where they could watch him than out and about doing God knows what. And, Fergusson had responded, they might as well do the same with Julia.

So, thought Colchester, I've come full circle. I have ended up where de la Fosse wanted to put me in the first place. (Without de la Fosse, of course: *he* had gone back home to something of a secret hero's welcome – although de la Fosse was the first to concede that he did not deserve it.) But, on the other hand, with Julia, and against all the odds . . .

'Now tell me what you can see,' her voice came over again.

Colchester concentrated on her face for a few seconds. Through the binoculars he could finally make out that she was smiling at him in the dark.

'I can see much more than you can,' he said to her.

Colchester packed away his binoculars, adjusted his jacket, left the bridge and began walking in her direction. He gave a final glance back over the lake. The birds seemed to have frozen into silence, as if they were hibernating for the rest of the winter.

'The Psychology of the Pheasant' was never going to be written at this rate.


Stanton went off to catch the tube back to Wembley, his little task complete for another month. His father would be there waiting for him, with his tales of the mythical giants, Uncle Sam and Uncle Joe.

Stanton had long since decided that, of the two, Uncle Joe was his favourite. Years ago, in Highgate, he had once met the man who – eventually – received all the letters he had been posting for so long. The man had told him it was better for him not to know his real name in Moscow, but rather to address him by the code name Victor.

Ever since, Stanton had often wondered what had become of Victor, and when the millennium which Victor had so confidently predicted was about to dawn.

He had been waiting such a long time.